PUFFIN BOOKS

THE YOUNG MAGICIANS

AND THE
21 HOUR
TELEPATHY PLOT

NICK MOHAMMED is an established actor with recent roles in *Ted Lasso*, *Collateral* and *The Martian*. He also played Piglet in Disney's live-action feature *Christopher Robin*.

Nick's television writing credits include his own series *Intelligence* for Sky, co-starring David Schwimmer, and *Morning Has Broken*, in which he co-starred alongside writing partner Julia Davis. He has also featured in a host of TV comedies including *Sally4Ever*, *Uncle* and *Stath Lets Flats*.

Nick is an Associate of the Inner Magic Circle and this is the second book he's ever written or read.

Books by Nick Mohammed

THE YOUNG MAGICIANS AND THE THIEVES' ALMANAC

THE YOUNG MAGICIANS AND
THE 24-HOUR TELEPATHY PLOT

Follow Nick on Twitter
@nickmohammed
#YoungMagicians

THE YOUNG MAGICIANS

AND THE
24-HOUR
TELEPATHY PLOT

NICK MOHAMMED

PUFFIN

To Anthony Owen,
who inspired magicians young and old

PUFFIN BOOKS

UK | USA | Canada | Ireland | Australia
India | New Zealand | South Africa

Puffin Books is part of the Penguin Random House group of companies
whose addresses can be found at global.penguinrandomhouse.com.

www.penguin.co.uk   www.puffin.co.uk   www.ladybird.co.uk

Penguin
Random House
UK

First published 2020

001

Text copyright © Nick Mohammed, 2020
Interior illustrations copyright © Noémie Gionet Landry, 2020

The moral right of the author and illustrator has been asserted

This novel is a work of fiction. In some cases, real-life names, characters
and places appear, but the actions, conversations and events described
are entirely fictitious. All other characters, and all other names of places and
descriptions of events, are the products of the author's imagination and any
resemblance to actual persons or places is entirely coincidental.

Set in 10.5/15.5 pt Sabon LT Std
Typeset by Jouve (UK), Milton Keynes
Printed and bound in Great Britain by Clays Ltd, Elcograf S.p.A.

A CIP catalogue record for this book is available from the British Library

ISBN: 978-0-241-33108-8

All correspondence to:
Puffin Books, Penguin Random House Children's
One Embassy Gardens, New Union Square
5 Nine Elms Lane, London SW8 5DA

5 P.M.

9 HOURS ON

President Pickle clutched his chest, leaning forward. His face, which was bright red at the best of times, was crumpled in agony, making him look a touch like an origami lobster that had been screwed up into a ball, reopened and then screwed up again for good measure. He fought back the stabbing knot of pain coursing through the lower parts of what used to be a substantial belly. How had it come to this?

He looked into the face of his beloved wife, Cynthia, who gripped his shoulders desperately, searching for an explanation.

'Edmund? What is it?'

Her glasses bounced on the garish string of beads just below her bosom. Which was the best place for anything garish, as far as Cynthia was concerned.

President Pickle gasped the words she never thought she'd hear him say:

'Get . . . Get me the Young Magicians!'

And, with that, President Pickle slumped forward on to the table, his face landing in a bowl of bright green pea-and-mint soup, splattering his fellow diners haphazardly, making them look like they had emerged from a painting class (but one where nobody was that good and everyone was actually very clumsy and only ever used bright green paint).

Cynthia's scream cut through the chatter in the dining room.

'Zack, Sophie, Jonny, Alex – get here this instant!'

1

8 A.M.

'Anything from the trolley?' shouted the bulbous man traipsing up the carriage of the 06:46 from London to Blackpool, bashing his cart heavily into everyone's ankles as he went.

'Yeah, have you got any plasters?' joked Jonny Haigh, rubbing the front of his long leg. If you want to picture Jonny's legs, think of a stork. In fact, think of a stork that has been hanging off a beam for the past fourteen years, with weights attached to its ankles. It was a fact of life that, when Jonny entered a room, his legs came in some time before the rest of him. He was used to it, which was why he could stay cheerful on the many occasions when his height worked against him. Like now, when the laws of physics meant that his legs absolutely *had* to stick out into the aisle of a railway carriage, making them easy prey for passing lunch trolleys, small dogs and anything else with a personal vendetta against his ankles.

Jonny's cheerful eyes danced between his friends: Alex Finley sitting next to him in the window seat, Sophie Yang opposite Alex, and Zack Harrison across from him.

The others smiled back, Alex still a little shyer than the rest, as if he couldn't quite believe smiling in public with friends was legal. In fact, since he had met these three particular friends, Alex had learned that smiling wasn't just legal, it was inevitable and in lots of cases actively encouraged.

Oh, and if you want to picture Alex think of a blond, tousled head of hair and large glasses, emerging from the collar of a smart, way-too-big school blazer with a crest on the pocket – not the same crest as the school Alex went to, it must be said, but that hadn't been top of Alex's mum's agenda when she bought it. She had bought it because she really hoped it would last him for at least another decade.

'*And look, there's plenty of room for you to grow into it now, dear,*' she had said the first time Alex tried it on and almost disappeared – though there was nothing magical about this particular disappearance. Of course, Alex did fully intend to start growing into it – any ... day ... now ...

It was great being together again after such a long time apart. It had been nearly six months since the Young Magicians had thwarted a devilish plot to steal the Crown Jewels and, even though they'd stayed in regular contact, this was the first time they'd properly got back together. And boy, did it feel good!

'No, we don't sell plasters,' the man finally answered, clearly not getting Jonny's joke. 'We sell a selection of hot and cold drinks, light refreshments – including pastrami-filled baps – teas, coffees, biscuits, cake and crisps,' he added monotonously.

'I'd love a piece of cake!' exclaimed Zack.

On a normal day, Zack put away enough breakfast to feed a small army and was still hungry by lunchtime. On this particular day, however, he had had to get up so early that it had been a choice between sleeping a bit longer or eating, but not both. He had gone for sleep, which meant making do with the last-minute cereal-based product his parents plonked in front of his bleary eyes. And that had now been a long time ago. Indeed, when Zack had learned what time the train was leaving London, he had been astonished and indignant to discover that the rumours were true and that every day did in fact have *two* 6:46s in it, which meant that a) he was now fully awake, from the tips of his toes to the top of his flat-top haircut, and b) unspeakably hungry.

'Chocolate or carrot?' responded the man tonelessly, like he'd been preprogrammed with only these two words.

'Sir . . . I'm fourteen years old!' said Zack indignantly, thinking this was answer enough (chocolate, in case you're wondering!).

But Mr Bulbous just stared straight ahead, unable to compute. Dealing with a response like Zack's had evidently not been part of his training.

'I tell you what . . .' said Zack, beaming up at the man.

The other three all sat up a bit straighter. They recognized that tone. Sometimes they used it themselves. Zack was about to do something tricksy!

It had been too long since they last saw their friend in action, working his wizardry on unsuspecting members of the public.

'I've written the type of cake I'd like on the back of this card. If you can guess it, I'll pay double, but if you get it wrong, I have the cake for free!'

Zack flashed a folded piece of white paper as the others leaned in.

'I'll give you a clue,' Zack prompted as the man blinked way more times than was really necessary. 'What I've written down is either chocolate or carrot!'

Sophie cocked an eyebrow at Jonny and Alex. If you want to think of Sophie, think *sharp*. Sharp haircut, sharp clothes, sharp cheekbones, sharp mind, sharp accent. (She came from the Lake District, which is north of Blackpool, and so she could have joined the train at Preston, just half an hour before 't'journey's' end. But she had missed her friends so much she'd gone down to London just so she could travel back up with them. She'll probably do the same but in reverse on the way back.)

Sophie had seen Zack use this 'Magician's Choice'* type ploy before, but the way he was doing it now seemed

* Magician's Choice, sometimes referred to as *equivoque*, is a verbal technique by which a magician gives an audience member (or, as in this instance, Mr Bulbous) an apparently free choice, but frames the

too straightforward. What was he up to? Sophie was an expert at mentalism, which some people called mind-reading (though not her because she knew there was no such thing), but she still couldn't tell on this occasion exactly how Zack was going to pull this off. His language and fair set-up seemed completely binding.

Careful to check that none of the other train guards were watching, though evidently intrigued, the man went for the counterintuitive option. 'Carrot!' he blurted, loudly enough to rouse the commuter sitting across the aisle, unsuccessfully trying to doze on this early northbound service, and who was now somewhat annoyed to have been woken up by the word *carrot*. He was doomed to go back to sleep and dream of root vegetables taking over the world, all the way to Blackpool. (This would upset him so much that it would be years before he could look a parsnip or potato in the eye again.)

Slowly Zack unfolded the paper to reveal the word *INCORRECT!* written in heavy, smug marker pen. Mr Bulbous the Ankle Basher shrugged irritably, patently unimpressed. He didn't have time for this childish nonsense – after all, he was only partway through Coach B.

'You said you'd written either carrot or chocolate. Deal's off.'

He was about to push the trolley on down the carriage, in search of more ankles and maybe even the odd knee or

---

next stage of the trick in such a way that each choice has the same end result – in this case, getting chocolate cake. Result!

two if things worked out, when he hesitated. It was just as he feared – the precocious boy hadn't quite finished.

'Ah, but if I turn the paper round –' Zack twirled it effortlessly between his fingers – 'you'll see this . . .' He held the paper aloft, revealing the defiant word *Chocolate* emblazoned across the back. 'You owe me a free piece of chocolate cake!'

The man huffed like a warthog, flaring his nostrils, and threw a napkin and a piece of chocolate cake at Zack, who grinned back at him.

'Thank you!'

The man trundled off, rousing the commuter dreaming about a root veggie apocalypse for the second time in five minutes.

'What if he'd said chocolate?' Alex asked quietly as he watched the man slope off.

'Let me guess!' Jonny interrupted, keen to show how much more he'd learned about magic technique in the last few months. 'If you open the paper the other way, it says carrot?'

Zack answered by unfolding the paper completely to show that it was otherwise completely blank.

'Hmm,' said Sophie, narrowing her eyes. 'Well, in that case, given that it was fifty–fifty, did you just get lucky?'

'You think I'd risk those kinds of odds on getting a free piece of chocolate cake?!' laughed Zack.

'Well then, come on, how did you do it?' Sophie demanded playfully. She'd missed this. Zack was infamous

8

for his tantalizing and drawn-out explanations. But, more often than not, the wait was worth it, even for a simple effect like this. Zack held up his right hand and gave them a thumbs up.

'Piece of cake . . . I just wrote down the opposite of what he said right in front of him while it was all happening!' he revealed.

Jonny stared. There was something odd about Zack's thumb . . .

'Oh, now, that's wicked!' he said. He grabbed Zack's thumb and pulled it closer like a particularly impatient doctor. Stuck to the end of it was something resembling the nib of a marker pen.

Sophie clapped a hand to her forehead. How could she have forgotten? A nail-writer, swami gimmick or boon-writer as it was sometimes known – was an essential part of any mentalist's toolkit. With a gadget like that, you could appear to make predictions about pretty much anything, at any time, and all secretly written right under the spectators' noses. It didn't get much better than that!

'Neat,' Jonny said as he continued to examine it. 'I guess you made it yourself?'

'Yes, and I'd just like us all to observe a moment's silence to honour the many marker pens that died to bring us this trick,' Zack said, bowing his head melodramatically.

'It sticks out a bit . . . Hmm . . .' Jonny thought out loud. This was Jonny at his best. Thinking up gadgets, or ways to improve existing ones, to make a magician's life easier was a particular strength of his. 'You need something like . . . a thumb tip, with a retractable flesh-coloured nib that doesn't catch the eye . . .'

'Yes please!' said Zack.

'But still – what if he'd seen you writing it down in the moment?' Alex pointed out.

Zack grinned confidently. 'There was never any chance of that because he was looking me in the eye. I kept his attention throughout. Right, Sophie?'

Sophie smiled and nodded. Misdirection – diverting people's thoughts away from what you were actually doing, so seamlessly that they never noticed – was a key weapon in any magician's armoury and Sophie relied on it pretty much all the time . . . both when she was performing magic and sometimes when she was not. Hold the punter's attention. Don't give them a chance to look where you least want them to.

'I must remember to take it off when I get changed, though!' Zack added, exposing a part of his T-shirt now almost completely covered by a thousand inky lines and smudges. 'Anyway, lady and gents, to the victor, the spoils!'

He took the cake in his hand, opened his mouth wide and was about to chomp down on it when Alex unexpectedly interrupted. It was unexpected because, when he was about to take a massive bite of chocolate cake, Zack wasn't really in the zone for interruptions – and it was also unexpected because he didn't expect such an interruption to come from Alex.

'Want to make this interesting?' Alex asked.

Zack paused and a slow, thoughtful grin spread across his face. They both could feel a magical duel brewing. Granted, not the Harry vs Voldemort type, but then this was *real* magic (well, as close to real as it would ever get for these four), and thus a lot more exciting.

'Go on . . .' Zack said, intrigued.

A pack of cards appeared in Alex's hand. He spread them into a pressure fan – a flat, perfect half-circle of cards – with a twitch of his fingers, just because he could and it looked good. Then, with another twitch, he swivelled them into a solid oblong pack again. Alex's hand flickered back and forth as he dealt four random cards, face up, on to the table.

'We each draw a card,' Alex said. 'The highest card gets the cake. Aces are low.' He swept the four cards up with a wave of his hand, put them back on top of the pack and started to shuffle.

Zack quickly reached out and took them off him.

'*I'll* shuffle,' he said. Alex smiled slightly.

'Sure, whatever.'

And that was when Zack knew he was going to lose because – like him with his choice of cake – there was an air of nonchalance about Alex, something that implied he was fully in control of whatever was about to happen. But Zack was so consumed with curiosity to find out how his friend might manage this that he suddenly didn't mind risking his cake.

Zack wasn't as adept as Alex when it came to cards, but he had been practising since they last met and one thing he knew he could now do was keep track of a card while he shuffled. Which was exactly what he was doing now. Alex would deal clockwise from himself because that's the proper way to do it – so the cards would go to Jonny first, then Zack, then Sophie, then Alex last of all. All Zack had to do was track the king that Alex had just dealt as he shuffled, and make sure it finished up being the second card from the top of the deck when he handed the pack back to Alex and he'd be sorted.

He smiled at Alex as he offered him the cards.

Alex held the pack in his left hand. His right hand flickered over the pack as he dealt the top four cards, face down, clockwise starting with Jonny, just as Zack had hoped.

'Showtime!' Alex said.

Sophie turned over her card: a two. She grinned and leaned back in her seat, saying, 'That's cool. I'm really not in the mood for chocolate. Jonny?'

His card was a seven.

Zack turned his card over confidently. An ace.

The *ace*! The lowest of all!

'But the deck couldn't have been prearranged because I just shuffled it! How?' he asked as a beaming Alex turned his own card over to show the king. Alex just slid the cake on its napkin over to his side of the table, then cut it in two with the plastic fork.

'I guess we'll never know. Split it with you?' he asked, smiling. A happily defeated Zack shook his head and held up his hands in surrender.

'You've earned it all, mate!'

Alex grinned and caused a pair of sunglasses to appear out of thin air with a flick of the wrist, popping them on to his small face like this was the start of a musical and he was about to burst into some cheesy song about holidays. (Which, for anyone who knew Alex, was pretty unlikely!)

'Oh, now *that* is cool!' Jonny exclaimed. 'How . . .'

'Ah, the blazer, right?' Sophie said, eyes wide. 'I wondered why you were wearing it on a Saturday.'

Alex just grinned more widely. Yes, the blazer. If life hands you lemons, learn to make lemonade. Alex had worked out that the massive blazer his mum made him wear had a serious upside: plenty of pockets and masses of space to hide things like multiple decks of cards, sunglasses (naturally) and tiny bunny rabbits – if Alex ever got into that breed of magic, that is, which was rather unlikely. Add to this the fact that Alex was the kind of kid who might arguably wear an oversized blazer on a weekend even when not at school . . . well, it was just too good an opportunity to miss for any shrewd magician.

'I've been working on it for ages,' Alex explained. 'It's going to be part of my new close-up routine – but I need a way of switching the decks without people noticing. Sometimes I have to do this –'

He flicked his wrist back and forth again, several times, before another pack of cards finally appeared in his hand.

'. . . which kind of gives the game away,' he finished. 'It would be cooler if it was all a lot more *seamless*.'

'I bet Jonny could come up with something for that too,' Sophie suggested.

'Hmm.' Jonny rubbed his chin thoughtfully. 'I'm sure I can rig up a feeder mechanism that will put whatever you want right into your hand, whenever you want it.'

'That would be so cool! Thanks!' Alex said happily. He had the highest regard for the technical skills of Jonny Haigh – the boy who successfully rigged up a one-and-a-half-mile-long zip-line from Euston to Buckingham Palace – and it knocked him out to think that Jonny would use those skills for *him*.

Meanwhile, there was a cake to eat. Alex picked up his fork again – and blinked in bafflement at the scattering of chocolaty crumbs on the napkin.

'You know how we were talking about misdirection and maintaining eye contact . . .' Sophie said indistinctly as she chowed down on the last of the cake.

The three boys gaped, and then they all burst out laughing.

It wasn't just that Sophie had nicked the cake from right under their noses without them noticing. She had *set them up* so that they wouldn't notice. First she had planted the idea, by pretending she wasn't interested in the slightest. Then she'd deliberately allowed them to be diverted on to other matters like Alex's blazer and feeder mechanisms for switching decks of cards – and, while they were all at it, she had just taken the cake – plain and simple – making it all so natural and obvious that they hadn't even noticed.

And this was the way it went for the next hour or so as the four friends continued to hurtle towards Blackpool, entertaining each other with a six-month backlog of tricks, ideas, MORE CAKE and a hell of a lot of general catching up. And wow, did they have a lot to catch up on! The last time the Young Magicians had been in such frenzied discussion was when they were standing in front of the Queen of England, explaining to Her Majesty exactly how a bunch of thieves were about to steal her precious Crown Jewels. Or not, as it actually turned out, thanks to the four's quick-wittedness.

The story now followed them about wherever they went, like some delicious perfume. 'Wow, isn't that one of the Young Magicians?!' (And you can read all about it in *The Young Magicians and the Thieves' Almanac*, in which our four heroes meet for the first time. Go on, you know you want to!)

Not that it had gone to any of their heads, of course. Zack, Sophie, Jonny and Alex probably had about as much combined ego as a horsefly (that's to say very little, apart from the one horsefly who flies about once a year blatantly thinking he or she is IT!).

What really counted was the way things had changed within the Magic Circle as a result of the Young Magicians. For anyone not familiar with it, the Magic Circle is for magicians what NASA is for astronauts. Kind of. Either way, the society was now indebted to the four, not least because of the Queen's rather generous (tax-free) donation, saving them all from financial oblivion. But the events had sparked an even greater change – not that it had been fully implemented yet, but a new-found respect for junior members was beginning to pervade the society in the same way that a warm breeze might disturb a winter's chill.

Of course, there were still older members who only accepted any changes through gritted teeth, who thought these younger magicians were invading their territory, but then proper change took time. Especially when dealing with the likes of HRH (His Royal Haughtiness) President Pickle and society treasurer Bill Dungworth, who often took about four years to change his tie, let alone something like his mind. (And his socks? Well, once a week or so – he wasn't an animal . . .)

Anyway, one such change (for the good) that had happened quickly was that junior members of the Magic Circle were now permitted to attend the Annual Convention (according to clause 5.50/1, subsection B of the newly amended constitution, subject to confirmation based on how well the whole thing went this weekend). And this was where Zack, Sophie, Jonny and Alex found themselves headed right now.

'I wonder what mischief we can get up to?' said Jonny, jiggling his eyebrows up and down to show that all kinds of intriguing possibilities were already running through his head.

'Don't get too excited,' said Sophie, smiling. 'We're heading to Blackpool, not Las Vegas!' Which was a fair distinction, though perhaps a little unfair on Blackpool. But, at the same time, Sophie casually reached into her pocket and brushed her fingertips against the edge of a piece of paper there. Oh yes, Sophie had her *own* reasons for looking forward to the convention.

'Something tells me we're bound to stumble across *something* to solve,' said Zack eagerly, relishing the prospect of another magical adventure with his three best friends.

'Yeah, magicians are a weird bunch at the best of times,' said Jonny. 'Put them all in the same hotel for a long weekend and surely all hell breaks loose!'

And, just as if it was listening in and agreeing wholeheartedly with Jonny, the train responded with a loud, two-tone *honk!*, which would have been even more effective had it emitted a rush of steam at the same time, but steam trains hadn't run on this particular branch of train line since 1964. FACT!

2

9 A.M.

'HI!'

Imagine a ball of expensive, brightly coloured, designer-label clothes wrapped round an explosion barrelling towards you at a hundred miles an hour, and you're in the cramped vestibule area of a train with nowhere to run.

That was how the four friends felt as the train began to trundle into Blackpool station. Except, they all realized at about the same time, it wasn't an explosion ball. It was Deanna.

It hadn't really occurred to the four of them until then that now junior members of the Magic Circle could come to the convention, they might not be the only ones taking up the offer. Jonny ran through the names of the other juniors in his head. There could be Max: *Yay!* There could be Hugo: *Hmm . . .*

'I'VE MISSED YOU SO MUCH!'

Deanna yanked Sophie into a hug so tight that Sophie's ribs began to creak. Alex, Jonny and Zack stood back with bemused expressions on their faces. Was this really the same Deanna from six months ago? The same Deanna who despised Sophie and who could go from zero to full-on nuclear meltdown in less than a nanosecond?

A middle-aged woman in exactly the same outfit was hovering in the background, trying not to get too involved. Sophie just had time to realize that this was Deanna's mum when:

'WHY DIDN'T YOU EVER WRITE BACK TO ME?!'

Ah yes, this was more like it! Sophie looked at the younger girl, trying to fathom what best to say, for not even a master mentalist like Derren Brown could predict the erratic behaviour of someone like Deanna.

'I've just . . . I've just had a lot on,' Sophie answered rather feebly.

She had frankly been overwhelmed and mildly disturbed by the sheer volume of letters Deanna had sent since the last time they met. Most were vague extensions of friendship, now that Sophie was somewhat of a celebrity. Some were ravings about who or what was Deanna's latest obsession at school (mostly boys, but there were several times when Deanna wrote exclusively about her sequined fidget spinner), some were the starts of bizarre works of fiction (Sophie presumed – *hoped*), and others were lists of things Deanna would like for Christmas and/or forthcoming birthdays and/or other times Deanna felt she should be at the receiving end of a gift, which in a typical year of 365 days was somewhere in the region of 363 to 365.

Notably, Sophie observed, none of her correspondence was about magic. Not that she would have paid too much attention if it was – for Deanna had about as much genuine magical skill and interest in magic as a tin of corned beef – but there wasn't a club in the country Deanna hadn't once been a part of and, while magic was still on her list of current fads, they were lumped with her.

The two girls looked at each other, Sophie biting her lower lip awkwardly, not knowing what else to say, and hoping she hadn't already started a chain reaction of almighty tantrums to mark the start of the weekend, like an explosion of ironic fireworks. Deanna breathed through her nose, closing her eyes, like a dragon preparing to break wind.

'It's fine,' she said with sudden, almost eerie, calmness. Then she grabbed Sophie by the shoulders and shook her. 'We can just catch up ALL weekend instead!'

Sophie did her best to appear delighted. Although, if truth be told, this was about as restrained as Deanna had *ever* been about *anything*, so perhaps things were improving. Slightly.

'Well, that'll be nice for you!' whispered Jonny as Deanna barged her way towards the train door.

'NO, *I* WANT TO BE THE FIRST ONE TO PUSH THE BUTTON!'

Sophie gave Jonny a friendly thump, not knowing which was worse: maintaining her position as Deanna's ultimate nemesis or the prospect of becoming her new best friend.

'There's Cynthia!' Alex said happily, peering through the window as the doors unlocked.

'Right, all junior members follow me, please!' Cynthia called as the first passengers began to appear on the platform. She clapped her hands loudly, accidentally catching her left thumb in the string of beads permanently attached to the ends of her glasses (and now semi-permanently caught round the end of her thumb).

Cynthia was in her absolute element. Not only was this the first time her beloved junior members were allowed (as an 'experiment' – see the latest council minutes) to attend the Magic Circle's Annual Convention, but Blackpool was where she and President Pickle had first met.

It was a good few decades ago now, of course, but the place still thrilled her, just like it did back then when she first rode the big dipper, her soon-to-be-hubby howling with glee (he'd had a sense of humour in those days) as he munched his way through several bags of crisps and candyfloss (before violently throwing up). Cynthia could still smell it in the air (not the sick) and it made her feel good. Something she hadn't felt in a number of weeks now, not least because of the letters:

those unfathomable,

sinister

and *terrifying* letters.

At first Cynthia had thought they were a joke. At least she told herself she thought they were a joke. It seemed to make the problem go away. But then they kept on coming. She'd tried to hide them – for President Pickle was prone to lolling around in bed until way after the postman had made his rounds, so perhaps he wouldn't see them. But then he'd stumbled across them while emptying the recycling (who recycles death threats?!). *He* hadn't thought they were a joke, though. He'd taken them deadly seriously, and his fears had fuelled the ones Cynthia had been trying to hide, and so the two of them had started to tumble into a tornado of paranoia and panic.

But now here they both were, back in Blackpool, back to putting on a show, back to pretending everything was fine.

No, she told herself, *everything* was *fine*. The Magic Circle was making progress. It was no longer staring bankruptcy in the face and it had got fresh talent in at the younger levels, to help carry the burden of running it and to take it forward into the future. And at the *very* youngest level there was enough talent to keep it going for at least another century.

As if to prove this, the very first youngsters to appear in the carriage door were her favourite four. The sight filled Cynthia with hope, pushing her fears away. For now.

'Mind the step!' she called as Zack, Sophie, Jonny and Alex hopped off the train and on to the breezy platform.

'I must say, it's *so* wonderful to see you four again,' she added a touch breathlessly. 'I mean, you *all*,' she corrected herself, quickly spotting Deanna.

Fortunately Deanna wasn't listening – she was already in some kind of disagreement with her mum about her strawberry-coloured (and possibly strawberry-flavoured) inhaler. ('*You* had it!' 'No, *you* had it!' 'Do you think I don't know who's got my inhaler?' 'Well, as it's yours, maybe you should be the one who –' 'WHY ARE YOU SO MEAN TO ME?' And so on. And then some. Et cetera. You get the point!)

Cynthia noticed Sophie cock her head slightly and look at her, a little askance. Cynthia bit her lip. None of the Young Magicians were stupid, but Sophie was the one Cynthia could trust most of all to notice something odd about someone's body language. Was she trying too hard? Had the girl spotted something in Cynthia that gave her away?

She snapped back into the moment and resumed ushering the remaining juniors off the train, accidentally including a small but rather stern businesswoman who frowned at the idea of being referred to as anything less than senior. Jonny looked up and down the platform, at the other disembarking passengers.

'Aren't there any older magicians here too?' he asked.

'Already at the hotel, dear,' Cynthia replied. 'President Pickle thought it would be best if you all came up on the Saturday, to –'

'Put up with us for as short a time as possible?' Zack said with a grin.

'Let you all have a good rest at home on a school night,' Cynthia corrected him gently, not quite meeting his eyes. 'OK now, just through the gate you'll see the society minibus. Steve's driving!'

Alex couldn't help but grin at the mention of Steve's name as they headed off towards the exit.

'Cynthia looks tired,' said Jonny quietly as they began walking along the platform, dragging their cases behind them.

'Mm,' Sophie agreed. She was sure she had seen something a little odd in Cynthia's eyes – a peculiar anxiety – just for a moment. Nothing she could put her finger on, though.

'Well, wouldn't you be if *you* were married to President Pickle?!' Zack joked.

'Probably just keen for us all to make a good impression at the convention,' Alex reasoned, enjoying the sound of the seagulls and the salty air blowing against his face.

None of them could argue with that. They knew their presence was a landmark victory for Cynthia. If this went wrong for any reason, then who knew how long it would be before such a trial were permitted again?

'I wonder who else is going to be here,' Jonny said as they went through the barrier. 'Lots of familiar faces probably.' His mouth twisted wryly. With their experience of the Magic Circle, 'familiar faces' could be a mixed blessing.

'I can think of one who probably won't be here,' Zack said sadly. 'Or at least won't be seen: Alf.'

'Oh. Yes.'

They all took a moment to think of Alf Rattlebag, the ghost who actually wasn't a ghost secretly living in the rafters of the Grand Theatre of the Magic Circle, and the most unexpected friend they had made the last time they'd been together.

'I don't know,' Jonny said, 'maybe he's found a hidden lair somewhere in the basement of the hotel here – that wouldn't be creepy at all!'

They all had to laugh and agree that yes, that would be Alf's style.

Their thoughts were brought abruptly back to the present as the minibus Cynthia had mentioned came into view.

'Well, *this* should be interesting!' joked Sophie as the four approached the rusty and battered contraption. It would have looked more at home in a museum dedicated to exhibiting ancient modes of transport that didn't really care for its exhibits. And with Steve Moore, the world's most embarrassing and least self-aware magician driving . . . 'interesting' didn't begin to cover the endless possibilities.

'Thank goodness they didn't offer to drive us up from London,' Jonny murmured, taking in the state of the vehicle.

'Nah. Not even President Pickle dislikes us that much,' Zack agreed.

And there was Steve, sitting in the driver's seat with an enormous grin splitting his bouncy face, still inexplicably dressed in a set of 'official' Oriental wizarding robes (which was how *he* referred to them).

'So who have we got here then?' Steve bellowed excitedly, like he was attached to a speaker. The four friends were the first to reach the minibus. 'We've got Zack, tick, Sophie, tick, Alan . . .' Steve suddenly honked the car horn while squashing his nose with the flat of his other palm, as if he'd just got the wrong answer on a quiz show. 'Incorrect! That should have been *Alex*, and finally . . . Ladies and gentlemen, please give it up for the tallest boy on the planet, it's Jonny!'

Steve held his hand down on the horn for a disconcerting amount of time, causing it to sound like a distressed gosling before fading out with a wheezy pop.

'Right, I might have broken that actually . . .' Steve repeatedly punched the horn, to no avail. 'Let's maybe keep that between us!' he said, winking at the four who beamed up at him.

You took your life in your own hands where Steve was concerned, but – wowsers – it was always fun. 'I thank you!' he added, semi-bowing, conjuring up a fistful of old gummy sweets and throwing them at the Young Magicians.

'How are you, Steve?' Sophie asked as she heaved her bag up the small flight of steps and on to the minibus, the poor suspension causing the bus to lean towards her like a teetering canoe.

'Oh, same old, same old,' blathered Steve. 'Very busy now that I've retired . . .'

'From magic?' asked Sophie, a tiny bit hopeful and a tiny bit worried. The world of magic would be a safer place if Steve retired, but also a lot duller.

'Oh no – from dentistry! That was my day job.' Not noticing her slightly stunned look, he continued. 'I'm sure I'll be performing magic even when I'm dead!' he snorted.

Sophie could well believe it, imagining for a moment the surreal idea of Steve emceeing his own funeral, his coffin no doubt some fancy box covered in magical symbols with dry ice pouring out of the sides; Jane – his wife – strapped to the underside, waiting for her cue to appear, but never quite getting the timing right and always making too much noise; Steve light-heartedly reprimanding her from beyond the grave.

'I must say everyone's really excited about having all you youngsters up here this year,' Steve continued as Alex tumbled on to the minibus, hurtling forward under the weight of his bag.

'Really?' said Zack, not buying it – Steve could be about as convincing as a bad ventriloquist pointing at his own moving lips when it came to hiding the truth.

'OK, well, maybe *excited* is a little strong . . . but Jane and I are pleased at least!' he confessed.

Zack gave him a loud high five. Sure, Steve and Jane were perhaps some of the worst performers the Magic Circle had ever produced, but – oh my – they were a wonderful couple and didn't have an unkind bone between them.

'Room for a little'un?' Jonny called in a mock Cockney accent as he finally stepped up, stooping low and twisting his body like a crumpled Fagin. Jonny's body wasn't really built for minibuses. Frankly, nothing with the prefix 'mini' really worked for him.

'So . . . how's, erm, your . . . Ernest?' asked Steve a bit more soberly, tugging Jonny's arm lightly as he passed.

The effect on Jonny was immediate. It knocked him back like it would if a little kid went up to a famous magician and said they'd seen the rabbits hiding in the hat right from the start of the act. He had known the question would come up eventually – he'd even thought about what he might say in response – but this didn't make it any easier now the moment had come.

'Erm . . . He's . . . he's doing fine . . . I think,' Jonny managed to utter, feeling his cheeks begin to glow like hot embers and his throat go dry. 'We're not really in touch any more.'

It was true. Jonny hadn't seen his grandfather since the day he, a respected elder member of the Magic Circle, had been arrested alongside the devilish child-impersonating Henry – or whatever his real name was – for his part in the Crown Jewels plot. True, Ernest Haigh wasn't a criminal in the strictest sense and he'd never meant for anyone to get hurt, but – despite his protestations six months ago – he had still manipulated the Young Magicians for his own gain. And, as his only grandson, Jonny had felt particularly betrayed.

Jonny took his seat next to the others at the back of the cramped minibus, hoping they hadn't heard. Hoping the moment would pass and that soon they'd be on their way.

'Everything all right, mate?' Sophie asked, instantly spotting that Jonny wasn't his usual cheery self.

Jonny half opened his mouth to answer, not quite knowing what to say. It had all just happened so quickly, he thought, with a touch of renewed bitterness. One moment he'd had a grandfather revered by the entire magic world, someone whose name implied a certain prowess, a kindly sort recognized as having amazing foresight about the future of magic and who had always been at the cutting edge of new technique; the next, he was the grandson of some devious puppeteer, whose magical abilities and past achievements were now overshadowed by his talent for masterminding and orchestrating a cunning plot to steal the Crown Jewels – a fall from grace of dramatic proportions.

'Ernest?' offered Sophie quietly. She didn't need her mentalist skills to read Jonny's tumbling thoughts perfectly.

The tall boy slowly nodded. *What was the good of clamming up about it all now?* he wondered. *I mean, if anyone's going to understand*, he thought, *it's bound to be these three*. After all, they'd been with Jonny at the time of the shocking revelation, and even shared that odd combination of anger, upset and betrayal.

'You . . . you can talk about it if you want,' said Alex. 'I . . . I find that helps sometimes,' he added kindly. Jonny looked at Alex, and then to Sophie and Zack, desperately trying not to cry, pulling a face caught somewhere between looking startled and swallowing a burp.

'You're not *him*, remember? Despite what happened, no one is going to judge *you* for what he did,' said Zack, who had known Ernest the best, after Jonny. He was determined that his friend would enjoy the convention, despite the skeletons it might dredge up. And, after all, Zack knew more than anyone what it felt like to be an outsider in the magic world. A false accusation about pickpocketing had followed him around like a cloud of bluebottles on the trail of a particularly tasty bit of horse dung secretly hidden in someone's back pocket.

'You're right,' reasoned Jonny, pushing back into his seat with his long legs. 'It's just going to feel a bit . . . different, that's all. Plus . . .' His voice trailed off like he was suddenly ashamed. 'Is it bad that part of me *enjoyed* the attention I got for being the grandson of a living legend?'

'You wouldn't be human if you didn't have feelings like that,' said Sophie with a reassuring rub of his arm. 'And – you know,' she continued, a mischievous glint in her eye, 'perhaps it's good for you to have been brought down a peg or two!'

Jonny threw his head back, laughing. 'Yeah, maybe that's a fair point!'

'And I'm sure we'll find plenty of stuff to take your mind off it once we get to the convention,' Alex added.

Jonny smiled. *Yes*, he thought, *perhaps everything will be OK after all*.

The four relaxed back into the tattered seats, trying to avoid the odd spiky spring that had begun to poke through the dark-green upholstery as they watched Cynthia escorting the remaining junior members through the car park towards the bus.

'Come on now, we can't be late!' Cynthia fumbled about her midriff for her glasses, before realizing they were still teetering on the bridge of her nose. She looked at her watch. 'Good golly, Steve's going to have to step on it!'

Zack grinned at the others, relishing the prospect of Steve trying to get the rusting minibus to move any faster than a tired limpet.

But Jonny was now gazing out of the window and his grin had become fixed.

'Oh,' he said in a flat tone. 'Joy.'

A wedge-shaped formation of boys was approaching, like a flock of efficient birds, or the RAF, looking as if they were on a business trip in their fitted suits, immaculately gelled hair, mirror shades on spotless faces, and *far* too many teeth between them. It was obvious which of them was the leader from the fact that he was the one at the head of the wedge, dragging his silver wheelie case behind him like someone else should be doing it for him.

Hugo.

'Urgh, this bus is disgusting!' His voice whined like faulty windscreen wipers, though not as much fun to listen to. 'Can't we all just get taxis?'

'Society funds won't stretch that far, I'm afraid,' Cynthia said pointedly. He stopped and stared at her.

'But the *Queen* gave us *money*!' he squeaked.

'And it's all been prioritized. It's amazing we even managed to find funds to keep this little thing on the road!' sang Cynthia.

She bashed the side of the bus fondly, causing it to bong like Big Ben announcing its decommissioning. Something rattled beneath Sophie's seat as the reverberation travelled back to where the four friends were sitting.

'And lovely to see you too, Mayhew, Charlie, Salisbury, Jackson . . .' Cynthia ticked the rest of Hugo's brigade of friends off as they reluctantly climbed aboard the minibus as if it were infected by the plague, hardly daring to touch the sides, all with the same uppity air of entitlement and all with their faces agog at the so-called transportation device before their eyes.

'Well, I'm texting Mummy!'

'Is that the latest iPhone?'

'What's that awful smell?'

'Where even *are* we – does this still count as England?'

Et cetera!

'They should be happy just to *be* here,' Jonny scoffed under his breath. He lifted up his chin in the manner of Hugo and his brigade of friends.

Hugo's eyes had settled on the four of them at the back. 'Oh look. The Young Magicians,' he said flatly.

The four friends innocently met the five identical sneers.

'We didn't see you on the train,' Sophie said pleasantly.

'*You* weren't in First Class,' Hugo said as though he were explaining something very basic to the school idiot. 'Anyway, you can be the first to know: you lot aren't the only ones who can give yourselves a name. We're an official group now too. Guess what we're called!'

'The Right Honourable Squad of Hugo Lookalikes?' Jonny asked. Hugo's face twisted scornfully.

'Class Act!' Hugo spoke proudly as if he were naming his first baby. The other boys smirked as Hugo tapped his head. 'Remember that name when you're scraping a living in the end-of-the-pier show.' He turned away as the Hugolikes made a great show of dusting off their seats before sitting down.

'No, that one's got rat droppings on it.'

'Can someone turn the air conditioning on?' (Yeah, good luck finding *that* button, Steve!)

'This is ridiculous – I'm texting Mummy again.'

'Is that the new iPhone?'

Et cetera!

'Do you think we've just been put in our place?' Zack asked, loud enough to be heard at the front of the bus.

'Come on, let's be having you,' Cynthia chirped, checking that she hadn't missed anyone. 'Max, do hurry up. We're going to be late!'

Zack, Sophie, Jonny and Alex eagerly pressed their faces against the window like they were tourists on safari, hoping to be the first to clap eyes on the rare breed that was Max.

'Max!' shouted Zack, spotting him coming out of the station exit and banging on the window loudly, doing nothing for the centuries-old glass.

The boy looked up and grinned. Max was one of the Young Magicians' favourites. He loved magic as much as he loved food, always gave every trick a good go, and was never one to judge. In fact, throughout the whole of last year's debacle, not once did Max cast any doubt on the four, despite the fact that it would have been easy – maybe even *beneficial* – for him to do so, just like everyone else had. No, Max was certainly one of the good guys. He had a kind of infectious innocence about him that just soaked into anyone he was with. And he had just popped into the station shop for a couple of quick (large) snacks, judging by the size of the plastic bags he was now carrying.

'Wow, someone's . . . grown,' said Alex, who it seemed had now been reduced to a third of Max's size in practically every direction. It was true that Max was certainly growing up – and out – fast, but the four were pleased to see he was still as baby-faced as ever as he bounded over.

'That's right, straight on to the bus, Max,' said Cynthia, a tad flustered, as Max hoisted himself up. The minibus heaved dangerously towards him like a lumbering hippo as he clambered in through the side door.

'Aha, lovely to see you again . . . *blaamrnsr* . . .' Steve made a strange wobbly noise, half covering his mouth, hoping to hide the fact that he'd blatantly forgotten Max's name. Zack, Sophie, Jonny and Alex grinned.

'How have you been, mate?' asked Zack, clapping Max on the back and helping him with some of his bags. (I mean, how much stuff had he *bought*?!)

'Amazing – look at this!' Max dumped the rest of his bags in the aisle and grabbed a small, slightly crumpled red hanky from his jeans pocket. He proceeded to push it into his bulging fist. 'Now watch . . .' he said as he slowly and melodramatically unfurled his fingers to reveal that the hanky had completely vanished. He beamed at the others like a baby elephant.

'That's wicked, mate!' said Sophie as the others applauded encouragingly.

(It's fair to say that our friendly four were perhaps being rather kind here. Not that Max's sleight of hand hadn't improved; it was just that the hollowed-out fake thumb (or 'thumb tip' as mentioned earlier) that made this trick possible was so obviously stuck on to the end of Max's real thumb – with the hanky squashed inside – that the whole thing stood out, quite literally, like a sore thumb! Oh well, A* for effort! Maybe that's one for Jonny to have a look at fixing too?)

'By the way, can I get your autographs later?' said Max suddenly. 'Everyone at school has been asking for them.'

'Oh, erm . . . sure, if you'd like!' said Jonny, already excited by the idea of dressing up his somewhat plain signature into a fancy, swirling autograph.

'Great! Right, well, I'd better sit at the front in case I get sick,' Max said breathlessly, grabbing one of his plastic bags and sitting down in the seat behind Steve. The air whooshed out of the seat like a drawn-out sneeze.

'I do love that kid!' said Jonny quietly, turning to the others, his earlier worries forgotten.

'Ah, there she is – finally!' said Cynthia, spotting Deanna and her mum running after the bus, having been held up searching for Deanna's strawberry-coloured and possibly strawberry-flavoured inhaler, which – if truth be told – she didn't really need any more, but she had kicked up such a fuss when the doctor had tried to take it from her that the lady eventually caved and insisted Deanna just keep it and use it as infrequently as humanly possible.

'*Please can I sit next to Sophie, please can I sit next to Sophie, please can I sit next to Sophie?*' Deanna was droning.

'I'm sure if you ask her *nicely*,' Deanna's mum panted, trying to keep up. As she was dressed in exactly the same outfit as her daughter, from certain angles you'd think it was just one person running towards the bus but with two heads, four arms and four legs.

'Oh!' said Deanna loudly, grinding to a halt as she clambered aboard the bus, spotting Sophie already squeezed between Alex and Jonny. She took a deep breath as before, trying to suppress her inner rage, which presently was something just shy of a giant supernova explosion. 'It's fine, it's fine,' she muttered. 'I'll just sit here with . . .' She scanned the rest of the minibus aggressively before turning to face Max, who already looked, inexplicably, somewhat travel sick. 'What's your name again?'

'Max.'

'Right, I'm Deanna, but I'm going to listen to my music now so please don't talk to me for the rest of the journey.' Deanna whacked on a pair of garish headphones, which had big diamond Ds blasted into each side, in case anyone should forget who these wannabe earmuffs might belong to, and cranked up the volume to max.

Max turned pleadingly towards the four at the back, patently terrified. Was this really what she was going to be like all weekend? Fingers crossed!

'Well, finally, that's everyone!' Cynthia declared, stepping up on to the bus. 'Are you coming along as well, dear?' she added, turning to Deanna's mother, who was waving at her daughter like a possessed seal, but getting nothing back.

'Oh, good grief, no, I'll be glad of the break!' she answered bluntly – well aware her daughter now couldn't hear a word. 'Have a great trip!' She ran back towards the station, victorious, leaping in the air like she'd just negotiated a business deal that had worked out *massively* in her favour.

'Well then,' Cynthia said to Steve, 'shall we see what she's made of?' She patted the dashboard of the minibus, causing a corner to ping off, and hastily squeezed into the little space left by Max and Deanna on the passenger seat – fastidiously doing up her belt, almost like she knew something about Steve's driving that the others didn't.

Steve reached down below the steering wheel and turned the ignition. The bus lurched forward alarmingly, interrupting a nearby seagull in the middle of its tasty midday treat of dropped chips mixed with old dog poo and making it screech out its disapproval.

'*Whoops!*' Steve caught everyone's eyes in his rear-view mirror. 'Which bright spark left this in gear, eh?!' He tried the ignition again, almost snapping the gearstick in the process. The engine belched and roared to life, leaving a carbon footprint the size of a brontosaurus in size thirteen wellies as a thick gush of black smoke belched out of the exhaust.

'Right, hold on!' shouted Steve over the noise of the engine as he slowly lowered the handbrake. 'The pedals are a little sensitive!'

The minibus shot out from its spot in the station car park like a sprung coil, forcing them all back into their seats as if they were on their way to the moon (whether they liked it or not).

'Mind out!' Cynthia shouted, clapping her hands over her eyes as Steve narrowly missed colliding with nearly every other car in the car park. This was like a giant, hair-raising game of pinball.

'Scream if you want to go faster!' Steve shouted joyfully. He was spending more time checking out everyone's reactions to his 'jokes' in the rear-view mirror than keeping an eye on the road.

'Left-hand lane!' Cynthia screamed as they screeched on to the main road away from the station at full pelt.

Zack, Jonny, Sophie and Alex jostled into each other like peas in a very turbulent pod.

'Red light!' screamed Cynthia.

'Other way!'

'Slow down!'

'Police!'

And so it went on until Steve finally got into his groove as they shot up the A583.

Sophie stared through the window as the view outside became increasingly bleaker, the grey of the town being replaced slowly by the patchy green and brown of moorland and peat bogs. She loved this kind of landscape. It wasn't massively dissimilar to the landscape of her hometown in the Lake District, but there was something about being so close to the sea and the clifftops here that made it feel even more otherworldly.

In the seat next to her, exactly the same scene was slowly blowing Alex's mind. His parents hardly ever travelled, so neither did he. For the first time in his life he could see for miles without a single building getting in the way. Just moor and sea.

'Wow . . .' he breathed.

'Whoa, what is *that*?' said Jonny, leaning heavily across the others to get a better view. Zack rubbed the grime from the crusted window and peered out, his eyes widening.

'Jeez, what in –?!'

It was a fairground. A funfair to be precise – Ferdinand's Fantastic Festival of Fun – though 'fun' wasn't the first word that sprang to mind. It clearly hadn't been open for a number of years judging by the dilapidated sign and the chained, rusting, wrought-iron gates that now closed off the entrance. The faded lettering and artwork looked more like the etched storyboards of a nightmare than a place people would enter voluntarily. And certainly not in the pursuit of 'fun'.

Alex tried to imagine the place full of life, the smell of fried onions, children bustling between the rides and screaming with delight or fear. He shuddered as his eyes fell on the entrance to the ghost train, which looked like some gateway to hell, made even more authentic by the real cobwebs and rotting woodwork that now unapologetically smothered the front.

'Let's hope we don't end up *there* this weekend!' said Zack, the glint in his eye suggesting that he probably hoped for the exact opposite. Sophie smiled knowingly.

'Hey, look!' shouted Jonny, leaning towards the other window, bringing his weight down on the bus's dodgiest and arguably single suspension spring, so that the entire back end of the minibus rocked alarmingly. And alarmingly rocking was not what any of them wanted to be doing right then, given how close they were to the cliff edge. A strip of barren moorland was the only thing between the road and a delightful – albeit treacherous – sea view.

They were coming up to a crumbling block of concrete about the size of a caravan. It was ugly and artificial, so it immediately made Alex feel at home again. There was a long black slit three-quarters of the way up one side that looked almost as inviting as the entrance to the ghost train at Ferdinand's Fantastic Festival of Fun.

'World War Two outpost!' yelled Steve like a tour guide, veering dangerously off course as he craned his neck to get a better look. Cynthia grabbed the side of the steering wheel before Steve could take them on a lethal detour.

'I've read about these places,' Jonny said eagerly as the stony outpost disappeared behind a blanket of heather. 'Apparently there's hundreds dotted all along the coastline of Britain, to defend against invaders – but I've never actually *seen* one. Cool!'

'Oh, come on, are we nearly there yet?' moaned Hugo, looking at his fancy watch and sighing heavily like this whole trip was a massive inconvenience. (Hey, Hugo, no one made you come, right?)

'Not long now!' called Cynthia as Steve took a sharp turn, frantically trying (and failing) to find the correct gear and causing all their stomachs to lurch – poor Max! But finally the minibus began to slow. The road turned to gravel, the suspension getting the workout of its life as the vehicle bounced up and down and jerked from side to side while Steve desperately tried (and failed – again!) to avoid the numerous potholes that were dotted about like craters on the moon.

'Oh, thank goodness,' Cynthia breathed as the minibus finally came to a standstill, partly because they had arrived on time, but also because she was still alive. With a conscious effort, she plastered her cheerful, friendly smile back on to her face and turned to the young magicians behind her. 'Here we are then!'

Jonny, Zack, Alex and Sophie looked out of the window and their jaws dropped.

'So you know how that funfair looked creepy . . .' Jonny said nervously.

3

10 A.M.

The minibus had stopped in the shadow of a building that looked like a cross between an old boarding school and somewhere that used to house the criminally insane during Victorian times.

A hundred small windows peppered the stark charcoal-grey front of the building, which looked like it had suffered several hundred years' worth of winter storms. The yellowing net curtains inside offered little welcome or comfort, wafting in the breeze even though the windows were screwed tightly shut, as if the place were haunted by a thousand ghosts all keen to get a good look at who had just arrived.

'This looks a bit like my house!' Hugo cried out, sounding the happiest he'd been since he stepped off his first-class carriage an hour ago. Yes, thought the others, they could well imagine Hugo and his intimidating family living somewhere like this!

'Well . . . welcome to Tudor Towers!' said Cynthia. 'So this will be your home for the next two days. All the various magical activities will be taking place here too, *so there'll be no need for anyone to venture off site.*'

Zack looked at the others, his eyes twinkling with excitement. Sure, this place might be the North of England's very own Alcatraz, but it certainly wasn't going to stop *them* from having a little *tour of the local area*! Ferdinand's Fantastic Festival of Fun, anyone?

'Indeed,' continued Cynthia, through slightly gritted teeth, staring at Zack and correctly interpreting his mischievous grin, 'it is *forbidden* for any junior member to wander off site. Let's not ruin what will hopefully be the start of many trips like this.'

Zack looked innocently back. After everything Cynthia had done for them, he didn't want to upset her. But surely it must be possible to sneak in a little extracurricular *something*?

Alex looked up at the oppressive building, the ivy growing up its sides like some green, clawing virus. Well, he'd survived worse encounters, he thought. And with Zack, Sophie and Jonny by his side, how bad could things ever really get?

'Oh, and before I forget,' said Cynthia, pulling out a scruffy canvas bag which smelled of compost, 'no phones allowed, I'm afraid.' She jiggled the open bag up and down. 'So I will be collecting them now, thank *you*.'

Deanna was the first to react, pulling off her headphones like they'd just given her an electric shock, having lip-read the whole thing.

'Try to stay calm, please, Deanna. Calm . . .!' Cynthia added quickly as Deanna began to swell like a whale sucking in its breath as the prelude to a massively deep dive.

'But . . . *why*?' Deanna wailed (different kind of whale, that!).

'One, because if a young person is going to lose anything, then the chances are it will be their phone, and we're not insured for that. Two, because you are here to learn from other magicians, not your screen. And three, so that no secrets leave the building – we can't have everything getting out on all these smart drones or whatever they're called.' Another jiggle of the bag. 'Come along now.'

'But how will I text Mummy?' cried one of Hugo's clan who – it seemed – would even resort to texting Mummy just to get him something from the next room, he was that lazy . . . and that into texting Mummy.

'Your mother has my number in case of any emergencies,' Cynthia answered briskly, passing the bag round. 'Pop it in now!'

'I actually don't even know where my parents are!' said Max, oddly upbeat, dropping his phone into the bag happily.

Alex cocked his head. He often didn't know where his parents were either, regularly coming home to a note on the microwave or freezer with instructions on how to make a lasagne-for-one using the very few ingredients kept in the brand-new cupboards. But, then again, at least they came back at night . . . Most of the time.

'Well, I mean, I know they're in Costa Rica somewhere!' Max clarified. 'Last I heard, they were about to go skinny-dipping off the coast,' he added, 'but I'm staying with my auntie who's a great cook so it's a win-win really.'

Now it was Jonny's turn to cock his head to one side, wondering why no one else seemed even remotely perturbed by this. The thought of parents going skinny-dipping. The thought of parents *telling their kids* they were going skinny-dipping. And the thought of parents skinny-dipping in what were obviously shark-infested waters. *EEWWW – poor sharks!!*

'Yes, please, Deanna,' Cynthia tutted as the girl stared at the bag, agog. Didn't people know that her phone was her LIFE!? 'If you're good, you'll be allowed five minutes on it this evening,' Cynthia added kindly, unaware that Deanna needed at least fifty hours of phone time per day if she were to be even remotely sated. Summoning up every ounce of energy, and with her eyes fixed on Cynthia all the time like she was already plotting her revenge, Deanna dropped her prized sparkly-cased phone into the bag.

'*And* the other two as well, thank you!'

You could see the wheels turning in Deanna's head.

Deny I've got another two!

How does she know I've got another two?

Hello – wife of the president of the Magic Circle – might just know a thing or two about concealing items!

Not going to win this one . . .

With an audible huff, like she'd just blown out the world's biggest birthday cake, Deanna produced another two phones from her stretched leggings pockets, dropping them in the bag and throwing her head back against the seat like she was a two-year-old who had just been refused milk.

'Fantastic!' said Cynthia. 'See, that wasn't so hard, was it?'

Yes, it was!

Cynthia now turned to Hugo and his group of cronies who shall henceforth be referred to as Class Act. Hugo smirked sideways at the Young Magicians, and pretended to pluck his phone from nowhere *out* of the bag. Neat trick, Zack thought: he was already kicking himself for not having got his own phone prepared for a similar type of act. It was just sitting in his pocket.

'Jonny . . .' he murmured. 'I want a gadget. Something that will store three or four identical mobiles up my sleeve and feed them out whenever I want them. So that when people think I'm handing over my phone, or putting it in my pocket, I can keep on producing it from somewhere else. We can work on the details.'

'I'll get on to it,' Jonny promised, immediately drawing up designs in his head, alongside the improved thumb device that Zack had requested.

Hugo's attempt at light entertainment was slightly spoiled when Salisbury unmagically pulled out a roll of bubble wrap, before encasing his thousand-pound phone as if he were handling an expensive piece of art during a house-move.

Cynthia waved the bag at the friends at the back of the minibus.

'Do you want to pass yours forward?'

Zack, Jonny and Sophie got out their phones, making sure they were switched off.

'Ooh, old school!' said Sophie, spotting Jonny's retro model.

'I like to think so!' said Jonny, giving it a quick peck before passing it forward. Zack turned to face Alex, who had begun to blush a little.

'My parents . . . said I don't need one. And that I should just use a public phone box if it's an emergency,' he said quietly.

'Well . . . that's even more old school!' said Zack cheerfully, not wanting his friend to feel embarrassed.

'Great. Well, now we've got that out of the way,' chimed Cynthia, 'all we need to do is work out who's sharing with who.'

The four suddenly sat up – surely this arrangement could make or break the whole weekend. Sophie began to feel queasy as Deanna turned to face her with a bright, desperate smile, holding up her hands to show that all eight of her fingers were tightly crossed, the ends a blotchy mishmash of bright pink and yellowy white.

'How has she even managed to *do* that?' whispered Zack, mildly disturbed.

'OK,' continued Cynthia, 'so Alex, Jonny and Zack, I've got you down in room two-oh-seven. Sophie, you'll be next door in room two-oh-eight . . . with Deanna.'

'YES!' shouted Deanna loudly, punching the air and almost instantly starting to hyperventilate. 'I can't wait, I can't wait, *I can't wait*!'

Sophie forced a weak smile, barely hiding her displeasure. Not that Deanna noticed.

'Hugo,' resumed Cynthia, 'and Salisbury and Charlie, you've been given the . . . Presidential Suite, it would seem – I'm guessing someone's parents must have phoned ahead to make that happen?'

'Yes!' Hugo agreed.

'It's a maximum of three per room, so Jackson and Mayhew . . .' She indicated the other two members of Class Act, who were slowly looking aghast as they registered the fact they would be in an *ordinary room*. 'You'll be in with Max, here.'

'Oh, cool,' Max said pleasantly. He held a paper bag out to the two tragic toffs. They looked at him as if he were a toddler innocently presenting them with a bit of roadkill. 'Would you like a jelly baby?'

Sophie twisted her body to face the others, looking a touch despairing. 'I guess I could just not *ever* go to bed, right?'

'Exactly, that's the spirit!' said Jonny, who was sure they'd find ways of sneaking Sophie next door with them if things got too desperate with Deanna. 'But, you never know, it might be the start of a blossoming friendship?' he added, trying not to laugh as he said it.

Sophie screwed up her face like she was eating a slug. Deanna may have softened a little, but an everlasting friendship – as Deanna seemed to be pushing for – still wasn't really on the menu.

Cynthia continued to fumble through several thousand pieces of paper, trying to fish out the relevant information on mealtimes, key allocation and what to do in the event of a hotel *inferno*.

'Well, I think that just about covers everything,' she said, finally taking off her glasses. 'Most importantly, have fun and please, please, please, if you do see anything *suspicious* . . .' Her face suddenly blanched as she aimed the final part of her speech towards the four at the back. 'Please do come and tell me about it first. Let's not have any repeats of . . . last time.* Well, what are you all waiting for? Let's make some magic!'

Steve gave a loud, explosive cheer, which caused Cynthia to fall back on the dashboard with such force that the airbag exploded out, catapulting her towards the back of the minibus with surprising grace. The only thing stopping her from a head-on collision was the soft cushioning of Max's snack bag that Zack had quickly and dexterously positioned between himself and the oncoming missile (aka Cynthia) just in time.

Yep, this was going to be a weekend *full* of surprises – Zack was sure of it!

---

* Cynthia is most probably remembering – though would rather be forgetting – the events of the last book in which – as well as meeting for the first time – our heroes become embroiled in a thrilling tale of theft, betrayal, skulduggery, royalty, pigeons and zipwiring. Oh – and magic. Obviously.

4

11 A.M.

The ivy-clad granite front of Tudor Towers loomed in front of them, and a damp sea wind gusted in their faces as they stepped down from the minibus. Now they were outside, they could see that the hotel was built right at the top of a slanting cliff. The door facing them was at ground level, but if you peered round the edge you saw that there were at least two more floors below, further down the slope towards the sea.

The inside of Tudor Towers did even less to calm their nerves than its Gothic exterior. The stark and airless reception was just bare tiles with no furniture apart from a large desk (which could well have been mistaken for a sarcophagus). Propped up in a chair behind it was what the four friends thought might be the training dummy used by apprentice undertakers at embalming class, or maybe even an Egyptian mummy borrowed from a museum, but in an inexplicably modern T-shirt. Fortunately it moved and turned out to be only the receptionist. Not that there's anything 'only' about receptionists – but you know what I mean.

Corridors led off from reception in three directions – left, right and straight ahead. The walls were a greying white, coldly lit like the lighting you might find in the freezer room at the back of a dodgy supermarket where the meat is kept, the marble floor causing their footsteps to pop and echo in odd directions as they all filed in.

'They reopened this place just for us. Isn't that nice?' said Cynthia breezily, consulting a plan of the hotel fixed to the wall and clearly trying to get her bearings.

'The real question,' whispered Zack ominously, 'is why was it ever closed?'

Jonny bit his lower lip theatrically, pulling a face. It was a very good point, though, he thought, his eyes travelling down one of the endless, deserted, bleach-white-tiled corridors that led off reception.

'OK, so the adults arrived yesterday,' he murmured, 'but where is everyone now?'

'They'll be here,' Sophie said confidently, deliberately keeping cool, but involuntarily feeling for the letter in her pocket once again.

'Now, everyone, line up so this adorable man can get you booked in and give you your keys, please,' Cynthia called. The junior magicians all shuffled into a rough sort of queue in front of arguably the least adorable man in the universe.

54

Deanna was first in line, followed reluctantly by Sophie. Deanna immediately sprang into Deanna-doing-a-trick mode, which to the uninformed observer could easily have looked like Deanna-having-a-fit mode: she leaped forward, pirouetted, shimmied her shoulders, rolled in a somersault and landed on both feet in front of the desk while at the same time reaching out for the massive rotary-dial phone that took up a large chunk of the desktop.

'I'll just . . .' she began brightly. The receptionist looked at her.

'Quickly use . . .' she said with a little less optimism. The receptionist didn't blink.

'*This?*' she squeaked in a small voice. The lack of sympathy in the receptionist's eyes could have dissolved galaxies. Deanna took her hand off the receiver as the receptionist silently handed over a pair of keys to room 208. Jonny and Zack grinned. Wow, this guy certainly knew how to put someone in their place!

Next up were Hugo, Salisbury and Charlie, who snatched the keys to the Presidential Suite as Hugo bleated out a smorgasbord of room requirements. The receptionist stared back like a velociraptor trying to work out which one of them to attack first, before getting bored and beckoning over those next in line.

Mayhew and Jackson forced a weak smile, while Max sucked happily on a lollipop he had produced from nowhere (his bag). He glanced up at his new roommates, flicked his wrist and a pair of lollipops appeared out of thin air (his bag again). Mayhew and Jackson glanced at each other, then down their noses at the sweets, both keeping their hands firmly behind their backs.

The queue trundled forward ... until finally it was Zack, Jonny and Alex's turn.

'Names?' the receptionist droned as they came up to the desk.

'Oh Lordy!' Jonny screamed a little too loudly. 'You're wearing our T-shirt!'

The receptionist glanced down. He was indeed sporting a Young Magicians T-shirt – something the four young people in question had had no idea existed until now.

The rainbow-coloured words **Young Magicians** were bursting through a cloud of stars above an outline of four unmistakable silhouettes.

'Yes,' he said as though he were talking about different types of cabbage, 'I'm your number-one fan. Names?'

Zack frowned.

'So you're our number-one fan, but you don't know our ...'

'Where did you even get that thing?' Sophie demanded.

'And why did no one tell us?' Jonny added.

'Oh ... dear ... yes ...' Cynthia looked embarrassed. 'You are just a tiddly bit famous in the magic world, I'm afraid, and some people want to, um ...'

'Cash in on us?' Zack finished.

'Yes,' said the receptionist, holding out room key 207 and rolling his eyes, like being part of a fanbase was a huge inconvenience.

'But people can't do that!' Alex protested in a shocked voice.

'I think you'll find they can, dear, and have,' Cynthia apologized. 'They're not using your faces, just an artist's impression of your outlines. I mean those silhouettes, legally speaking, could be anyone.'

'Plus, this one's home-made,' butted in the receptionist, before realizing how creepy that sounded and continuing with the justification: 'I have a degree in clip art.'

'Anyway, we must get on,' said Cynthia, handing the boys their key and leaving the receptionist as starstruck as a positively disinterested woodlouse meeting Justin Bieber for the fifteenth time. 'President Pickle will be formally opening the convention in the ballroom at eleven o'clock, and we mustn't be late because, because . . .' Cynthia hesitated. 'Well, you know what he's like!' She gave a short, sharp laugh before catching herself, her face suddenly darkening again. 'So, once you've found your rooms, get to the ballroom, quick as you can.'

'There's that look again,' whispered Sophie to the others as they headed off. 'I wonder what's bothering her?'

'I know what's bothering me,' Zack muttered. 'That T-shirt! What else are people selling with us on?'

'Don't we want to wait for your roommate?' Jonny teased. Sophie grabbed his sleeve and frogmarched him grinning down the corridor, heading away from reception. They stayed close together, hoping to avoid Deanna, who was now in hot pursuit, struggling noisily through the constricting corridor with her many suitcases like she was travelling with an entourage but had accidentally gone and packed them all by mistake.

'OI! Somebody help!' she shouted, which – for all it was irritating – certainly made the surroundings feel a little less intimidating, her petulant voice piercing through the sterile atmosphere like a cheerleading team arriving in Transylvania.

'What room are we in again?' said Jonny as they approached a lift at the end of the corridor, which looked like it hadn't been used since the 1950s and smelled rather like that too. On either side of it, staircases disappeared up to the next floor.

'Two-oh-seven,' answered Zack, entering the lift and scanning the various buttons, whose numbers shone out in a deep bloodcurdling red, as if they had been penned by Dracula on one of his days off. (Or maybe that should be nights off? Discuss!) He reached out to press the button for the second floor.

'Anyone would think you're trying to get away from me!' Deanna squealed behind them. She had caught up and now grabbed the metal scissor gate to prevent it from shutting, just in time from her point of view and just a moment too soon from the others'.

'Oh no, not at all!' Sophie managed to stammer, somewhat startled and spotting some of the old wildness back in Deanna's eyes. Her neck was sticking out towards them like a disgruntled turkey. 'I just . . . haven't seen these three in ages and . . .'

'Yes, well, you haven't seen *me* either!' retorted Deanna, still not quite getting it. 'Anyway,' she continued, 'all my bags aren't going to fit in there, so . . .?' She looked pointedly at Zack, Jonny and Alex in turn like *they* were the ones who needed to do something about this.

'Wow!' muttered Jonny, almost impressed by the sureness and audacity of the girl. Part of being a good magician was showing total, unswerving self-confidence and Deanna had that part down pat. It was just the actual, you know, *magic* part of being a magician she struggled with.

'Should we . . .?' Jonny extended one of his long fingers back out of the lift.

'It's fine. Go,' Sophie said eventually, half to herself and half to the others. 'I'll just give you a knock in five minutes, OK?'

Zack, Jonny and Alex dutifully nodded, filing out of the lift like a well-whipped chorus line. 'Five minutes *exactly*!' whispered Sophie as Jonny brushed past, not wishing to prolong her 'catch-up' with Deanna any longer than necessary.

'*Please let me press the button, please let me press the button, please let me press the button!*' squealed Deanna, piling in with her bags like this was the first time she'd ever been in a lift, or indeed the first time she'd ever pressed a button (at least since exiting the train doors earlier that morning).

'We'll see you in a bit then, roomies!' said Jonny playfully as Sophie and her pained expression vanished behind the clattering scissor gates.

'You'll pay for that later!' Zack teased. He imagined Sophie getting her own back by trying out some devious new hypnotic ploy when Jonny was least suspecting it. 'A hypnotist scorned and all that!'

'So . . . what *do* you think is bothering Cynthia?' asked Alex thoughtfully as the three of them began to lug their bags towards the barren-looking stairwell.

'I've no idea,' said Zack honestly. Now he was coming down from his irritation at the unauthorized YM™ merchandise, he had to admit that the question was tweaking his antennae for mystery. 'But something tells me it won't be long before we find out!'

'Excellent!' said Jonny, clapping his friend on the back, clearly hungry for another new adventure. 'Right then.' He put his foot on the first set of steps and raised his head up towards the countless landings. 'Race you to the top?'

Jonny bolted like a startled gazelle, leaping up the stairs three at a time, swinging his bag in one hand and using the other on the banister to hoist himself round the tight corners. Zack and Alex looked at each other in amusement, not moving a muscle.

'Let's just let him win,' said Zack quietly as Jonny called out a running commentary of his progress from above.

Alex nodded, smiling. Wow, it felt good to be back!

'JONNY WINS AGAIN! WHOOP WHOOP! THREE CHEERS FOR – Er, guys?'

Sophie knocked on the boys' bedroom door approximately four minutes and forty-five seconds later, having been granted early release from a distracted Deanna, who was now scouting their rather monastic bedroom for plug sockets in which she planned to charge her hair straighteners, her 'Shimmer and Shine Float & Sing Palace Friends' thing – whatever *that* was* – along with her 'Num Noms Lip Gloss Truck Playset'† which Sophie was sure didn't actually require charging, but she wasn't going to start asking questions now.

From there, the Young Magicians – glad to be a full pack again – navigated their way back down to reception, which appeared even more stark now that it was completely empty and silent, almost as if the pale floor had sucked up all possible sound along with any living occupants, apart from the somewhat dead-looking receptionist. For a hotel with a society convention going on, the place was eerily empty.

'OK . . .' Sophie looked at the different passages leading off in different directions. 'Cynthia said we need to get to the ballroom.'

* This actually exists!
† Yes, sadly this exists too!

'We could ask this guy?' Zack sauntered back over to the reception desk. The receptionist sat there, still in his T-shirt (which Zack scowled at), perfectly motionless, gazing blankly into the distance and totally failing to acknowledge the fact that Zack even existed.

Zack cleared his throat. 'Erm? Hello?'

The receptionist's eyes were still fixed on something only he could see in the distance. Zack tentatively waved a hand in front of him, wondering if he really might be seeing his first-ever dead body.

The man's head suddenly swivelled to face him.

'Just thinking happy thoughts,' he said, the same way a doctor might tell you that you only had twelve hours to live. 'Can I help you?'

'Er . . .' Zack began.

'Over here, Zack!' Sophie suddenly called, and Zack sidled gratefully away.

Sophie had found the hotel floor plan fixed to the wall. She saw immediately that you couldn't just follow your nose in Tudor Towers. The three upper floors, with the bedrooms, were comparatively easy. But the ground floor was a maze of offices and function rooms and places that weren't highlighted, presumably because the guests weren't meant to go there. Not that that would stop the Young Magicians!

Then a voice billowed out from somewhere unseen. 'Will you please stop telling me what I can and can't do, dear!'

It was a voice the four of them hadn't heard in a good while. A voice that took them straight back to their adventures six months ago. A voice filled with a strange mix of pomposity and cowardice.

'President Pickle!' whispered Alex, half excited, half scared. For even though the President of the Magic Circle had a lot to thank them for (restoring the state of the club's finances and getting them well in with the Queen, no less!) President Pickle had acted ambivalently to the news. As if this had somehow happened by chance and were to be temporarily celebrated – yes – but then quickly forgotten about to make way for more interesting and grander things that ideally didn't have a bunch of interfering kiddies at the centre of them.

'Hide!'

Zack leaped back into the middle of reception, before realizing there wasn't really any place to hide. Except for the large, tomblike reception desk, of course, but that had . . .

He blinked in surprise. The receptionist had vanished. *Oh well, what the hell!*

He made a dash for the desk. 'Come on!' The others glanced at each other, then piled in behind.

It wasn't like Zack felt they necessarily *needed* to hide; they were – after all – just looking for the ballroom. But then President Pickle had a way of making all children feel as if they were up to no good and, as far as Zack was concerned, that was all the prompting he needed. They'd lived up to President Pickle's somewhat skewed expectations thus far!

'I just wish you'd get some help, that's all,' said Cynthia's voice. The words tumbled out between little sniffs. The four looked at each other as they crouched uncomfortably behind the marble desk, Jonny folding his limbs into the space where the desk chair would usually go to prevent himself from being seen.

'Please stop all this incessant mollycoddling, dear. I'll be perfectly fine – we know everyone here. It will all blow over, I'm sure!'

They heard President Pickle stomp into the reception area and stop to catch his breath.

'But look . . .' Cynthia went on. They heard the sound of rustling paper. 'Have you seen the latest one? It only arrived this morning. You can see what it says . . .'

'Silly sausage scaremongering, that's all!' President Pickle snapped, followed by the unmistakable noise of paper being ripped up.

'To hell with all of it!' he announced. They heard him turn to go, footsteps squeaking on the tiled floor.

'Just let me see if they can do some digging,' Cynthia begged, following after him. 'They're as good a set of detectives as any!'

Zack gawped as the others looked at each other excitedly. Was Cynthia talking about *them*?

'Absolutely. No. Way!' shouted President Pickle, like the tolling of a grandfather clock. 'Even if it means never eating anything again, I won't turn to a bunch of . . . *children* for help. The whole idea is preposterous!'

Yep, thought Zack. *They certainly* are *talking about us.* They had been right to hide after all!

'But you *will* still be going ahead with . . . everything we discussed?' pressed Cynthia.

'Yes, yes. Now come along – we're going to be late!'

The four of them stayed low, waiting for President Pickle and Cynthia to disappear down one of the austere corridors. The reverberations of their heartbeats made them physically buzz with excitement.

'What on earth do you think *that* was all about?' said Sophie in a hushed voice, slowly peering over the edge of the desk and making sure the coast was completely clear.

'I don't know,' said Zack, 'but it sounds like President Pickle is in some kind of trouble and needs our help. Or that's what Cynthia thinks anyway.'

'Which he's blatantly *delighted* about!' added Jonny sarcastically, vaulting over the desk like a giant frog and giving a mock bow in appreciation of his efforts.

'Do you think . . . he's in *danger*?' asked Alex, who certainly wasn't the greatest fan of President Pickle, but didn't like the idea of harm befalling anyone. And what exactly did they mean by *still going ahead with everything*?

'Who knows?' said Zack. 'But it certainly explains why Cynthia's been looking so downbeat.'

Eight squares of torn-up paper were being blown by one of the hotel's many draughts across the floor. He scooped the pieces up in a couple of swift movements.

'Now let's see what this was all about . . .'

Zack crossed over to the desk and laid the bits out.

'That might be, um, private?' Alex ventured, though he crowded forward with the others to make out the writing on the paper jigsaw that Zack was deftly assembling.

'Cynthia obviously thinks it's something we can help with, so . . .'

Zack laid the final piece in place and they all leaned forward to read it.

It was eight lines of handwritten text.

Straight down the side.
See the old has-been?
Why does he still go on?
A sad relic of better days?
Enjoy the memories!
I doubt they will last much longer.
Deal yourself out, or we will.
Easy! See you at the banquet.

The four friends stared at it.

Sophie felt a shudder of spine-tingling excitement run through her. The words were simple, pretty even, like some old cheeky limerick, but there was an unnerving, malevolent tone behind the second-to-last line: *Deal yourself out . . . or we will*. What did *that* mean?

Zack tilted his head on one side to see if it read any differently the other way. It didn't.

'OK,' Jonny said, 'so someone's calling him a has-been and a relic . . . but that's – you know – kind of fair enough. It's hardly mega-evil. What's got Cynthia all het up?'

'I don't know, but we can worry about it while we walk,' Sophie said suddenly, checking her watch, 'because if we don't get a shift on we're going to be late.' She quickly scanned the plan of the hotel, tapping her fingers against the wall, and traced a course with her finger, instantly committing it to memory. 'OK, this way to the ballroom.'

Zack stuffed the bits of torn-up mystery into his pocket as the four of them trotted down the same corridor that President Pickle and Cynthia had taken. It ran along the edge of the building, and the rain outside began to lash against the thin windows so heavily that Alex could swear it was leaving pockmarks in the glass.

'Nice weather you have up here in *t'north*!' joked Jonny, overtaking Sophie with a grin.

'Almost as nice as you!' she said, catching his arm in a friendly way. 'This way!'

They swung left and plunged down a second corridor, right into the very heart of the building. Alex worked out that they must be behind the lift and the stairwell.

'Down here!'

They reached a small set of stairs and sped down to the level below. They had entered the part of Tudor Towers that was built further down the cliff. Even though they'd only descended one floor, Zack could swear the air felt danker. At the bottom they dashed down a further corridor, which appeared to widen out with every step.

How had Sophie managed to memorize the route? Alex was starting to grow a little breathless and was remembering the time they'd all got lost inside the cavernous Magic Circle library when they were last together.

'We're here!' said Sophie, slowing to a stop as they came out into a wide lobby and approached a wall studded with several sets of double doors. She struck a pose and gestured at the doors with both hands, like it was the denouement of a trick, which – given the amount Sophie had had to memorize in such a short space of time – it kind of was.

Jonny grabbed a set of handles and pulled them apart, causing a gust of warm, musty air to waft back into their faces along with a wall of chatter.

'Ah,' said Jonny, smiling. 'So *this* is where everyone is!'

The four Young Magicians had to squint as their eyes adjusted to the dazzling white light that made the ballroom shine like the inside of an industrial oven. It was a room of impressive proportions. Zack noted the distinct lack of windows on all sides and figured it was surrounded by other small rooms. At the opposite end was a raised stage, much wider than it was deep, whose maroon curtains drooped apologetically, not quite meeting in the middle. A large, oppressive, gold-crested lectern had been placed in front of the gap, almost like it was trying to make up for the lack of fabric.

In between the doors and the stage, the floor was filled with tables covered with white tablecloths, each one with four or five seats round it. The ceiling boasted a network of medium-sized chandeliers, all of which seemed to be switched to their maximum setting, making Alex feel a bit like they were stepping inside a giant microwave.

Sophie swept her eyes over the crowd and felt for the letter in her pocket again. Was its sender here? And would Sophie have the nerve to say hello if she was? Her heart was beginning to pound again.

She spotted several of the council members milling about at the front, all looking rather self-important as they busybodied between the hundreds of members present, handing out name badges and convention brochures and giving everyone polite nods of recognition, which really just hinted at acknowledgements of their own assumed superiority.

Zack suddenly got the feeling he was being stared at. It was the way two people were hovering in the corner of his vision. He glanced over at them quickly, but in another flicker of movement they chose that exact moment to look away.

Jonny smiled at the murmuring sea of grey hair beginning to take their seats. The only splash of colour came from the silk handkerchiefs being sporadically produced off to one side by Steve and Jane, who applauded and guffawed like they'd not performed this and a hundred other similar effects today a thousand billion times already – and seemingly all for their own amusement.

'Wow,' said Zack, spotting Cynthia and President Pickle up ahead, briskly navigating their way forward and inefficiently zigzagging between several rows of tables, 'President Pickle sure looks . . . different!'

It was true. Not that any of the four were particularly prone to passing judgement on anyone's appearance, but now they got their first proper look at him, without the reception desk in the way, the transformation from the last time they had seen the man was drastic.

Gone were the portly belly and quivering jowls that wobbled and creased every time he spoke. Gone were the rosy red face and big rubbery lips that caused him to look like an inflated schoolboy. Instead, presented before them was a shell of the man they once knew. It was as if someone had taken his vital organs and a huge amount of guts, cast them to one side and then tried to (unsuccessfully) readjust his skin and bones to fit the new shape. But you could see the dramatic change in President Pickle's drawn expression too, as if he carried with him a new heaviness – despite the weight loss. Like the change hadn't come about in a positive or natural way, but some kind of sacrifice had had to be made.

'Is he . . . unwell, do you think?' asked Alex, who could see the other members blatantly wondering the same thing as President Pickle journeyed towards the lectern at the front, their faces all brimming with concern.

'I mean, he wasn't *that* well before, to be fair,' said Jonny, remembering President Pickle's love of rich foods and fine wines, and not quite deciding which of the two versions was the more healthy-looking. 'Didn't he mention something about not eating?'

Cynthia had now turned to face the partly seated crowd, casting her eyes about the ballroom, hunting for the junior members who peppered the scene like flecks of accidental tissue left in a dark load of washing. Hugo and his flock didn't stand out much, blending in perfectly with the gloomy suited members' attire like they'd all got the same invite to the same funeral. Cynthia finally caught the eyes of the four at the back and gestured vigorously for them to take a seat.

'This way,' said Sophie, spotting a table with four empty spaces at the back of the room. Among the general chatty hubbub, as they made their way over, Zack's ears suddenly pricked up as he caught the phrase 'Young Magicians –' And then again, from another direction. He whipped his head round and stared about him. Was he imagining it, or were people now nudging each other and pointing them out?

At least he couldn't see anyone wearing another of those ghastly T-shirts . . .

Sophie suddenly stopped dead in her tracks.

'Whoa . . . Everything all right?' said Jonny, colliding with her melodramatically.

'It's her!' said Sophie, her voice cracking slightly and the colour draining from her face, which would have been a cause for concern – especially for someone as stoic as Sophie – save for the simultaneous smirk creeping up both of her cheeks. 'It's Belinda Vine!'

'Who?'

'Belinda Vine! I mean, of course I knew she'd be here, but actually seeing her . . .'

'Who's Belinda Vine?' Zack asked casually. Sophie stared at him.

'*Who's Belinda Vine?* Didn't you check the programme before we came?'

Zack shrugged.

'I'd have come to this even if it was a non-stop weekend of Deanna trying out new routines, providing it meant we all got to be back together. So this Belinda's pretty cool then?'

Sophie shook her head helplessly. 'She's a legend!'

Belinda Vine! It wasn't just that she was clever, talented, striking in her own distinctive way . . . On the other side of the Atlantic, Belinda had pulled herself way up from her humble origins and blazed her own trail in the male world of American magic – something that Sophie admired greatly! And, as if it weren't enough being a lone female in this community of mostly geriatric men, her performances were always impeccable and frequently floored even the most astute audiences. She'd even been known to fool some of the best minds in magic at conventions across the world with her mind-reading act, which was so brilliantly devised and so beautifully performed and so tantalizingly impossible that it could almost have passed as the real thing. Indeed, despite watching and re-watching countless performances of Belinda's act on the web, Sophie *still* had no clue how she achieved some of her mental miracles.

Then, just a year or so ago, Belinda Vine had announced that she was crossing the Atlantic: '*My work is done back home and a girl needs fresh challenges to stay on top.*

Look out, men (and women!) of Europe, Belinda is on her way!' And here she was, just fifty metres away at the other side of the room, laughing heartily, looking stunning in her perfectly fitted red dress, her long ginger hair exploding from the top of her head and waving gracefully down her back – almost like she was underwater – as she swung her head to and fro to take in the room, perfectly at ease.

'And she wrote to me,' Sophie went on. She pulled the letter from her pocket. 'Care of the Magic Circle. She said she'd heard of me and was looking forward to meeting me . . .'

'Cool!' Jonny was actually impressed. 'So what's the problem?'

'Now I'll actually have to *meet her*!' whispered Sophie as they continued towards their table, her legs feeling a little squishy.

'You know, I didn't have you down as the starstruck type,' said Jonny, enjoying the moment, not used to seeing Sophie so overcome.

'Why's that?' said Sophie, as quick as a flash, and sounding a bit more like her usual self. 'Because I didn't react like this when I first met you?'

Zack and Jonny laughed loudly as they finally sat down, causing a few of the ageing members at the tables in front to turn round – or at least try, their necks creaking slowly – as they cast sour looks at the four, shaking their heads like broken nodding dogs.

'Thanks so much for having us!' Zack said genially to the disapproving audience members, with an elfish twinkle in his eye. Ah, it was good to be back.

Alex elbowed him lightly as he spotted Cynthia glaring over at them from the front, biting her lower lip, clearly desperate for her juniors to be on their best behaviour and not to attract any unwanted attention. Or at least none of the naughty negative kind.

So, for once, Zack obeyed. They'd made it this far – making mischief could wait, he reasoned. Well, for the time being, at least! He straightened himself up, straining his neck over the hundreds of bobbing heads patiently waiting for things to begin.

A spritely middle-aged fellow, dressed like a teacher who was trying a bit too hard to be cool – jeans, trainers, a T-shirt and baseball cap (hugely unnecessary!) – got up on the stage and gambolled over to the lectern. He was wearing a gigantic sticky label that named him ERIC DIVA.

'Well, what a pleasure, what a treat, what a delight, what *fun* it is to see you all!' he crooned into the microphone. 'People from every nation, gathered here together!'

Sophie glanced around. Every *nation*? *Really?* she thought. Despite some promising 'initiatives' (as Council liked to refer to them) at the Magic Circle, the society was still as infamous for its lack of diversity as it was for its lack of gender equality. Sophie sat back in her seat, bemused.

A few of the councillors cheered, shooting glances at the rest of the membership who all joined in on autopilot, many of them not really knowing what was going on.

'And obviously just to say, on a more personal note, how proud it makes me feel – as this year's convention organizer – to have *so many* youngsters in the crowd!'

'*So many* is a bit of an exaggeration, isn't it?' said Jonny in a low voice, trying not to move his lips. Cynthia gave the man a polite nod, probably wishing for him not to dwell on the matter, aware that – for the vast majority of members – the news of juniors being present (apart from the famous Young Magicians, who to some minds were like honorary old members) was probably as unwelcome as a cat at a dog's hen do. And maybe even in some cases the first time certain members were receiving the news at all. In spite of this, Eric Diva continued.

'Indeed, let it be sung from the rafters that these junior members are the future of magic and we welcome you, one and all. Especially the famous four at the back!'

He suddenly gave a jubilant wave to Zack, Sophie, Jonny and Alex, causing the entire room to effectively swivel on its axis as everyone twisted and turned – some more noisily than others, all at random speeds – to get a good look at the Young Magicians, who now sat looking and feeling a little like rare pieces at an exhibition, not quite knowing how to react. Even Jonny, with all his casual bravado, only managed the smallest of cursory waves. The room slowly heaved its way back to facing the front as Eric Diva continued to beam at the four friends.

'*Big, big, big, big, big* fan!' he mouthed, and brought his hands together towards his chest, forming a heart shape, holding it there for a disconcerting amount of time and causing Jonny to let out a giggle like a tickled toddler – this guy was a hoot!

Sophie was withholding judgement. Who exactly was Eric Diva? He certainly wasn't present at the Magic Circle six months ago. And now, just like that, he was in a position of responsibility. That must have taken some serious greasing . . .

'Anyway,' continued Eric, addressing the whole room once more, 'you'll be seeing a lot more of me over the course of the weekend, I'm sure, so please don't be afraid to say hello!'

'Well, I'm already a *bit* afraid!' Zack joked quietly, flashing the others a grin.

'Anyway, let's get things formally under way, shall we? Ladies, gentlemen, *youngsters*! Please welcome your president and mine: Mr President Edmund Pickle!'

The council members at the front started a long, sonorous handclap. The other members began to join in, Cynthia motioning for all the juniors to do the same, like she was slowly egging them on. The clapping began to intensify, the pace quickening dramatically as President Pickle slowly clambered up on to the stage and headed towards the lectern, his body still somewhat tense and so unbelievably pinched.

He finally faced the front, causing some of the more bootlicking members to stand and bow needlessly as he nodded at them all, though still with a whiff of uncharacteristic nervousness, Sophie noted. Slowly he raised and lowered his arm like he was conducting some giant orchestra. The crowd began to diminuendo into silence. Like the eerie calm before an execution . . .

President Pickle looked out over the crowd, his eyes roaming from person to person before sweeping towards the back of the room, darting up into the corners of the ceiling and then back towards the front, checking out the wings either side before focusing on the lectern he was now leaning on rigidly, gripping the sides like a terrified vicar at a pulpit. He seemed to mumble something to himself before summoning the reserve to stand up straight, pushing out his chest like a well-groomed yet evidently malnourished pheasant, a touch of the regal returning to him.

Ah yes, thought Zack, trying to work out exactly what was troubling the man just by looking at him, *this is a bit more like the President Pickle we know and – ahem – love.*

'Welcome to the Annual Convention! A place for us to discuss ideas, to learn, grow and consolidate as a society, to celebrate our rich and bountiful history and to stamp out any bad blood. Most importantly of all, we are gathered this weekend to elect the officials who will carry us into a new and prosperous magical year. I hope you are all looking forward to it as much as me . . .'

He trailed off, confronted with the horrible possibility that maybe he was right, and that everyone *was* looking forward to it as much as him, which was to say not at all. Not in the slightest. Not this weekend.

'Anyhow . . .' he murmured, trying to find his groove. 'Another year, another convention! How time flies. It doesn't seem like five minutes ago that I . . . that I . . .' The man suddenly lost his train of thought, fumbling for a piece of paper in his inner jacket pocket before righting himself again and remembering what he was saying. 'That I stood here last time.'

A few of the members grumbled a strange appreciation of how quickly the years seemed to pass by nowadays, like a whole twelve months could go by unnoticed by just taking the briefest of afternoon naps . . . and then it was back to the Annual Convention!

'Now a few of you will have noticed my – er – my change in appearance,' said President Pickle, clearly trying to sound upbeat. 'And some of you have even been so kind as to point it out and ask after my health, so I ought to set matters straight . . .'

The four sat up, wondering if they would be given a clue as to what was so evidently unsettling the man. They had heard him insisting to Cynthia that everything was fine. But now?

'So let me assure you that it's only a temporary state of affairs while . . . Well, no one needs to know about that!'

He cast a look over at Cynthia, who was massaging her hands so vigorously that Zack could swear he could see steam rising from them.

'It does mean, sadly, that I'm off the booze, and the food. Which is . . . well, a *huge* shame. I hear this place does a marvellously gloopy and exquisitely sticky sticky toffee pudding! But no, not for me this weekend, thank you very much!'

He laughed awkwardly, before trailing off. Was it Jonny's imagination or was President Pickle starting to get emotional?

'I can't even remember the last time I was allowed sticky toffee pudding.' President Pickle's eyes seemed to mist over, like he was in some strange trance, his mouth starting to droop, heavy with saliva. 'Lettuce is what I get now. Scrubbed within an inch of its life, all pale green and tasteless, wilting and silly. Not even allowed to cover it in bacon and cheese just in case someone has p–'

Cynthia suddenly coughed loudly enough to snap President Pickle out of his food dream or whatever this was. He mumbled something to himself again, clearly in two minds about . . . something. Sophie looked over at Cynthia, who had now locked eyes with her husband, clearly trying to impress something upon him, nodding tightly, her hands held closely together over her neck and chin. If it wasn't for Cynthia's manner, Sophie could still have believed that this was just President Pickle feeling sorry for himself over a touch of indigestion: he could – after all – raise self-pity to a new art form. But, with Cynthia behaving as she was, Sophie knew something was desperately awry.

President Pickle stared back at his wife, chewing his lower lip, evidently completely at sea and still incomprehensibly, mindlessly hungry. He cleared his throat again, unfolding the piece of paper he'd taken from his pocket, pushing down on the creases to stop it from closing, taking his time . . . making a point.

'So . . . as many of you are aware, I have been president of this magical society for nearly a quarter of a century.'

A few of the crowd began to applaud, but President Pickle silenced them with a waft of his hand, like Dumbledore turning out a light.

'Many people have joked – often inappropriately – that you get less than that for murder. The truth is, twenty-five years is *such* a long time that that joke no longer applies any more.'

'Sounds like he's saying goodbye?' said Zack. 'Or giving in to something.'

'Or some*one*,' offered Sophie, her mind ticking.

The thought of President Pickle giving in to anything that he didn't want to didn't really compute. And when he did – like letting younger members in – then he certainly wasn't one to make a public affair out of it.

'No way!' said Jonny, clapping his hand over his mouth to stop the sound from coming out too loudly.

Alex shifted in his seat as he craned his neck even higher. Was President Pickle really about to announce his retirement? For the Magic Circle that would be like ... like ... He couldn't imagine what it would be like. A bit like the Queen announcing she was stepping down, maybe, and handing her crown over to one of the corgis.

Sophie spotted Eric Diva poised like a concerned parent off to the side, biting his fingernails. What on earth was going on?

President Pickle continued. 'So it would seem that there are *some* who believe twenty-five years is more than long enough ... That I should now fizzle out and away like some defunct firework and pass into the realm of past-presidency.'

He took another long deep breath while staring down at the paper still held firmly between his fingers.

'And I agree – to a certain extent. It has been quite an impressive innings, even if I do say so myself ...' The man paused for an obscenely long amount of time. '*However*.' The whole room suddenly shifted as one. 'I will not be bullied, beaten or broken. I will not bow down and beg. I am the President of the Magic Circle and it is I and only I who decides when my time is up. Do you hear me?'

President Pickle had started to bellow as the blood began to drain from Cynthia's face. *No! No, no, no!* Hadn't those horrible letters made it very clear that he must step *down*? That if he didn't go ahead with it, there would be *dire consequences*? But President Pickle was now on a roll, cheered on by the growing army of supporters in the crowd who were now whooping loudly, like he was leading them into battle.

'Once a president, always a president, that's what I say! Anything else just takes the pickle!'

Zack, Sophie, Jonny and Alex looked at each other, not really knowing what to say. Evidently Cynthia had expected her husband to be announcing his retirement from the Magic Circle's top job. And, by the looks of it, President Pickle had been partway towards making that decision too. But then – for whatever reason – something had changed his mind. He was here to stay. Or at least not going to go down without a fight!

But you could sense it a mile off, Zack thought. Despite the seeming overwhelming support and overzealous cheering, dotted somewhere between the slight glances between council members and the loud coughs emanating from the crowd – though a lot of that could arguably have been the flu – was the whiff of disapproval and disappointment. The thought that perhaps, had the man stepped down, something or someone better might come along. But *who* exactly that person or persons might be was – as yet – unclear. And what exactly did the president mean by saying he *wouldn't be bullied*? Was someone forcing his hand? Zack rubbed his left eyebrow thoughtfully.

The clapping took a second to spread from the stuffy Pickle fanbase, who were evidently delighted by what they were hearing, to the corners of the room, like a semi-toxic virus, growing and mutating all the time . . . Some choosing to whoop, whistle and cheer if their vocal cords could still hack it, others resorting to a wheezy moaning noise, which could easily have been mistaken for disapproval if it weren't for the beaming smiles the sound was emanating from.

But there was one thing about the whole affair that was abundantly clear, and the four Young Magicians at the back of the room clocked it a mile off. One person in the room was the very last to start showing his appreciation, even though he was trying so desperately hard to prove otherwise.

Eric Diva.

'Anyway, there you go, nothing to see here!' blathered President Pickle into the microphone, putting an end to the commotion all of a sudden. 'I now declare the sixty-eighth Annual Magic Circle Convention open – have fun!'

He magicked his infamous gavel out of his reedy midriff and slammed it down on to the gold lectern with such force that sparks sprayed out, as if to prove beyond any reasonable doubt that there was still life in the old boy yet. President Pickle chanced a fleeting glance at his dear wife, who had now turned the colour of wallpaper paste. He grinned at her sheepishly: a strained, haphazard, *oh-hell-what-have-I-just-done?* type of grin.

Indeed, President Pickle, thought an ominous somebody in the crowd. *What. Have. You. Just. Done?*

5

12 P.M.

The four Young Magicians stayed in their seats as the hordes of members trudged out of the ballroom on the hunt for yet another giant mug of tepid tea and perhaps a couple of stale Viennese swirls. That was what magic conventions were *really* about, right?

Sophie spotted Belinda Vine in conversation with a couple of adults, nearer to the exit than she was; it was impossible to get to quickly without making a scene by pushing her way through the people in between. She had just plucked up the courage to try and make contact when Belinda reached the door and left the room.

President Pickle climbed down from the stage like a tiptoeing stick insect, which is a description no one would ever have thought of applying to him before.

He's so thin! The four friends weren't the only ones to think it.

President Pickle moved straight over to his wife who looked like she might a) shout something rather rude at him, b) hug him despairingly or most likely c) a repetitive combination of the two, but in no predictable order. They moved over to a side door, along with the other council members.

Eric Diva was the last of them to go. Just before disappearing, he turned back to the room, grinned at the Young Magicians, clicked his fingers, winked and gave them a double thumbs up with index fingers stretched straight out. It was probably well intentioned, but it also looked a little like he was pretending to shoot them.

'Well, that all seemed rather . . . eventful!' said Jonny as the crowd began to thin, though not quite as drastically as President Pickle. 'Do you think that happens every year?'

'Or maybe just once every twenty-five years,' Sophie said, still trying to work out what they had just witnessed.

'He's . . . he's certainly hiding *something*,' said Alex, though still none the wiser as to exactly what.

'Well, in that case, I suspect it's only a matter of time before we find out!' Zack exclaimed optimistically. 'But, in the meantime, where shall we explore first?' He picked up one of the convention brochures and started flicking through it. 'Oh wow, so it looks like this friend of yours, Belinda Vine, is headlining the Gala Show tonight!'

Sophie casually plucked the programme from Zack's hands and not so casually scanned it hungrily, wide-eyed.

MAGIC CIRCLE

68th ANNUAL CONVENTION

11 a.m. Opening address by President E. Pickle, Ballroom

12 p.m. Dealers' Hall set-up.
Seminar: '"What about the poos?" The best animals to hide in your clothes, and where'
Buffet Lunch, Montpellier Room (junior members, Syd Little Memorial Pantry)

1 p.m. Dealers' Hall and Exhibition open.

2 p.m. Seminar: 'Privacy implications of mind-reading and body language'

3 p.m. Auction

4 p.m. Interactive workshop: 'Ways to make your assistant disappear – whether they like it or not!'

5 p.m. Grand Convention Banquet, Montpellier Room

6 p.m. Seminar: 'Bullet catching – the pros and cons of using live rounds'

7 p.m. Gala Show, Ballroom – featuring Belinda Vine!

7 a.m. Breakfast, Montpellier Room

8 a.m. Annual General Meeting, Ballroom

9 a.m. Dealers' Hall and Exhibition open.
Seminar: 'Insurance cover for smashed watches and other breakages'

10 a.m. Seminar: '"But that's offensive!" Arcane stage rituals in a multi-faith society'

11 a.m. Interactive workshop: 'Stage patter for the tongue-tied and terminally shy'

12 p.m. Seminar: 'How not to get burned: legal advice for the unfortunate assistant'

'I think our wonderful friend Sophie here may be in lurve!' Jonny joked, making odd, slurpy, smoochy noises that reminded Alex of the sound guinea pigs sometimes make (sometimes). 'So what's the big deal with Belinda? Why have we never heard of her before?'

'That's not her style,' Sophie said immediately. She knew that Belinda was a magician's magician who pretty much exclusively performed at conventions like this. It was where she was at her best, turning the tables on traditional methods, leaving well-respected magicians floored by her devious techniques that she never revealed. Ever. Many magicians regularly sought to share their secrets – often for very large sums of money – but not Belinda Vine. There was an intrinsic purity about her and her magic, so that anything less would be seen as selling out. And it was this clarity, this depth of character and commitment to her craft that was the real fuel behind Sophie's infatuation. The lady was a bona fide superstar in Sophie's eyes. If Sophie wanted a role model, Belinda was it.

'Shall we check out the Dealers' Hall maybe?' asked Alex, his eyes lighting up like a pair of fireflies at the prospect of a hall *full* of freshly printed books, tricks, props, magical apparatus and who knew what else!

'Well, it doesn't *technically* open until two p.m., Alex,' said Zack, pretending to sound quite teacherly, 'but – then again – things like that haven't stopped us before, have they?!'

Zack bounded up from his seat as the others quickly followed, racing out of the ballroom and into the lobby-like area at the back, their faces beaming.

'Anyone have a clue where the Dealers' Hall might be?' said Jonny, looking for some sign, but only seeing more endless grey-white walls spreading out at every angle. There was no point following the crowd – they were all heading in different directions.

'Sure, let me just consult my map,' said Sophie casually, closing her eyes and placing a hand to her forehead.

'And what map might that be, Sophie dearest?' asked Jonny, bemused, suspecting Sophie must be having him on. 'Oh . . . wow.' He remembered the intent way she had stared at the floor plan in reception for a couple of seconds, and suddenly realized. 'Did you genuinely memorize the *whole* thing?'

'*Cooooooooool!*' said Zack, mightily impressed by the speed at which Sophie must have committed the plan to memory.

'Yep! This way!' said Sophie suddenly, opening her eyes and going back into the ballroom. 'Even better – I memorized a short cut!'

'I mean . . . how . . .?' Alex asked as the four went back through the double doors into the ballroom, weaving their way through the network of connected seats towards the front.

'I've been studying memory palaces,' Sophie explained as she clambered up on to the stage, through the welcoming

88

and perfectly child-sized gap in the curtains. 'It's a way of committing really complicated stuff to your memory and remembering it just like that.'* She clicked her fingers. 'This way!'

She headed out through the stage-right fire exit officiously marked QUIET! (UNLESS IN THE EVENT OF A FIRE, IN WHICH CASE SHOUT 'FIRE!').

'You'll have to show us how to do that,' said Zack as the four of them skipped down a flight of dimly lit concrete stairs before emerging into what was pretty much an identical backstage area, just one floor below.

Sophie smiled. 'When we've all got a moment, no problem. And here we are!'

The Young Magicians peered through the stage curtains, conscious of the chitter-chatter coming from the other side. The Dealers' Hall wasn't officially open yet, but the dealers themselves were there, still setting up, chatting, talking shop, sharing stories about the latest rip-off gadget they were all happy to bad-mouth, but even more happy to sell to any semi-interested punter.

What met the four's eyes was a glorious sight, an undeniable feast for the curious eyes of any aspiring magician.

* Memory palaces – also known as the Method of Loci. This is a way of enhancing your memory by visualizing information instead of just trying to remember stuff. Be warned: 'loci' is Latin for 'places' and nothing to do with Norse gods. Sadly.

The hall was pretty much the same size and shape as the ballroom, one floor up. But, whereas you could at least see the ballroom floor upstairs, here all that could be made out was a vast grid of tables and stands with a criss-crossing web of paths running through it, barely the width of an adult, like a giant snake slithering across the room, trying to find its way out.

Bunting with fluttering flags hung from corner to corner and, if there weren't quite the 195 countries Sophie had been thinking of, they could see there were a good few nations present. Each table and stall displayed a collection of magical apparatus, a vivid mix of props, cards, books, DVDs, old posters, large colourful boxes with mannequins positioned resplendently inside, silk scarves, and banners with freshly printed logos, advertising personal tuition, discounts on rare and bewildering gadgets, and free top hats with every purchase.

All four gasped in awe at the amount of magic on display. It was as if they had dived into a living, breathing magic catalogue. Alex mentally ticked off the various pieces he recognized: cups and balls, chop cups, dice-stacking cups, ghost tubes, dove pans, sympathetic silks, mirror boxes, sliding die boxes, Gozinta boxes – and that was just on one table! Then there was the raft of stuff he hadn't even heard of before. In fact, in many ways, this set of artefacts was even more interesting than the first – who knew what these gadgets and gizmos could accomplish?! Not that Alex had a lot of money to spend. But he had made a point of saving up as soon as Cynthia had been in touch with the news that junior members were going to be allowed to attend the Annual Magic Convention, which promised a hall – an entire *hall* – dedicated to selling magical equipment.

Jonny, Sophie and Zack looked at Alex fondly, enjoying the delighted expression on his little round face. Much like the vast underground library in the bowels of the Magic Circle headquarters back in London, this was a place you might gladly and legitimately lose yourself in.

Then, one by one, their faces fell. A woman was pinning up the backdrop on her stall over to one side, next to a table covered with a white cloth. The backdrop was a large poster showing a design they all recognized because they had last seen it on the T-shirt being modelled by Mr Taste himself, the hotel receptionist.

On the table were piles of more T-shirts and rolled-up posters, presumably the same as the one on the backdrop.

'They're selling the things!' Zack hissed.

'Cool!' Jonny whispered, and clocked the outraged looks from his friends. 'I mean, that's absolutely disgraceful! We are definitely going to have words.' He smiled. 'Anyway, my grand–' He stopped himself, quickly shaking his head like he was trying to physically jiggle off the thought.

'It's all right to still think of him, Jonny,' said Sophie softly.

'Absolutely,' said Zack. 'Just because of the way things turned out doesn't mean you and him didn't have *some* good times.'

Jonny thought for a few seconds before answering. It was true, he thought: his grandfather had fallen from grace, but that didn't rewrite history. That didn't suddenly eradicate all the times they'd shared a special moment or the times they'd laughed together, or the times Ernest had shown Jonny something truly magical with that inimitable twinkle in his eye as the coin vanished, or the cane he was using to prop himself up disintegrated in a haze of glitter and confetti, or the time he joyfully ridiculed the way large parts of the magic industry had gone nowadays.

'I was about to say,' said Jonny slowly, 'that Granddad always thought half the stuff magic dealers sold at conventions was a load of overpriced claptrap. *His* words – obviously!'

'Oh well, he was certainly right about that,' said Zack, with another dark look at the Young Magicians merchandise stall. He peered back through the curtains and spotted a pair of colour-changing sunglasses that had about as many zeroes etched on to the price tag as there were promises that the trick could 'be performed surrounded' and didn't use electronics, magnets, fine wire, palming or indeed any skill. Yeah, right!

Then . . .

'Oh, now *there's* a face I haven't seen in a while,' said Zack all of a sudden. Alex followed his friend's gaze towards a rather ostentatious stand with a banner in glowing letters reading DAVENPORT'S MAGIC STUDIO. A hobbit-like man with heavy bags under his eyes was setting out his wares, still with the same haunted stare as when they'd last encountered him: Alton Davenport. Alex shuddered, remembering the last time they'd seen the man. It had been only moments before creepy Henry, a key figure in the Crown Jewels conspiracy – SEE BOOK ONE! – had sprung out on them beneath Charing Cross Station, apparently beaten up and disfigured. Alex shook the unfortunate image out of his mind.

'It'll be nice to wind him up again!' Jonny whispered.

'Oh, but I bet there are some real gems to be found hidden among the rubbish!' said Sophie, a little too loudly, and causing some of the dealers to raise their heads. She ducked, hiding herself behind the saggy curtains that smelled of a decaying Santa's Grotto.

'What I meant to say,' said Sophie, a little more quietly, 'was take a look at the stuff on *that* stand, for example.' She nodded towards a small, slightly rundown kiosk off to the side of the room, less gaudy than the rest, and appearing a little out of place among the more commercial stalls being set up. It had the Stars and Stripes flying from a small flagpole.

'If it's proper and authentic stuff you're looking for, well, you can practically smell the history coming from over there.'

'Sorry, that might have been me,' said Jonny, pretending to look sorry save for the huge grin dolloped across his face and the fact that he never missed an opportunity to make a joke about letting off accidental smells.

It was true, though – the kiosk in question seemed to have been dressed in original red drapery with yellow tassels, almost like an oversized Punch and Judy stand. On the sides of the tent-like structure hung several posters, each showcasing a different Edwardian magician, almost like this was a portal to some bygone era. Even the table positioned in the centre of the stall looked as if it had been plucked from another world. On top of it sat a rich collection of magical curiosities – collapsible birdcages, wands and watch-winders – that seemed to shimmer in the light, enticing the four of them in.

'Wow,' said Zack, squinting slightly to try and focus. 'Is that an original poster of Ron and Nancy Spencer?'

'Who?' said Jonny, racking his brains and jutting out his lower lip – he'd certainly heard those names mentioned to him before, perhaps by Ernest one time, but why they were such important figures in magic history presently escaped him.

'Only one way to find out!' said Sophie suddenly, crouching low and moving swiftly through the curtain and down on to the hall floor, successfully squeezing under one of the tables before beckoning to the others.

Jonny, Alex and Zack followed slightly more clumsily. Jonny attempted to 'cascade' himself off the raised stage like a slinky spring before commando-rolling his way into Sophie's hiding place to join the others, like a rather inefficient game of Sardines. Then it was on across the hall floor, out of sight, their only points of reference now being

94

the legs of the table stands that swamped the room and the legs of the dealers milling about chirpily, excited by the prospect of selling their favourite tat.

The Young Magicians crept quietly under the stretch of tables towards the aged kiosk at the end. The poster that Zack had pointed out now was coming into sharper focus as they approached.

Alex studied it as they crawled closer. It was not unlike some of those they'd seen six months ago that adorned the corridor walls outside the entrance to the Grand Theatre of the Magic Circle. It was easily as tall as Alex – a lot of people would say that's not hard, but the point is it was unusual for a poster – the canvas slightly fraying at the edges but otherwise in wonderful condition. The price to own the rare piece was hidden from view, or perhaps deliberately absent so that one had to 'enquire within', which was often code for 'it's highly unlikely you can afford it, please *don't* enquire and leave NOW'.

At the very centre of the poster was a lady in an evening gown – presumably the titular Nancy – who stood beneath an immaculate proscenium arch, flooded with light, her body facing away from the audience, as she held a graceful hand up to her forehead. To her side and slightly more downstage was (presumably) Ron, a tall, confident man with a splendid handlebar moustache dressed in finest top hat and tails. One of his arms gestured towards the magicians milling around; the other held a small trinket, perhaps a locket, which he

was staring at intently as if he were willing it to come to life and speak.

'I wish we'd been around to see stuff like this,' whispered Sophie, basking in the shadow of the poster that really did reek of some brilliant magical past.

'Sorry, who exactly *were* Ron and Nancy Spencer?' asked Jonny, trying to fathom exactly what was happening in the poster.

'Oh, only the greatest mentalist couple that ever lived!' said Sophie. 'They travelled the world with their Minds in Harmony telepathy act.'

'Telepathy?' enquired Alex. 'You mean talking mind to mind?'

Sophie shuffled into a small vacant spot beneath the neighbouring table, crossing her legs like one might at the beginning of a story. She smiled at the three boys who had now huddled even closer together in front of her, eager to know more.

'Are you sitting comfortably? Then I shall begin!'

Alex, Zack and Jonny sat – less comfortably, in Jonny's case, with his knees round his ears – and let Sophie's words sink in, each of them picturing the scene in their own way. Feel free to do the same. Ready? Then we shall begin.

It is 1926. The occupants of the Grand Theatre of the Magic Circle sat in stunned silence. How had she known? How had the legendary Nancy Spencer perfectly described the small object that her husband Ron had borrowed from an audience member and now had concealed in his hand from a considerable distance away? How had she *known*? And in such inexplicable detail too, like she was seemingly seeing the object through her husband's eyes. As if the two of them had some kind of *telepathic* connection.

Of course there were many who didn't believe that Nancy had been registered as blind at birth, aware that this made the act even more impossible, thinking that this was just a brilliantly constructed piece of backstory with which the dynamic duo could sell their act to even the surliest of sceptics. But no, it was true: doctors, physicians and opticians from

97

across the globe would examine Nancy's eyes live onstage every night, many travelling thousands of miles just for the chance of finding some evidence of deception. They had all been forced to confirm the simple and sad truth of it: Nancy was completely and utterly blind, and no amount of conjuring could change that grim reality.

Still, even had Nancy her eyesight, that couldn't explain the fact that – despite facing the other way, and with no mirrors present and without the benefit of some hidden camera or other (not that the occupants of the Grand Theatre of the Magic Circle in 1926 knew about those futuristic devices yet!) – she somehow knew *exactly* what object her dear husband held in his hands. Even when he had journeyed way up into the gods, making use of the theatre's newly installed amplification system so he could still be heard, leaving Nancy standing alone onstage – all eyes focused on her perfect frame – even *then* she was able to speak in unfathomable detail of the object clasped tightly between her husband's fingers. An engagement ring, a book – by Dickens, the red bookmark currently placed at page 372 – a locket containing a picture of a lady named Anne who is standing next to a pony, a small key connected to a purple purse . . .

And so it went on, until audiences began to believe that perhaps the two really *did* share a telepathic gift, one that defied the laws of physics and nature – for there was no other explanation. Surely. Of course, the magicians in the audience thought they had it sussed, that Ron and Nancy were somehow communicating via code, or that he was able to secretly get the message to her by means of some special device. But then what about those times when Ron merely picked up an object and didn't say a single word? No, that had baffled even the most well-versed magicians of the day.

*Stooges,** others would cry – surely everyone who handed Ron an object was in on it, and Nancy was just recalling some predetermined order of objects from memory? But no, anyone – literally *anyone* among the hundreds packed into the theatre, and they came in their droves – could hand Ron an object, and Nancy would get it right every single time. There was no identifiable solution. And, since Ron and Nancy had both passed away some time ago, their beautiful secret – if indeed there ever *was* a secret to be learned – had been buried with them and now only existed in stories like these. Trapped and extraordinary – almost undoubtedly how they would have wanted. That is, until someone worked it out!

Alex, Zack and Jonny sat, enraptured, as Sophie finished off her tale. None of them had heard anything like it! And to think such brilliant magic was being performed nearly a hundred years ago. Alex liked to imagine that, if Ron and Nancy Spencer were still alive today, they would have

* Stooges: the unsung heroes of so many magic tricks. To everyone else they may look like unsuspecting members of the public, having magic performed before them. But no, they are in on it up to their necks and know exactly what's going on. They are part of the misdirection to fool you, the *real* unsuspecting member of the public. Apart from YOU, that is, dear reader . . . who is much too smart to be taken in by such buffoonish witchcraft.

approved and enjoyed the company of the Young Magicians and their passion for bold, brilliant and bewildering magic.

'I know this might sound like stating the obvious,' said Jonny, his head cocked to one side to avoid lifting the table he was sitting gawkily beneath and giving their hiding place away, 'but I really do *love* magic!'

'I'd love to know how they did it!' said Zack, clearly already trying to find a weak spot in the description, searching for a solution but finding none.

'Well, no one's sussed it in a hundred years, so good luck, mate!' said Sophie, winking.

Surely Sophie knew better than to goad a magician like Zack with something like this! Solving unsolvable magical mysteries was Zack's bread and butter. But then even Zack, with his wickedly divergent brain, couldn't claim to have any clue as to how Ron and Nancy Spencer had given the impression of harbouring some telepathic power, especially back then when the best modern technology had to offer was a rudimentary microphone – no keyhole cameras or smartphones with retina HD displays allowed here, thank you very much. Yet hadn't there been *something* in Sophie's description of the effect that had stood out to him for some reason, that hinted – as always – that they were perhaps looking in precisely the wrong place for a solution . . .?

A *bing-bong* sound, like that which might indicate the seat-belt sign on board a jumbo jet coming on to signify heavy turbulence, interrupted Zack's train of thought, causing the four to sit up – Jonny banging his head on the underside of the table noisily in the process.

To their amusement, the sound had actually been made by the bonkers Eric Diva, who not only enjoyed the sound of his own voice, it would seem, but also enjoyed the sound of announcing his own voice!

'*Bing-bong!* Will all conventioneers please note that a buffet lunch will be served at one p.m. in the Montpellier Room – great, wicked, thanks, bye! *Bing-bong!*'

Zack, Jonny, Sophie and Alex looked at each other hungrily. LUNCH!

6

1 P.M.

The fancily named Montpellier Room was back at ground level in the main part of the hotel. When they got there, they found it was actually as sterile a room as the countless others they'd come across these past few hours. It was as if the atmosphere of reception were a fungus, spreading in every direction along the passages leading out from it. The room's walls were another hostile shade of white, with patches of yellowing damp spreading out from the corners like angry tentacles. Directly opposite them, at the back of the room, were a series of French doors which rattled and creaked as the storm continued to rage outside, like the weather was doing its best to make itself known, the trees swaying from side to side like angry fists.

But it was the smell that was the most striking thing about the room. It smelled of absolutely every cuisine going all at once – a bit like an overused slow cooker. Or as if every school dinner in the country had been squeezed into one room – *that* smell!

The four Young Magicians ambled between the small circular tables that had been set out haphazardly – like someone had tried to break a world speed record when laying them out – towards the side of the room where a hundred steaming trays were bubbling away enticingly.

Zack and Jonny scoured them hungrily with their eyes.

'Where to start?' Jonny wondered.

'Maybe a bit of everything?' Zack suggested. 'Race you!'

'Challenge accepted!'

They started to load up their plates. Jacket potatoes, spaghetti Bolognese, chilli con carne, ham and eggs, Thai green curry, CHICKEN LASAGNE!

The room was starting to fill up now as some of the more vocal members shuffled in, already complaining about this, that and the other, both hungry and tired from a day of . . . well, so far doing nothing but complaining, with many now raising an additional eyebrow at the sight of the Young Magicians.

Alex's face started to burn as he tried to focus on loading up his plate with every morsel of food going, regardless of the clashing combinations.

Sophie kept her eyes peeled for Belinda Vine as she approached the food counter. She still intended to take Belinda up on her invitation of meeting – but it would have to be in the right way at the right time, and who knew what bad impression she might make if she were eating the wrong thing? Sophie pondered for a second what dish Belinda might choose – probably something quite light, Sophie figured a little sheepishly as she eyed up the giant portion of sausage and mash set inside an even more giant Yorkshire pudding and which came with its own jug – its own *jug* – of rich, velvety onion gravy.

Oh, and then there were the desserts: treacle pudding, chocolate gateaux, toffee sundaes – poor President Pickle, thought Sophie, imagining the man melting into a deep pool of his own saliva should he clap eyes on such a delectable bounty as this.

Seeing all the food laid out brought him back to mind – and the mystery of whatever was bugging him, and the tantalizing riddle of that torn-up note that obviously meant so much to Cynthia and nothing at all to the Young Magicians. There was no sign of him, but then he wouldn't stand a chance against this lot! No, this certainly wasn't the place to dabble in a *light snack*. Maybe Tudor Towers had its perks after all!

Sophie picked up a large serving spoon and was about to help herself when a thin, firm hand gripped her shoulder. She turned, coming face to face with a beaming Eric Diva who looked like he'd just got into a cold bath.

'I am *so* sorry! I should have said in my announcement. *Bing-bong!* Junior members have a separate dining area in the Syd Little Memorial Pantry – this room is just for the adults!'

'Oh . . .' said Sophie, casually putting down the serving spoon, a little embarrassed, but not as much as Jonny and Zack, who had just finished loading their plates with every single item going – even all the desserts.

'*Riiiiiiiiight,*' said Jonny, trying to style it out and hastily return all the different morsels to their respective serving trays without drawing any attention – kind of difficult, given the sheer volume of food he'd taken!

'Oh, but you know what,' said Eric Diva, a little too hastily, like he'd planned to amend his comment all along, 'as it's *you* four – *go ahead*!'

Jonny sighed and began the rather arduous task of reclaiming the items of food (plus the relevant sauces) which had now travelled from the serving platters, to his plate, back to the serving platters and now back to his plate – making one hell of a dribbly mess.

'In fact,' continued Eric Diva, 'maybe I could join you?'

'Er . . . sure,' said Sophie, not quite knowing whether she should seem grateful or a bit deflated.

'Excellent – two secs!' Eric Diva darted off like a startled fox as Sophie turned a trifle apologetically to the others.

'Maybe he'll know what's going on with President Pickle,' whispered Zack, never one to waste an opportunity to gather information.

That's true, thought Sophie as she reacquainted herself with the food on display, her tummy growling happily.

The four quickly took their seats at a table close to the jangling French windows, somewhat glad of the breeze forcing its way through the gaps, diluting the various pongs of the room, which had started to grow stronger as more and more members piled in.

Zack smiled as he noticed Alex produce a pack of cards. This was how Alex filled even the briefest of quiet moments – with practice, practice and more practice.

Alex shuffled the cards like a mini-maestro, before dealing them into a pile on the table. Zack raised an eyebrow in surprise as Alex dropped a couple of cards, not used to seeing a grandmaster finger-flicker like Alex stumble, especially when performing such a simple operation as a standard table deal. But then Zack had learned all too well that looks could be deceiving. Maybe that's just how Alex *wanted* it to appear.

But enough wondering: there was food to be eaten. Zack reached for the salt and pepper, sprinkled a sprinkle on his food, put them back and happily picked up his knife and fork. Then he frowned, put the knife and fork down, and slowly picked the saltcellar up again.

It was a squished-up human figure, a caricature like a toby jug. But it was still recognizable. A flat-top haircut, a jacket and a big grin, exactly like . . .

'You're kidding!' he wheezed. 'We're *condiments*! How much are these people rinsing us for?!'

He was interrupted by Eric Diva plonking himself down with a small plate of salad and some sliced avocado. *Where's the fun in that?* thought Jonny, who had reluctantly had to fit his meal on to *two* plates in the end – though he was already regretting having baked beans and Thai green curry swimming in the same gloopy pool.

'Wow, what a treat getting to share a table with the Young Magicians!' said Eric.

Zack handed him the saltcellar without comment, but sporting a somewhat menacing scowl. Eric Diva took it, his eyes widening.

'Wow! Not authorized?'

'Nope,' countered Zack. 'And we've seen more stuff like it.'

'OK – well, you certainly have to look out for that. You need an agent, someone who will safeguard your image against unauthorized piracy.' He studied his fingernails with a display of modesty that was almost but not quite convincing. 'Of course, I'd be happy – no, honoured – to take the job on . . .?'

Zack opened his mouth to answer, but Sophie got there first.

'Can we think about it?' she said quickly.

Eric Diva smiled and nodded in approval. 'No, absolutely – always read the small print! Just bear me – the *offer* – in mind,' he said, positively glowing and throwing a salad leaf into his mouth like a particularly cool rabbit. 'So tell me . . . what have you been up to lately?'

'Well,' began Zack, 'we're still at school obviously.'

'No, of course, sure!' Eric Diva laughed noisily, and quite unnecessarily. 'I meant in the world of solving magical mysteries – *obviously*!' Sophie detected a stray note of impatience in his tone that seemed somewhat out of line with the man's stand-out breezy exterior.

'We did wonder,' began Jonny, pausing for a second to slurp up an extra-long piece of spaghetti, the sauce gathering prominently around his lips, 'what on earth President Pickle was going on about during his opening speech?'

Eric Diva nodded, like he was deeply troubled, or at least trying to give the impression that he was deeply troubled.

'It was very strange, wasn't it? I hope he's OK. Though I won't deny there are some on Council who would rather see him go, to make way for – well – fresh blood like yourselves.'

Alex didn't quite like the way the man referred to them as *fresh blood*; it felt a bit . . . creepy. But, then again, perhaps that was because Alex was now eating an overly filled strawberry jam doughnut, the red gooey contents oozing out of the end theatrically, making him feel a touch vampiric.

'So how did you get into magic?' asked Sophie, having finished her plate and pushing it forward, a habit she'd inherited from her father – apparently. Not that she could really remember who her father was, but that's what her mother had told her he used to do.

'Well, you've probably spotted there's a bit of performer still left in me?' mused Eric, leaving a slight pause which could only suggest that he was looking for some kind of affirmation.

'Yes!' answered the four in unison.

'That was always my first love. I started in the bingo halls and basically worked my way down from there! Did the cruise ships for a while, bit of magic here and there, some cod impersonations, bit of ventriloquism – and I was *so* rubbish at that, frankly, it was just embarrassing – bit of gambling all my earnings away. Whoops!' He grimaced at them like these weren't particularly happy times.

'But then something clicked and I finally got into my thick head what you all worked out years ago, I expect – that to be good at anything takes time and application, even if you have a natural gift to start with, which I certainly didn't. So I put in some decent practice, I managed to find my way out of that rut, and – well – here I am today: your convention organizer extraordinaire!' He sat back, looking a touch proud of himself.

'Well, good for you!' said Jonny, warming to the strange man a little. It had to be no mean feat organizing a convention for a few hundred complaining magicians, booking acts from all across the world, negotiating their fees and trying to turn a profit. And, for all his bluster, Eric Diva seemed to be managing just fine. Not that the four of them had attended any conventions previous to this, but *they* were all having a good time at least.

A shadow fell over them as a soft, sultry Southern US accent delicately split the air like a sweet perfume. 'Why, hey, guys!'

Sophie froze. No, surely not! Not here, not when she probably still smelled of jacket potato!

But yes. There she was. Belinda Vine, towering over them, looking magnificent in her clinging red dress, like some glorious mermaid (but with legs). She grinned at the four of them as Sophie tried not to fidget and blush. Sophie looked in desperation at Zack, Jonny and Alex who – for all their previous nonchalance – also seemed thunderstruck now that the prospect of actually meeting this magical superstar had become a reality.

Sophie very quickly rearranged the tufts of hair on her fringe that she'd gelled expertly into several spiky peaks that morning, as her thoughts tumbled. What if Belinda hated the lot of them? What if she was actually saying hello to someone else – that was always spectacularly embarrassing and happened spectacularly frequently! What if . . .

'Belinda!' Eric Diva rose smoothly to his feet, hand held out, like he was a gentleman aboard the *Titanic*. 'So good to meet you in the flesh at last, after all the emailing back and forth! Eric Diva, and let me introduce you to the newest and brightest stars in magic. Belinda, please meet Sophie, Jonny, Alex and Zack.'

All four Young Magicians shot to their feet as Belinda offered her hand to each of them, Sophie frantically trying to dry her palm on the cuffs of her jumper before holding out her hand in return.

'Sophie Yang!' Belinda smiled and gave Sophie an extra-firm handshake. 'You got my letter? It's such a pleasure!'

'*Mrkglphm*,' Sophie said.

'And you boys too. Eric has told me so much about you . . . via email,' said Belinda, smiling at them warmly. 'He said if anyone's ever gonna be able to work out my act, it's you guys!' The four of them grinned, blushing with pride as Belinda let out a deep laugh that caused her fiery hair to tremble and shimmer. This was high praise indeed. And no one felt it more than Sophie.

'So . . . how are you finding the UK?' Jonny asked, going strangely tingly when Belinda smiled in answer.

'Well, I do love it here, Jonny. Just the thought of performing for you all at the Magic Circle – it's gonna be such an honour. So all you guys super-dig mentalism, right?'

Sophie felt her throat go dry.

It was Zack who piped up first. 'Well ... no one performs mental magic in our group better than Sophie.' Alex and Jonny nodded emphatically, glad – for once, in Jonny's case – for someone else to steal the limelight.

Cheers, Zack, thought Sophie, both flattered by the compliment and terrified by what might come next.

'Awesome! I thought I caught that special glint in your eye,' said Belinda, twinkling and pulling up a chair. They all slowly sat back down together. 'So you gonna show me something or what?'

Oh no! thought Sophie. Surely Belinda wasn't asking for a demonstration – this lady knew every trick in the book. There'd be no fooling *her*!

Eric Diva rubbed his hands together like an overexcited child, dragging his seat closer to the table – too close, Jonny thought – as Sophie toyed with her paper napkin, her face uncharacteristically pale.

'Well ... I don't really have anything prepared, so this might not work, but ...'

Sophie caught herself, suddenly conscious that this was a classic line enjoyed by many mentalists, used to deliberately wrong-foot the audience member into thinking there was a chance this could go wrong, that this wasn't fully tried and tested, when in fact the performer was in complete control and had even planned to say this very line. But of course *this* audience member knew the real truth all too well. Hell, even someone like Jonny knew about this sneaky verbal set-up before performing a trick!

(No offence, Jonny!)

(None taken, Sophie!)

Sophie took a deep breath as Belinda gave her a slight nod of encouragement, smiling at her knowingly. *Come on*, Sophie thought to herself, *these opportunities don't present themselves every day – it's worth a go.*

'OK, what I'd like you to do is think of a drawing . . . something that I couldn't guess, but nothing too complicated either. Do you mind drawing it while I look away?'

Sophie handed Belinda the napkin, then fished out a pen from her pocket and slid it over to her.

'You can show it to the others if you'd like. Or not!' continued Sophie, her nerves starting to dilute a little as she got into her stride. And why not? After all, she practised this stuff almost every day. There was no point pretending this was new to her. And, from Belinda's little secret smile, she sensed that the older woman knew it too. *Come on, Sophie, you can do this!*

Zack, Alex and Jonny drew closer, both excited about what Sophie might be about to do and nervous on her behalf. Screwing up in front of your idol would be a major bummer.

Belinda thought for a while, staring at the napkin before drawing. 'OK, done,' she said, snapping the lid of the pen shut. She flashed the drawing at the others, making a point to check there was no way Sophie could see, that there was no reflection or anything else that might help her out.

Zack looked at the sketch quizzically: a set of false teeth, which Belinda had clearly and boldly underlined several times. Interesting choice!

'And please make sure it stays hidden from view so that I can't see it,' said Sophie.

Belinda neatly folded the drawing and hid it under one of Jonny's dinner plates.

'OK, all hidden away,' she said, clearly enjoying herself.

Sophie turned fully back round and stared into Belinda's large, bewitching eyes.

How on earth *is she going to do this?* thought Alex. Surely this was . . . impossible? But then wasn't that the point?! It would be a waste of time demonstrating something Belinda had seen a million times over. If Sophie got this right, wasn't that basically *proof* that mind-reading existed!

Sophie cleared her throat. 'So I'm getting a sense that . . . Are you thinking of . . . a face, or a mouth maybe?'

Sophie paused as they all stared at her, trying not to give anything away. But this was undoubtedly along the right lines . . .

How did she *know*?

'Yes, I'm pretty sure you're thinking of . . . a set of false teeth?'

It was Jonny who erupted first, causing a couple of neighbouring diners to almost choke on their Arctic roll as he and Alex and Zack jumped up from their seats as if several billion volts of electricity had just hurtled up their bums.

'What? No way. NO WAY!' he screamed as the others gasped, wide-eyed, patting Sophie on the back and laughing incredulously.

And none laughed more than Belinda Vine. 'That, my girl, was pretty darn impressive – well done!'

Sophie was speechless, not least because she'd managed to pull off something so bold that the others would probably de-friend her if they knew how it worked! (*No chance of either of those things happening any time soon – don't worry, Sophie!*) But she couldn't have hoped for a better reaction, for it confirmed a lot of what Sophie knew about Belinda – that not only did the lady love seeing this kind of reaction from audiences, but that she and Sophie were going to get on very well indeed!

'I mean, I mean ... How?' stuttered Eric Diva, his mouth still agog. He had remained uncharacteristically quiet throughout the performance, his brain clearly working overtime trying to catch Sophie out. 'I am honestly ... speechless,' he said conclusively, with perhaps just a hint of jealousy, his eyes turning to Belinda.

Not that *speechless!* thought Zack.

'Well ... didn't I say they were a clever bunch!' he added, as proud as punch again and dabbing his mouth with a serviette. (Completely unnecessary when all you've consumed is a salad, Eric!) 'Well, I'd best check that everything is in place in the Dealers' Hall – the demonstrations will be starting shortly.'

The four clocked each other knowingly. If he wanted a progress report on the Dealers' Hall, then all he needed to do was ask!

'See you shortly, bunnies!' He sprang up from the table like a catapult, causing the same two neighbouring diners to have another cataclysmic collision.

Belinda rose from the table as gracefully as a swan before looking back down at them, her beaming smile radiating warmth. 'I look forward to seeing you all around. And congrats again, Sophie, that was awesome . . . and bold!' Belinda winked as she spun away from the table, causing the very same unfortunate couple to have yet another near-fatal incident, this time involving one of their spoons and all four of their eye sockets. Plus, chunks of now-unidentifiable Arctic roll.

Sophie sat back in her seat and turned her face to the ceiling, sighing with happiness.

Right then, Sophie, how in the name of Dunninger* did you do *that*?

---

* A brilliant mentalist born at the end of the nineteenth century who would have *massively* approved of Sophie's daring method!

7

2 P.M.

Zack, Sophie, Jonny and Alex headed out of the Montpellier Room, leaving behind all of its peculiar smells, and back down two levels towards the Dealers' Hall. They wanted to browse the place legitimately this time, maybe even spend a few hundred pennies, and that meant they had to enter the proper way.

The friends squatted down next to the wall to take the weight off their feet as they joined the queue. Alex absently produced his pack of cards again and Zack was curious to see him go through the same sequence of moves – apparently trying a simple deal but obviously getting something wrong along the way, whatever it was.

Deanna suddenly appeared behind the four friends, firing out questions like a bubble machine before any of them had time to respond. 'How did you get to eat in there? What did you have to eat? Was it nice? How do you know that American lady? Can I walk round the Dealers' Hall with you?'

'Sure!' said Sophie, who had a newly acquired bounce in her step following her brilliant display of talent in front of Belinda Vine.

'Oh!' answered Deanna, who, it seemed, had grown accustomed to being constantly rebuffed by Sophie. She paused for a second, trying to work out how to react before finally shouting, 'AMAZING!' at the top of her voice. A few of the greying members ahead scowled at her in annoyance as the queue began to move forward.

Scowl all you like, thought Sophie – this was turning out to be a cracker of a weekend! (Plus, if Deanna's atypically upbeat outburst was cause for a scowl, then who knew what expression these grouchy fellows reserved for when she *really* kicked off! Now *that* would be a sight to see!)

The four friends smiled in delight once more as they entered the Dealers' Hall, now brimming with life, the tables even more densely laden with goods than before as the members gathered in every nook and cranny available to marvel at the various magical wares on display, squeezing themselves between the tables like hungry cattle on market day.

'I am going to spend *so much* money in here!' Deanna exclaimed with a dreamy look in her eye. And with that she disappeared into the throng.

'Whereas we,' said Jonny, rubbing his hands together and itching to get a closer look at some of the more extravagant props, 'are here to get the best price going and to have bags of fun – what are we waiting for?!'

'Him apparently,' answered Zack, spotting Eric Diva leaping up on to the raised platform much like he had done earlier that morning one floor above in the ballroom.

'OK, brilliant, great stuff!' Eric said wheezily, making a play of pretending to count all those in the room that he milked for way too long. 'Perfect – I *think* that's everyone accounted for! So we're delighted to welcome dealers from all over the world this year. Do try and support them if

you can. They are after all – like me – failed performers and need every penny they can get!'

The joke hung in the air like mouldy dung.

'Well then! Come on, dealers, get to it!'

He flapped the backs of his hands towards them as the members began to jostle between the various stands, their fingers twitching hungrily, many keen to catch a glimpse of the latest magical gizmo or whatnot that soon every magician on the planet would own but likely never use – the gadget destined for some back drawer or other where it would sit and disintegrate over the next hundred years, an entirely different kind of vanishing act.

'Which stand do you want to visit first?' said Jonny excitedly.

'Guess,' Zack said grimly, and they trooped over to the rip-off Young Magicians merchandise stall they had spied earlier. The woman they had seen before was sitting in a chair, reading a magazine. She glanced up casually at first, then bolt upright as she clocked who they were.

'Well, this is a nice surprise!' She pushed a pile of T-shirts and magic markers forward. 'Any chance you could sign these?'

'No,' Zack said bluntly. 'Who gave you the right to use our faces?'

'Faces?' The woman made a big show of studying the poster behind her, and the T-shirt designs. 'Can't make out any faces here . . . just silhouettes and shapes – could be anyone!'

The Young Magicians stared at some of the other unlicensed goodies on display. Along the front of the table was a row of action figures. They came in four distinct styles, one clearly taller than the other three . . .

As if in a dream, a horrified Zack reached down and picked up a fully – well, at least partially – poseable Zack Harrison.

'*This* has a face!' he said, scowling. The woman took it, inspected the little head and then peered into his own face.

'No resemblance at all if you ask me!'

'So why are you selling them?' Alex asked. He handled the smallest figure cautiously. The glasses were way too big, like he was out of a cartoon . . .

'Is there a law that says I can't make my own figures and sell them?'

'They're *us*!' Zack squeaked in frustration.

'Says who?'

'Says . . . us!'

'Plus, they don't do anything magical . . .' Sophie added.

'True . . .' the woman acknowledged, clearly already plotting how she might adapt them.

'So why are you selling them at a magic convention if they're not us?'

'Is there a law that says I can't sell –?'

'Oh, this is nuts!' Zack snapped. Sophie put a gentle hand on his shoulder.

'Come on, let's not give her any extra publicity. People are here to buy magic, not . . . *these*.'

Zack gave the woman a final glower as Sophie led him away, followed promptly by Alex, followed less promptly by Jonny, who lingered just long enough to ask in a quick whisper, 'How much for the tall one?'

'Five quid.'

A note and a Jonny Haigh action figure quickly swapped hands. Jonny slipped it into his pocket.

Across the room, Sophie saw Belinda Vine waft gracefully into the room, as elegant as a scented breeze. She caught Sophie's eye and gave a distinctly friendly wave that Sophie gladly returned. She continued to watch as Belinda turned towards Eric Diva, giving him the briefest of nods before continuing her journey into the thick of the Dealers' Hall, members parting before her like the Red Sea. Hmm, was it Sophie's imagination or did she catch something in that small look to Eric Diva that hinted at something more than just an email acquaintance? Those two knew each other already, she was sure of it. But why would they pretend never to have met?

Jonny had caught them up.

'OK,' he announced optimistically, 'I want to get three laps of this entire place under our belts before the hour is out! Shall we start at Davenport's?'

The four of them headed over towards the Davenport's Magic Studio stand, carving out a pathway through the wash of suits, Jonny's head sticking up above the crowd like a curious and beaming buoyancy aid.

'Hey, Alton!' said Zack loudly as they approached.

Alton rolled his eyes, so much so that for a split second all Alex could see were the white bits, causing him to look even more inhuman than he already did. He let out a prolonged, nostril-inflating huff.

'If you're not here to spend any money – and let's say at least thirty quid – then you're going to have to move on. Sorry, goodbye.'

'Oh, now, that seems a little steep, Alton,' said Zack, smiling warmly. 'We just want to check out your latest tricks.' Zack knew how to wind up Alton impeccably. In fact, he and Jonny almost regarded it as a light sport, getting the greedy man to demonstrate effects – always hugely overpriced, and always way above Alton's skill set – just to watch him fall at the first hurdle.

'This looks interesting,' said Jonny, picking up a small blue box.

'Linking ropes: thirty pounds,' said Alton in a heartbeat and not taking his eyes off Jonny. 'You either pay now or put it down. I don't care if you're famous.'

'Neither do we!' said Jonny, pretending to think about it, but evidently with no intention of spending such vast amounts of his well-earned pocket money (and not least because he didn't have even *close* to that amount on him). 'Perhaps if you were to *demonstrate* the effect for me, I'd be more inclined to buy it.'

Alton blew his cheeks out once more, like life was just one massive inconvenience.

'And you're *definitely* going to buy it?' Alton asked, his little tongue poking out of the corner of his mouth like a Chihuahua.

'Sorry, but isn't that missing the point?' enquired Sophie, a little bemused by the man's tiresome attitude. 'Isn't the whole reason for a dealer demonstration at a convention like this that you – the *dealer* – *demonstrate* the goods and then we – the *customer* – decide whether or not to buy them?'

For whatever reason, whether it was out of irritation or boredom, Alton didn't respond. Instead, he snatched the small box out of Jonny's hand, and began opening it recklessly, all podgy fingers and thumbs, as bits of rope and several tiny disc-shaped magnets fell out of the base and on to the floor. Alton stooped to retrieve them, cursing loudly, as several rolled away behind someone else's stall.

'No prizes for guessing how *this* trick works then!' said Zack quietly.

Alex couldn't help but grin. Wasn't the Davenport's Magic brand meant to be one of the most highly regarded in the country?

'OK, just give me a minute.' Alton pored over the instructions, fiddling with the ends of the orange rope, trying to surreptitiously fix the magnets into place without the four noticing (FAT chance of that happening now, Alton!). Finally, after a lot of grunting and sweating, he was ready to begin. He gave them a strange waspish smile, like he'd read somewhere that this was what you were meant to do when about to perform a magic trick.

'OK, so here I have two completely ordinary loops of bright orange rope.'

'Perfectly, perfectly ordinary,' repeated Jonny, trying not to laugh. Alton made a weird shaking move with his left hand, about as subtle as a velociraptor attack.

'However,' he continued, 'if I jiggle them about a bit . . .' He accidentally dropped one of the pieces of rope on the floor, cursing even more loudly as he crouched to pick it up again. 'You'll see they are now linked together.' The four Young Magicians stared at Alton as his shoulders sagged. Alton, it would seem, despite coming from a rich family of magicians, cared as much about performing good magic as he did about his unwashed, greasy hair.

'Is . . . that it?' offered Alex quietly. He wasn't prone to sounding sarcastic, but then it was rather difficult not to, given what they'd just witnessed.

'Yes, of course that's it!' snapped Alton. 'Thirty quid.' He held out a grubby hand presumptuously.

'But it's just a piece of rope with magnets on the end!' said Jonny.

'Who said it uses magnets?' the man scoffed back, narrowing his eyes at the four of them.

'But we just *saw* you screw them on, Alton,' said Zack, growing increasingly bewildered and wondering whether Alton might be finally losing it from having spent too much time underground and out of direct sunlight.

'Well, this one comes with free tuition,' Alton huffed, thinking this was enough to explain the inflated price tag. He extended his hand even further, rubbing his fingers together, exasperated.

'Tuition? By you?' asked Sophie, hardly believing her eyes and ears.

'Of course by me!'

Alton thwacked his hand on the table in frustration, so heavily that he caused an intricate display of thumb tips to cascade away from his stand and on to the floor, like a million Tom Thumbs had just met their bloody fate. The Young Magicians leaped out of the way of the torrent.

'Right, if any of those get lost, you're paying for them!' Alton vowed angrily as he scrabbled round their feet to retrieve the items.

'Oh, cool!' Alex exclaimed suddenly, which was so unusual – for Alex or in fact for anyone watching one of Alton's so-called demonstrations – that all activity briefly paused while Alton stared suspiciously up at him from the floor.

Alex was holding up a small tube the size and shape of a lipstick.

'Glue!' he said happily. 'I could really do with some of this for a trick I'm working on.'

Alex had forgotten the first rule of trying to buy something from a dealer, especially when that dealer was called Alton Davenport – don't show you're interested. Ever!

'Now *that* is a quality product,' Alton agreed, rising smoothly to his feet like a liquid-metal Terminator. 'A snip at ten pounds and that includes training.'

Alex's face fell. He could afford it, just, but had really hoped to spread that amount over a few purchases, not blow it all on . . . well, glue!

'Training in how to use glue?' Sophie demanded, sounding even more incredulous than before. 'I mean, how is it different to what you get in a stationery shop? Apart from the price?'

'It's semi-permanent,' Alton announced as though that were meant to be a major selling feature.

'Is that a good thing?' she asked.

'Yes, it is,' Alex murmured sadly.

Jonny couldn't bear the look on Alex's face. He moved his mouth close to Alton's ear.

'Hey, Alton, I'll make you a deal,' he murmured.

'Hmm . . .?' Alton asked, side-eyeing him warily.

'Sell him the glue at a reasonable price, or we hang around your stall until closing time.'

Wheels almost visibly turned behind Alton's eyes as he processed the offer. Then he looked into Jonny's eyes and saw that the tall boy was in total, not to mention deadly, earnest. Meanwhile, Alex was holding out some coins without a lot of hope.

'I can pay two pou–' he began.

The coins vanished as quickly as if they had been part of a trick. When Alton wasn't actually trying to do magic, whenever money was to be swiped, he was pretty damn good.

'Special discount rate for convention-goers,' he said. 'Two pounds, done. Deal?' he added to Jonny.

Jonny smiled.

'Deal. C'mon, guys, three laps, remember?'

They were gone before Alton could reconsider. Thankfully, Hugo and Class Act were en route with notes billowing from their suits like a traditional Greek wedding, so Alton would soon get over it.

The Young Magicians spent the next fifty minutes racing round the rest of the room, Jonny keen for them to at least *attempt* their three-lap target (which was soon to prove a statistical impossibility) and insisting on a rather strict schedule. Or summarized more precisely:

- **2.10 p.m.** – Le Slie's Magic, Paris. Purchases – 0. Encounters with Deanna – 1. Favourite trick – one where a signed card appears inside a tin of baked beans.
- **2.15 p.m.** – Impractical Magic. Purchases – 1, made by Alex: a four ace type routine using fifteen gaffed aces and a hell of a lot of sleight of hand. Encounters with Deanna – a thankful 0. Favourite trick – the Seven-Blade Wrist Chopper!
- **2.20 p.m.** – Nästan Mirakulös (Almost Miraculous), Stockholm. Purchases – 0. Encounters with Deanna – 9 (wouldn't go away). Favourite trick – one where a

closed fist produces a jet of water – really quite messy. And way too loud.

- **2.25 p.m.** – Vanishing Ink. Purchases – 1, made by Jonny: some actual vanishing ink, which he promptly lost. Favourite trick – a small pamphlet on being able to detect whether someone might be lying or telling the truth. Might come in handy one day! (Additional purchase made by Sophie.)

2.30 p.m. Alcatraz Magic Supplies, San Francisco. Purchases – 1, made by Zack: a set of metal lock picks with a mental note attached to get some guidance and basic tuition from Alex. Encounters with Deanna – a dizzying 2, her having caught up with them in the crowd. Favourite trick – the Unbreakable Bottle, but which was currently undemonstrable owing to it being broken.

- **2.35 p.m.** – Guy Tornado's Illusion Design. Purchases – 0. Encounters with Max – 1, who appeared to be haggling over an origami illusion, but was concerned that they didn't quite have it in his size. Favourite trick – the Amazing Incredible Appearing Gorilla!

- **2.40 p.m.** – Magic Trix, Japan. Purchases – 1, made by Zack: a gimmick-free way of performing Pen Through Anything. Favourite trick – a toss-up between the Self-balancing Samurai Sword and the Self-working Self-tying Self-inflating

Self-resetting Shoelace. (Does NOT come with English instructions.)

- **2.45 p.m.** – Mercury Magier, Berlin. Purchases – 0. Encounters with Hugo – 1, who was trying to pay for his purchases using a variety of contactless credit cards and Bitcoin, having exhausted all of his cash at Davenport's. Favourite trick – Glitter Cannon From Nowhere.

- **2.50 p.m.** – Hilda's Fancy Dress, Auckland. Purchases – 0. Encounters with Deanna – 1 (although somewhat terrifyingly dressed as a nun). Favourite trick – n/a. Encounters with Hugo – none up close, but across the room they saw him, Salisbury and Charlie staring with shrieks of envy at the knock-off Young Magicians stall ('Why doesn't anyone want to sell pirated tat of *us*?!') and trying to persuade the stallholder that there should be a range of Class Act merchandise too. She wasn't having any of it.

- **2.55 p.m.** – Le Slie's Magic (round two). Purchases – 1, made by Sophie who simply *had* to know how one manages to get a signed card inside a sealed tin of beans. Encounters with Deanna – 0 (thankfully still being caught up inside her nun outfit). Favourite trick – see Sophie's purchase.

- **3 p.m.** – Ye Magick, New York. Purchases – sadly 0, partly because there was no one manning the stand, but also because the ancient poster of Ron and Nancy Spencer was practically priceless. Favourite trick –

Ron and Nancy's deliciously diabolical telepathy act, of course!

'*Bing-bong!* Well, it looks like the dealers will all be able to eat for at least another week!' Eric Diva had hopped up on to a small podium and his voice echoed over the hum of noise in the Dealers' Hall. 'Some probably more than others, by the looks of it – isn't that right, Alton?!'

Like before, the somewhat misjudged comment hung dreadfully in the air. Not that Eric Diva seemed to mind!

'On saying that, I hope you haven't spent *all* your money just yet because it's now time for the Annual Auction . . . Once again, please give it up for his eminent grace, the inimitable President Pickle!'

8

3 P.M.

President Pickle strode defiantly into the centre of the Dealers' Hall and on to a small platform, next to a stand covered in a wispy black cloth that boasted shapes of various and weird proportions beneath it. Zack tried to guess what they all were from the shapes, but it wasn't easy.

'Do you think he's going to do an act?' he murmured. Jonny held up crossed fingers and shuddered.

He looks a little more sure-footed, at least, thought Alex. Though beneath the pomposity there was arguably still a faint but fearful flickering of the eyes, like the man was still on the lookout for something . . . or someone, but doing his best to plough on regardless – like the captain of a ship plunging into the dark night, wondering what that big icy-looking thing ahead might be, but what the heck, let's keep going because what's the worst that could happen?

Cynthia appeared at his side, still looking a little bleak. The room hushed as President Pickle withdrew his infamous gavel.

'Well, it's high time I put this to good use again!'

He whacked the gavel down on to a wooden block, and a deafening pop rippled through the Dealers' Hall like a shockwave.

'I really wish he wouldn't do that!' said Jonny, wincing and rubbing his ears. But then, as they'd become only too aware six months ago, banging down his gavel was one of President Pickle's favourite pastimes. And it would seem, despite his thinned appearance, the man certainly hadn't lost any power in his right arm.

The echoes died away and Sophie spotted several members surreptitiously pop in a set of earplugs. *Now that's planning ahead!* she thought.

'So, as many of you will have heard by now,' President Pickle continued, 'our dear friend and treasurer Bill Dungworth passed away last week.'

The four looked at each other in shock. They'd only ever had quite odd encounters with the decidedly ancient Bill Dungworth previously, and he'd not so much as said a proper hello to them, but he was clearly a part of the Magic Circle furniture.

'I dread to think how long Bill was a member,' said President Pickle, scrunching up his face and clearly struggling with the maths – partly because maths was not his forte, but also because the number was so huge! 'Well, anyway,' he resumed, 'it doesn't really bear thinking about, does it? The same will become of us all one day . . . I imagine . . .'

He looked down suddenly, acutely aware that he was standing in the centre of a large room full of people staring up at him. He shot a glance at Cynthia, clearing his throat nervously before standing up straight again.

'Anyhow, good old Bill only went and donated his entire personal collection of magic props to the society in his last will and testament, and so it seems fitting that we auction them off this afternoon in his memory.'

President Pickle whipped away the wispy black cloth from the stand to reveal a whole host of conspicuous (and mostly rotting) magical items. A few of the nearby members coughed loudly as a cloud of dust heaved into the air. Cynthia dusted down her jacket politely.

'I don't think many of these have seen the light of day for a good while,' said President Pickle, trying to make this sound like a positive. He picked up a wooden duck, the paint peeling away from its body, as though it had some rare tropical disease.

'So who wants this!' he exclaimed with a beaming smile. 'It's an Educated Duck* for all those at the back. Shall we start at – say – thirty pounds?'

* A wooden duck with a hinged mechanism that allows the duck to lean forward and select a chosen card from a deck placed in front of it. Made famous by the late, great comedy magician Tommy Cooper.

What is it with everything being priced at thirty pounds? thought Jonny in frustration.

Alex looked round the room as everyone, including all of the dealers present – many of whom were selling a reproduction of the same item, with fresh paint too, for way less – just stared straight ahead.

'Oh, now, come on!' bellowed President Pickle, who was clearly putting his troubles to one side for a moment and enjoying himself. 'This is probably a hundred years old. It's an antique!'

Yes, thought Zack. *Doesn't the man realize that's precisely why no one wants it?!*

'OK, twenty pounds,' sighed President Pickle, like this was now a bargain. The Young Magicians looked round the room again as no one so much as raised an eyebrow.

'Surely not!' exclaimed President Pickle. 'A tenner?' he strained, hardly believing himself. 'Come on now. It's even been painted with good old-fashioned lead paint . . . Oh marvellous, is that a hand?' Everyone turned to follow his gaze as President Pickle began to raise his gavel excitedly. But no. Much to everyone's disappointment, it was Alton slicking back his oily hair. He quickly yanked his hand down again before President Pickle could claim to have flogged the entire auction off to him.

President Pickle exhaled loudly, looking desperately disenchanted. 'Well, I guess *we'll* just have to take it home with us,' he stated sadly, and tossed the heavy duck to his wife, who welcomed it with not-so-welcome arms. 'I'll pop thirty pounds in the biscuit tin or whatever at some point when I next get a . . .' He tapered off, clearly with no intention of paying such a princely sum for the unwanted, mutilated mallard.

'OK, on to the next item. Fire from palms! Let's start the bidding at – shall we say – thirty pounds?'

Jonny let out a loud guffaw.

'Was that somebody bidding?' President Pickle queried, scanning the room optimistically at the sound of Jonny's laugh.

Everyone remained still and silent, especially Jonny, who sucked in his cheeks so hard that his eyes bulged and didn't so much as blink.

'No one?' continued President Pickle. 'Not one single person wants this old set of fire from palms that used to belong to Bill Dungworth? Oh dear.'

Sophie quietly squeezed Jonny's hand while nodding towards the stand of items next to Cynthia. This was going to be one long, drawn-out auction! She glanced over the mix of props and paraphernalia on display, in all their varying states of decomposition:

– Bill in lemon . . . As in a *dollar bill*, rather than Bill himself – that wouldn't have been nice for anyone. Asking price – yep, you guessed it – a sweet £30! Not sold.
– Needle through thumb . . . Asking price: £30. Not sold.

- A painting of John Nevil Maskelyne, presumably painted by Bill himself back in the day, but who clearly didn't really know what the man looked like. Nor what a human being really looked like, by the appearance of it . . . Not sold.
- Giant three-card monte set . . . Not sold and dreadfully creased in all the wrong directions.
- Rice bowls complete with a one-tonne sack of old rice . . . Not sold and riddled with bacteria.
- Eating Razorblades instructions written by Bill when he was in his teens, with the side note 'untested' . . . Definitely not sold for obvious reasons.
- Himber wallet . . . Not sold (inexplicably glued shut).
- Ventriloquist's dummy . . . Not sold. Paintwork even worse than the Educated Duck's, and lower jaw and one eye missing.
- Quick-change bag . . . Not sold, and not so quick any more.
- Dagger chest . . . Not sold and undoubtedly lethal.
- Card case . . . Sold! Sorry, NOT sold.
- Chinese linking ring set . . . Not sold.

And the list went on. The crowd were now starting to grow restless, many still wearing their earplugs and so presumably none the wiser about what was being sold (nothing) and what was being tossed over to Cynthia, who was now getting increasingly worried about where they were going to house all of this mouldy magic kit.

The auction finally drew to its excruciating end as President Pickle held up a moth-eaten copy of a first-edition *Abracadabra** magazine, so much in tatters that it could have been a publication about practically anything. He tossed it over to Cynthia – it having been successfully not sold like the rest of the items – and the pages fell apart on their brief flight over, meaning that all Cynthia caught was a thin spine of paper and a couple of rusty staples.

'Well, thank you, Bill – wherever you may be,' intoned President Pickle grandly, seemingly forgetting that the auction had just been a complete and utter disaster. 'Even though your body may have departed this earth, take solace in the fact that your props still live on.'

Jonny brought both hands to his mouth, trying not to laugh.

'And now to end with a minute's silence.' President Pickle slammed down his gavel even harder than the last time – having not had the pleasure of doing so during the entirety of the auction.

Zack, Sophie, Jonny and Alex bowed their heads. Jonny squeezed his eyes closed, desperately hoping he wouldn't be taken by a fit of the giggles, at least for the next minute, as the room fell silent. As funny as the situation was, Bill had still been a man. A person. Now dead. You had to show some respect for that.

* *Abracadabra* was a British weekly magic magazine whose publication life spanned sixty-three years. The first issue was published on 2 February 1946, the year in which Bill allegedly turned sixty.

Now his eyes were starting to water – not with tears, just with the pressure he was putting on them. He didn't want to wipe them in case anyone thought he was actually crying. So he began to blink as fast as he could, trying to clear them.

And that was why Jonny was able to catch the sudden movement in the corner of his vision. One tiny little flicker – the first spark of white that marks the start of the avalanche.

Jonny's eyes flew open. He drew in a breath. His lungs filled. He shaped his mouth to shout the words, but Eric Diva got there first.

'WATCH OUT!' he screamed, without even an introductory *bing-bong*, as a million things seemed to happen at once and the room began to shimmy and shake all around them.

Eric Diva began running full pelt away from Le Slie's Magic stand, which had begun to lean dangerously on to the stand behind it (Impractical Magic), whose shelves collapsed, sending a host of props flying.

Jonny watched as a pair of oversized dice arced through the air, one landing smack on to another stand (Almost Miraculous), which began to topple and teeter treacherously, while the other landed on Alton's foot, causing him to step forward involuntarily on to the sea of thumb tips he'd spilled earlier, resulting in him slipping into the stand next to him (Vanishing Ink). The room was now awash with a series of increasingly loud bangs and crunches as stand after stand began to collapse around them, a domino rally of upright box illusions gathering momentum, sending magic equipment flying into the air.

Alex ducked as a dove pan narrowly missed his jaw, emptying its contents of red ribbon like it had just been shot.

A large set of handcuffs from Alcatraz Magic Supplies catapulted past Zack like a set of nunchaku, twisting and spinning aggressively as panic began to spread across the room like wildfire.

Sophie watched in horror as Guy Tornado's Illusion Design spun into the Young Magicians knock-off table, sending the action figures flying (result!). The wave of destruction was heading right towards them, but they were trapped – everyone was! So intricate and complex was the table layout in the room that without clambering on top of one another there was no way out: all the usual pathways were now full of magic rubble.

Zack turned just as a Zigzag Lady illusion toppled on to a Head Chopper, which in turn hurtled into the Magic Trix, Japan stand, sending the large samurai sword hurtling into the air and right towards where President Pickle was now standing stock-still, frozen with fright, his mouth agape. The sword lurched and almost fell as it passed through an explosive spray of confetti and glitter emanating from Mercury Magier's stand, which also seemed to rouse several of the costumes from Hilda's Fancy Dress stand, making them look like they had all come to life all on their own. But an extra-thick cluster of glitter hit it and sent it on its way.

The sword oscillated terrifyingly, like it was being handled by an expert swordsman, prone to showing off, as it kept on towards President Pickle. Sophie watched, agog, as it sliced through the poster of Ron and Nancy Spencer, still maintaining its trajectory. The whole room fell quiet, save for the faint whistling sound of the oncoming samurai sword.

President Pickle closed his eyes.

9

4 P.M.

'*Arooga, arooga* . . . I mean *duck*!'

Eric Diva screamed as he hurtled through the air. President Pickle opened his eyes and looked at the duck that was still standing oddly proud atop the pile of junk that Cynthia was holding, and wondered how on earth a peeling, decrepit old magic prop was going to save him from certain death.

And then Eric Diva cannoned into him, knocking him to the floor and all the breath out of his body, just as the sword flashed through the space where he had been standing.

The sword struck the podium point-first and embedded itself in the wood, where it trembled, quivered and slowed down before finally dropping to the floor with a *clunk*, as though it were taking a bow after its spectacular little show and then standing aside when it saw that the audience really weren't cheering.

'Edmund!' Cynthia screamed. She threw the pile of non-auctioned tat into the air like a bride might throw her bouquet and ran towards him, just as the additional clobber hit the crowd. She knelt in front of her husband, her dangly glasses swinging so hard that they almost took one of his eyes out, and hugged him hard to her bosom, so that he thought that even though he had magically escaped death by impalement then surely his time had come by means of bosom suffocation.

'Was that . . . for real?' Alex asked. Jonny stood on tiptoes, which gave him a clear advantage over the milling crowd, like a giraffe standing on its hind legs amid a herd of goats.

'If it was, it was . . .' His voice trailed off in wonder as, with his eyes, he traced the trail of destruction and carnage in wiggly lines round the hall, back to where it had all started with Le Slie's Magic stand. If it had been set up, then it had been planned down to the last split second. There would have to have been hidden springs, pulleys, levers in a complicated line all around the hall to make everything tip or fall at exactly the right moment. In his head, Jonny was already planning how *he* might have done it. Setting off a train of events like that – making it all happen in exactly the right way at exactly the right time – would be crazy but undoubtedly *amazing*.

In fact, a lot of the audience were looking around, trying to work out what had just happened. This was a magicians' convention after all, and everyone knew that things were very rarely exactly as they seemed. There was always the chance of some massive set-up going on – that this was just a piece of staging for some even more spectacular payoff.

'No,' Sophie said quietly, correctly reading Jonny's mind before turning to watch President Pickle peel himself free of Cynthia. 'Neither of them is that good an actor. This was for real.'

There was certainly no sign that President Pickle was in on anything. One look at the man's staring eyes and heaving chest and clammy face told you that this had come as much as a surprise to him as to everyone else.

Eric Diva picked himself up, dusting himself down like a film star who had performed the perfect stunt.

He held out a hand to help President Pickle totter to his feet.

'It could have been someone trying to intimidate him,' Jonny stated, remembering the threats they knew President Pickle was getting. Even if they were weird threats that didn't apparently make any sense. Maybe this was what they were building towards?

'Or someone might have been trying to dispose of him altogether,' Zack said grimly. Sophie winced.

'That's one heck of a leap from sending him weird notes, Zack,' Sophie said.

'I know, I know. But that sword was *so close*. If that was just intimidation, they were cutting it pretty fine,' he added with a grin.

Cynthia slowly stood, no doubt still fazed by what had just happened, but conscious that she still had a job to do. She clapped her hands together.

'Well, that could all have been a lot nastier!' she said, with a vaguely passable attempt at breeziness (eight out of ten for effort, three out of ten for conviction, Cynthia). 'Now then, grown-ups, the next workshop is about to begin,* so if you could all make your way to the . . .' She scanned the crowd of faces, then gave a sort of *oh, whatever, just sort yourselves out!* flap of the hand. 'Junior members, however, please return to your rooms until Council has deemed this whole area safe again.'

She saw the crestfallen looks – not just from the Young Magicians, but from Deanna (half de-nunned, but still struggling with her wimple†), Hugo and his minions and Max, who had rather impressively managed to break the 'no food in the Dealers' Hall' rule with a bag of toffees, but was trying to surreptitiously hide them now that he noticed the president's wife looking at him.

Even Eric Diva looked a little stumped.

'And who's going to do that?' he asked, wondering wildly whether he'd factored this into his convention-planning procedures and protocols still-to-do list – but then who could have predicted *this*?

---

* Interactive workshop: 'Ways to make your assistant disappear – whether they like it or not!'
† Do look it up. Sounds like it should be rude, but sadly it's just a nun's headdress.

'Council's official Health and Safety officers – they're all fully trained for this kind of ... thing,' which even Cynthia knew was stretching the truth by several thousand miles, the training itself consisting of merely a few email attachments which more than half the Health and Safety officers openly admitted they hadn't even the technology to open.

Cynthia looked across the hall. The four friends, and a lot of other curious magicians, followed her gaze. Steve and Jane were in their robes, still chatting noisily and paying no attention to anything. Had they even seen what had just happened?

Cynthia stamped her foot to get their attention and repeated loudly, 'Council's Health and Safety officers. Please can you conduct a risk assessment!'

Wow, thought Jonny, both terrified and delighted in equal measure by the prospect of Steve and Jane being the ones in charge of everyone's physical safety. *I guess that was why they chose Steve to drive!*

'Absolutely, of course, ma'am. We'll get right on it!' replied Steve, not quite knowing what he'd just signed up to.

Jane – correctly interpreting Steve's flamboyantly ambivalent face – poked a cautious hand up.

'Sorry, what did you just ask us to do again?'

'Cynthia's got a point,' said Sophie, scrunching up her face in frustration. 'I don't fancy hanging around anywhere there's swords flying about accidentally.'

'One hell of a *point*!' Jonny grinned. (Never one to avoid a terrifically tragic pun.)

They turned to go, picking their way through the debris of magic props – wands, hats, Bill Dungworth's ventriloquist's doll, lying where it fell like some contorted body after Cynthia threw the pile of junk into the air, an escaped rabbit nibbling at the corner of a tablecloth, packs of identical cards, semi-identical cards or seemingly semi-identical cards that were definitely not marked – left over from the chain of collapsing stalls.

'Ow!' Deanna complained. 'Can you believe anyone would make a costume like this?'

They were all in the boys' room now – Jonny, Zack, Alex, Sophie . . . plus a somewhat disgruntled yet startlingly undeterred Deanna. It was either bring her with them, or let her wander blindly about in her semi-nun state around Tudor Towers, like a nightmare, and no one had the heart to do that – not to her and not to anyone else in the hotel that might be unfortunate enough to be party to such an encounter. In her struggle to get the wimple off (shout out to all those who now know what a wimple is – welcome, friends!), she had managed to jam it completely over her head.

Sophie and Alex were grappling with the top end, trying to help. Sophie because, well, she was a girl, and Alex because there wasn't a lock he couldn't pick, so you'd have thought the clips and pins on a comedy religious item of fancy dress would be peasy.

'So this is a tough one,' Zack said.

'Uh-huh,' mumbled Jonny, barely looking up from the designs he was scribbling on a pad of paper.

'I mean, Cynthia said she wants us to help, but helping President Pickle is not exactly top of my to-do list.'

(Let's be honest, it wasn't even at the bottom of Zack's to-do list. It was probably several million miles *below*

Zack's to-do list, which would actually place it somewhere in the Mariana Trench.)

'Yup . . .'

'*Ow-w-w-w-w-w!*' screamed Deanna from the other side of the room, now practically bent in half and struggling to breathe as Sophie heaved with all her might with one foot on a shoulder (Deanna's shoulder to be precise).

'Why did you dress up as a nun anyway?' Sophie demanded.

'A nun? What's a nun?' Deanna exclaimed as Alex gave the wimple an extra-big tug, which didn't so much answer the question as just give rise to a load more extra questions such as a) how has she never come across the concept of a nun before? and b) given a), why did she then choose to dress as one?

'But whatever we think of President Pickle,' Jonny said, finally looking up to face Zack, 'we know Cynthia wants us to help, and she's done so much for us. Don't we owe it to her?'

'Yeah,' Zack admitted unhappily. 'We probably do.'

With a final scream from Deanna, she, Sophie, Alex and – crucially – the wimple all shot off in different directions.

'Free!' Deanna exulted, like she'd been held prisoner in a pyramid for several centuries. Her mouth dropped open as she caught sight of herself in the mirror. 'Where's my hairbrush?' she said in a small voice that a ventriloquist might use to insinuate their dummy is trapped in a box.

'Oh, I think it's in our r–' Sophie started to say, before being cut off by the sound of the door slamming shut in an instant and Deanna's footsteps racing down the corridor. Then racing some of the way back again, on remembering that she and Sophie were only in the room next door.

'–oom,' Sophie finished.

She and Alex picked themselves up and wandered over to Jonny and Zack.

'What have we missed?'

'We were just saying that Cynthia obviously wants us to help, so we should,' said Jonny.

'Even if President Pickle is utterly against the idea,' Zack added, with a twinkle in his eye. 'Which, you have to admit, is kind of a plus.'

'So where do we start?' Alex asked. The four friends looked at each other blankly.

Alex had hit it on the head. Their only clues to use as a starting point were an overheard conversation, a weird sort of riddle that President Pickle had torn up, and a near-accident involving a flying sword, which might or might not have anything to do with the rest of it. Where do you go from there?

Where indeed?

10

5 P.M.

'So is it . . . safe?' Sophie asked Cynthia.

The four friends were at the entrance to the Montpellier Room, which was set up a bit like a wedding reception, but one where they'd not properly budgeted and had run out of money halfway through making some big decisions. Thankfully, there didn't seem to be any of this 'young magicians have their own eating area' nonsense for the Grand Convention Banquet.

'Our Health and Safety officers have given the area the thumbs up!' Cynthia said proudly, though Sophie could make out just the tiniest twinge of uncertainty, presumably owing to the fact that Cynthia knew it was Steve who had conducted the inspection and that anything which received a thumbs up from him was to be taken lightly, or at least with huge quote marks. 'Not a dangerous cutting implement in sight!'

Jonny leaned over the crowd of young magicians now gathered and listening to Cynthia attentively.

'Just a couple of hundred table knives to worry about,' he said with a grin, 'or did Steve and Jane miss those?'

Cynthia's smile wobbled.

'I'm *sure* those are all *perfectly* safe. Now then, here's what I'd like you to do. I want all young magicians to split up – you're chiefly here to learn from our esteemed senior members, remember – so maybe see if they can show you some tricks in between courses. And there are a *lot* of courses . . .'

I bet there are, thought Zack cheekily, who occasionally wondered whether magicians were in fact a special breed of hyena. Snarly, smiley and always ready to eat at any given opportunity.

'And please sit at a different table, each of you,' Cynthia finished. 'We don't want some tables bombarded with youth; there'll be complaints!'

'She wants us to split up?' Alex said as they moved on into the Montpellier Room, a touch of his term-time nerves returning. He had learned a long time ago that there was safety in numbers. If in doubt – and he usually was, in a crowd – then hang together.

'No, it's a good idea,' reassured Sophie. 'We're here to learn after all, and if we all share what we've learned afterwards then we'll each learn four times as much!'

Alex nodded reluctantly. Sophie, as always, made a good point.

'Plus,' said Zack mischievously, 'that way there's only a one-in-four chance of any of us getting lumped with Deanna.' Which everyone had to agree were the best possible odds, short of not seeing her at all that afternoon, but which was verging on impossible given the sparkly dress she had changed into, a kind of polar opposite to the nun's habit she had found herself in earlier, and which contained seven different linings and had cost the lives of several now presumably extinct small animals to make.

'Well, here we go,' said Zack, disappearing into the room now filling up with packs of magicians all drooling at the prospect of more food and – *oh no, what's this boy doing here?* – entertainment.

Over soup (which is genuinely one of my favourite ways to start a new paragraph), Alex sat next to a friendly lady who showed him how to do a coin roll. He could already do the basic move, where the magician makes a coin roll back and forth across the hand, but this lady had the effect down to a T. It was almost as if the coin had come to life!

Sophie was hoping to sit on the same table as Belinda Vine, but sadly there wasn't a space. However, a rather creepy gentleman who smelled a bit like hot dogs taught her what he believed was one of the greatest effects of all time: write down a number (as long as it's sixty-five) and get your audience to pick five numbers between one and twenty-five at random – and the five numbers will always add up to the number you wrote down (as long as it's sixty-five). (And providing no one has seen the trick before. And providing the numbers chosen between one and twenty-five aren't in fact random but pre-selected.)

Over dessert, Zack learned how to bend a spoon in a way that looked like he was really bending a spoon when in fact he was just making it look like he was bending a spoon. Having said that, it didn't stop the doddery magician teaching him the effect actually bending all the spoons on the table in order to explain to Zack exactly what bending a spoon would look like if you really did bend one.

And, while Jonny didn't get to play with knives or samurai swords, he did enjoy being shown how to cut a volunteer's necktie in half with a pair of scissors – and restore it to full health (and – importantly – length) over the cheese course.

Eventually the meal came to an end and the Young Magicians began to drift back together. On her way across the dining room, Sophie heard a familiar fruity voice from a nearby table.

'So, Salisbury – this one? No, quite right. How about . . . this?'

The Toffee Apples were all gathered at a table of their own, plus Max, who was tucking into a bag of something big and ignoring everything else. Charlie and Salisbury listened raptly; Jackson and Mayhew had their attention split between Max's bag and Hugo, who was evidently mid-routine, having laid out several rows of cards, face down, and was idly twirling a pen in his hand. He stopped and scowled up at Sophie as she passed, in case she eavesdropped on his hard-won expertise, but she just smiled and moved on.

'That's old . . .' she murmured to herself.

Alex had shown her that one. And, despite its age, you couldn't deny the clever sideways thinking of it.

The volunteer chooses a card while the magician looks the other way. Then the magician's assistant indicates the cards one by one to the magician, but using a code that only they know. The code can be anything. It could be the card next to the third card that the assistant points at is the card chosen by the volunteer. It could be the only card that the assistant taps in one corner.

When Alex had shown Sophie, also using a pointer like Hugo (his pen), he had casually moved the pointer a bit further down the edge of each card every time he chose a new one. When he had finally reached the bottom corner of the edge, that was the one . . .

Sophie paused and frowned.

'Oh, my giddy aunt!' she gasped, and broke into a run, pushing her way through the tables towards the others. They saw her coming and looked up in alarm.

'The note!' she said to Zack. 'The torn-up note! Have you still got it?'

'Uh – yes, I think so.' Zack pulled the crumpled scraps out of his pocket and spread them on the table. 'Why?'

'Put it back together . . .'

Zack's hands moved quickly as he pieced the riddle back together, still as baffling as ever. Sophie ran her eyes down it, quickly, once, and her face went pale.

'It really is a threat!' She *knew* she hadn't been wrong when she sensed the underlying malice. Sophie craned her neck towards the top table. 'We have to tell him . . . And right now!'

'Tell him what?' Alex asked. He looked again at the lines of writing.

Straight down the side.
See the old has-been?
Why does he still go on?
A sad relic of better days?
Enjoy the memories!
I doubt they will last much longer.
Deal yourself out, or we will.
Easy! See you at the banquet.

'Straight down the side!' Sophie explained as the others looked at her, baffled. 'It's an instruction . . . It tells you how you're meant to read the letter. Read the first bit of each of the following lines.'

'See,' Zack began . . . 'Why. A. Enjoy.'

'Not the *words*, Zack, the *sounds*. The first syllables.'

'OK.' Alex took over. 'See. Why. A. En. Eye. Dee. Ee.'

Jonny's jaw dropped.

'You just spelled out *cyanide*!'

'And it ends ... *See you at the banquet ...*' Zack groaned.

Cynthia's scream cut through the chatter in the dining room.

'Zack, Sophie, Jonny, Alex – get here this instant!'

Every voice, every clink, every slurp fell silent as the gaggle of magicians – old and young, plus Deanna – simultaneously turned towards the high table where President Pickle and other high-ranking members of the Council sat.

Everyone at it had been noisily drilling into all sorts of food, as lions might dive into a gazelle, apart from President Pickle, who just sat there, bolt upright, like a very hungry rabbit, toying with the same bowl of soup for all four courses and salivating as the car headlights came towards it at 70 mph.

But the president wasn't bolt upright any more. For, in that split second, he had collapsed forward into a perfect 90-degree angle, lying face down in his bowl of soup.

'Oh my God, they got him!' Zack whispered, horror-struck. The threats had been real!

The four friends leaped to their feet and immediately ran to the table, in answer to Cynthia's summons.

But President Pickle stirred and lifted his face halfway out of the bowl as green gobbets dripped all around him, like a soggy beast slowly rising from a swamp.

'Yes!' Zack shouted. 'He's alive!' Then he saw how everyone was looking at him and remembered they weren't meant to know about the notes or any impending doom. 'I mean, um, of course, why wouldn't he be? I'm just, you know . . .' He pulled a desperate grin. 'So happy . . .'

'Stop talking now,' Sophie whispered curtly.

'Thank you,' he whispered back.

'Edmund! Darling! Look!' Cynthia gushed, like all this was perfectly normal. 'The Young Magicians are here! Just as you requested!' she added with a look that suggested she was just as surprised by her husband's final, desperate incantation (see the very start of the book if you wish, dear reader, and then skip right back to this place henceforth, thank you very much).

President Pickle gestured them closer.

'Find . . .' he wheezed, his lips still bubbling with pea-and-mint slobber. 'Find who's doing this to me.'

'You mean trying to harm you, sir?' Sophie asked delicately.

President Pickle opened an eye, which seemed semiglued shut. 'Even more important,' he gasped, 'find . . . out . . . who's stopping . . . me from . . .' His voice faded away in a muffled sob.

They leaned in closer to hear the rest, and he seemed to gather strength. 'From . . . *eating*!' he screamed before plopping right back down into the half-empty bowl of soup like a frog doing a belly flop.

11

6 P.M.

The handwriting on the paper was in neat copperplate, all squiggles and wiggles, so that Jonny actually had to squint to see what it was saying behind all the decoration as he read the verse out.

> *'Pickle's our most pompous president,*
> *But to bet for much longer I'm hesitant.*
> *If he doesn't retire,*
> *He'll attract our ire*
> *And soon in his coffin be resident.'*

Jonny uncrossed his eyes with a conscious effort.

'So it wasn't just the cyanide note. This one basically says that if he doesn't step down, it'll make them angry and he'll end up dead.'

President Pickle had plucked a wad of letters from an

inside pocket, neatly wrapped in a ribbon, and handed it over before Cynthia could escort him away from the table, still doubled over and gripping his stomach as if ferrets were gnawing away at it from inside.

The Young Magicians were now back in their room, commencing their investigation in the brief pause between the banquet and the Gala Show.

'Maybe they're just trying to starve him out,' said Zack. 'Make him too afraid to eat. Listen to this one.'

'I say, I say, I say, what's the difference between arsenic and Pickle's neckties?'

'I don't know! What is the difference between arsenic and Pickle's neckties?'

'There isn't one – they're both completely tasteless!'

Hope you're watching what you eat, Pix.

'So more poison,' Zack finished.

'There's a definite theme here, isn't there?' Sophie said, trying not to sound sarcastic. 'He gives up being president, or he gets poisoned to death. Talk about a Magician's Choice! There's slightly more at stake here than chocolate or carrot cake. Even if they're only bluffing about the poison.'

She shivered, like she had when she read the first note. There was something in these notes, like an echo hiding behind the words that only certain people could hear. Whoever wrote this really did not wish President Pickle well.

'It's certainly done the job of scaring him,' agreed Alex, thinking of Pickle's rumpled figure. Once, the man had filled his clothes so successfully that every button had been replaced at least twice a year, but now his dark blue suit hung on him like a malnourished scarecrow.

'You can see why Cynthia was upset,' Sophie said, 'and why he didn't want us involved.'

'Hmm, yeah,' Zack grunted.

Of the four of them, he had the least reason to like President Pickle. The man deserved to have his picture in the dictionary under 'pig-headed'. For once he had an idea in his head it was there to stay, and the more you tried to show him that he was wrong, the more convinced he became that he was right. Zack had suffered from being labelled a thief for a whole year, all because of President Pickle's stubbornness. So it followed that the more anyone tried to force President Pickle into resigning, the more he would put his foot down and stay.

Maybe putting him off his food was the cleverest thing to do, Zack thought. It was hitting him in the one place he could be hurt without actually finishing him off. But it was conniving, torturous and calculated and – to that extent – Zack didn't like the sound of whoever was behind these threats one bit. Even if they did share a common dislike of President Pickle.

'So, now we're authorized to do this, where do we start?' Sophie said with a twinkle in her eye that officially marked the start of their next mission. 'I know who my money would be on, if I had to guess.'

'Eric Diva,' said the other three in unison.

'He looked like he'd just been dropped into a cold bath from one thousand metres when President Pickle said he *wasn't* going to retire,' Jonny added, immediately realizing that such a fall wasn't survivable. (Or maybe it was? Given the right gear and set-up ... Jonny's mind immediately began to weigh up the possibilities and he quickly pulled it back to the matter in hand.)

'But, if it's him, why save President Pickle's life from that sword?' Alex whispered. Alex was too used to being on the receiving end of unpleasantness from kids at school twice his height and half his intellect not to feel President Pickle's humiliation and pain, but then something about all this just didn't add up.

'I mean,' he went on, 'if Eric Diva doesn't want President Pickle to be president, then a tragic accident would be the way to do it. No one would ever suspect him. Why go to such great lengths otherwise?'

'Maybe he just wants to scare President Pickle into resigning.'

'Well, in that case, we've got a little over thirteen hours to work it out,' Sophie said. Everyone looked at her.

'Thirteen hours?' Zack remembered the Crown Jewels case taking much longer than that. He hadn't realized there was time pressure. 'How do you work that out?' he asked.

'Because that's when the AGM is,' Alex reasoned. 'If he resigns, they'll need to elect a new president – and the AGM is when all the Magic Circle officials get elected.'

'Well then, we should get cracking!' Jonny took a single step towards the door – which, with his legs, took him most of the way there, if not a notch further – before he realized they didn't actually have a plan yet.

'There's the Gala Show coming up,' Alex said. 'We need to be there, and we need to keep our eyes peeled. Maybe someone will try something, or maybe someone will just give themselves away –'

'But this time . . . the Young Magicians will be there to stop them!' Zack vowed with a huge grin.

The others looked at him oddly.

'No offence, mate, but President Pickle hates you, and you know it . . .' Jonny began.

'So why are you so eager to help all of a sudden?' Sophie finished. Zack smirked, and began to tick things off on his fingers.

'One, I just don't like whoever's sending those letters. They're mean, and I hate mean people. Two, it's a mystery and I love mysteries. And three . . . Oh boy, three! Three . . .'

They waited eagerly, and Zack's smile grew impossibly wider.

'Three, it will *so* tick him off if we solve it!' He beamed at them, hands held out like he'd just pulled off the most amazing trick and was now waiting for the applause, just as a formality.

'That does make sense,' Jonny agreed, 'in a bizarre, Zack-like sort of way. I mean, Zack-logic doesn't always follow everyone else's . . .'

'I do use a superior system,' Zack agreed.

If they saved President Pickle's life, he would never live it down!

12

7 P.M.

The ballroom was packed when the four friends arrived. Jonny spied four seats together, at a table with a mousy-looking couple in their mid-thirties, and they started to push their way there before Deanna or anyone else could waylay them. As they headed over, they noticed Hugo, Salisbury and Charlie at one table, and Max, Jackson and Mayhew at another, sharing out a packet of biscuits.

Well, Zack thought, *at least some good has come out of this convention!*

They reached the table, and the couple there gave them a cheery wave as they drew closer. At first Alex thought the couple must be brother and sister – it was an easy mistake to make. They wore matching cashmere jumpers and fake grins, as if they were a little afraid to be here and trying hard not to show it. The man also had an extra-large gold crucifix around his neck, so big it could have been a prop. He leaped to his feet as they pulled their seats back and pumped their hands so vigorously that the crucifix came loose and dangled wildly in the four's field of vision.

'Hi! Clive and Victoria Gore!' Clive announced in a Canadian accent. 'And you're the Young Magicians! Gee, this is great!'

'Heh. Yeah. That's us,' Zack said weakly. He was running out of polite smiles and acknowledgements at being recognized.

Victoria giggled before placing a protracted kiss on Clive's lips, her eyes – bizarrely – still trained on the other four. Crikey, if this weekend wasn't turning out to be weird enough as it was!

Alex stared as he turned a bright, burning red.

'B-but . . . aren't you . . .'

'Brother and sister? No! Married,' Clive added. 'But some people say we do actually look quite alike!'

'*Bing-bong!*'

Eric Diva was onstage, doing what he did best.

'Hello, ladies and gentlemen, how wonderful to see you all here tonight! Especially after the events of this afternoon. The near miss, let's call it! Wow, wasn't that something!'

Sophie noticed that the near victim of the near miss was only sitting a few metres away from him. President Pickle's grin was as fixed as a frozen skeleton's. Full marks for tact, Eric!

Well, if Eric Diva were hiding anything to do with the earlier debacle, Sophie thought, he certainly wasn't afraid of talking about it. But then maybe that was a double bluff. Or not. *Grrr.* What were they not seeing?

'Anyway, welcome to the Gala Show. We're here! We've made it! A place for our peers to prove their prowess of prestidigitation and . . .' He trailed off, a little helpless as he tried to think of another word that also started with P and that could top 'prestidigitation'.*

'Anyway, a few safety announcements,' he continued, filling the void like a plug. 'In the event of a fire, the emergency exits are – well, actually there aren't any, so we'll have to magic our way out of here. Good luck, ha ha!'

Yes. Way to warm up an audience, Eric, thought Alex. *Make jokes about everyone dying a horrendous death while piled on top of each other inside this strange place.*

At last Eric Diva did himself a favour and came to the end of his spiel. 'Anyway, enough of me. To open our fantabulous proceedings, all the way from Vancouver, please welcome Clive and Victoria Gore, aka the utterly astonishing, the utterly ravishing *Resurrectio-o-o-n*!'

He held his hand out to the table where the Young Magicians were sitting. Absolutely nothing happened. The Gores had their eyes closed and hands clasped together, deep in prayer.

'Jonny – sorry!' said Eric Diva, getting his attention. 'Do you want to give them a nudge so that we can begin, please?'

---

* Which is a very long fancy-pants word for 'being a magician'.

Jonny delicately prodded Clive in the cheek, causing him to open his left eye a crack. He was evidently a little miffed at having had his conversation with the good Lord interrupted, but smiled politely all the same, conscious that – despite what he was feeling – the good Lord wouldn't want him to go BALLISTIC at this mild intrusion.

The couple got to their feet and sidled nervously towards the stage as Eric Diva moved off to the side.

'OK,' said Clive, 'so one of the main things we like to do before a performance is to pray.'

'Yes, we find it's the best thing to help focus the mind and prepare the body before going onstage,' Victoria added, clasping her husband's hand for encouragement.

The four Young Magicians looked at Cynthia and President Pickle, seated at the nearest table to the stage, their expressions indifferent, clearly not wishing to overly endorse this idea nor reject it outright.

'So if we'd all like to bow our heads,' said Victoria in a soft voice.

Oh right . . . they were actually going ahead with this!

Clive and Victoria reached the stage and knelt down side by side, facing the audience, their hands held aloft.

Sophie looked round the room as everyone slowly bowed their heads. She raised her hand.

'What do you do if you're not religious?' she asked confidently. Victoria looked at Sophie pitifully, like she'd just announced she had a terminal disease, biting her lower lip before eventually deciding on her answer.

'You just go along with it anyway, dear daughter of Eve.'

Unconvinced, Sophie bowed her head about halfway, though not before sneaking a sideways look at Zack, who mouthed at her, *'Me neither!'*

Cynthia shot them both a warning glance from the front, raising her eyebrows. *Behave, you four!*

'OK, let us pray . . .' said Clive solemnly from the stage. 'We pray that the performance we're about to give in front of our valued colleagues of the Magic Circle today goes well and that we don't make any mistakes.'

'Hear our prayer,' added Victoria solemnly as a coda, in case the Almighty had any trouble knowing when her husband had come to the end of his sentence/latest request and was about to start the next.

Clive continued piously. 'We pray that these youngsters – who have been granted the freedom to attend the convention this weekend – may learn from us such that when they come of age in a few years' time they too will be offered full membership of the Magic Circle and may flourish like us.'

'Hear our prayer,' repeated Victoria humbly.

'We pray that everyone's performances at this convention go well. Even for those non-Christians.'

'Hallelujah, praise Jesus!'

And then as a quick addendum Clive rattled off, 'We also pray for Steve and Jane in their performance as Ying and Yang today and hope that their accents are good and the balloons don't pop or anything like that.'

Clive and Victoria kept their arms aloft in silence for several seconds before finally opening their eyes and getting to their feet again. 'Do you wanna press play?' said Clive to Eric Diva quietly, not wanting to ruin the reverent atmosphere.

Eric Diva catapulted offstage and came back with a battered tape recorder, which was probably worth a lot as an antique.

A honky-tonk piano started to play noisily out of the speakers, crackling with too much reverb, playing heavy major chords: the opening few bars to 'Shine, Jesus, Shine'. Clive and Victoria took their places either side of the stage area, blowing each other a kiss and getting into position, ready to give the performance of their lives.

And . . .

Oh – my – God! Sophie and a lot of others thought, quite literally, over the next few minutes.

The room looked on, gobsmacked, as Clive and Victoria smoothly, flawlessly, seamlessly, extraordinarily re-enacted a handful of classic scenes from the Bible using a couple of dog-eared magic props.

'The virgin birth!' Clive announced, gesturing grandly at his wife.

Victoria produced a red handkerchief out of nowhere.

So far, so normal, thought Alex, who had several spare hankies stored up the large sleeves of his blazer for just this sort of occasion.

Then Victoria drew the hanky across her outstretched hand – and suddenly there was a life-size baby doll perched there, way too big to have been cached up her sleeve, or folded in the hanky, or any of the other ways the stunned Young Magicians could think of making something appear from nowhere. Sophie took an instant vow never to pre-judge anyone ever again. The whole meek-and-mild, mousy look had been the very best weapons-grade misdirection concocted by a pair of absolute masters.

'Hot under these stage lights, isn't it, dear?' Clive said. He produced a glass of water out of thin air. 'Water? Or . . .' he added, 'something a bit stronger?' He waved a hand over the glass, and the water became red wine.

'No thank you, darling,' Victoria said reprovingly. 'You know I'm trying to cut back.'

She wagged a forbidding finger at the reddish liquid, which obediently turned back to water again.

It went on. Clive presented a wicker basket to the audience. Victoria plucked five small loaves out of thin air, one by one, and juggled them – well, jiggled them about is perhaps a more accurate description – while Clive got President Pickle to verify that the basket was empty. Then Victoria tossed the loaves one by one into the basket. Clive swung the basket at the audience and a whole cloud of loaves flew out towards the tables. Jonny caught one with a long arm, and broke it into four pieces so they could all taste a bit. It was definitely a small loaf, brown, wholemeal, slightly seeded. Very nice actually!

Clive celebrated the applause by holding out a hand and twirling Victoria round, a bit too vigorously. Victoria's

hand slid out of his and she staggered away across the stage with a small shriek.

'Sorry!' he cried loudly. 'My hands are just a bit sweaty in this heat. Can you think of a way to keep us together?'

'Oh, I think so,' she agreed, producing a large hammer and a six-inch nail from nowhere.

'No!' Jonny whispered. 'Absolutely. No. Way!'

Victoria and Clive held their left hands out, flat, one on top of the other. Clive took the nail and held it point down above his hand. Victoria hefted the hammer and gave the nail a single, solid *thwack*. The nail passed bloodlessly through their combined hands. They tried to tug their hands apart, just to show that they really were joined together by the medium of carpentry. A murmur of surprise and respect rippled round the crowd.

'Is that . . . a trick?' a boggled Alex asked, uncertain of whether he'd witnessed miracle or madness.

The overzealous hymn came to a hollering climax as the couple formed the sign of the cross with their combined bodies. Then, without even appearing to try, the nail was gone and they were separated.

'Ladies and gentlemen, we've been Resurrection. Thank you, God bless and goodnight!' Clive announced, and they left the stage together to the silence that only comes when the audience is too stunned to applaud.

But then the applause did come – a bit determinedly from Cynthia at first, but then spreading round the room. The Young Magicians joined in enthusiastically. Cynthia looked around, encouraging every youngster to applaud, though even she – you could tell – was somewhat weirded out by the offering! *Well, at least it was original*, thought Cynthia, sighing.

Victoria gave the Young Magicians a wink, a far cry from the little mousy figure that had begun the show, as she and Clive passed them en route to the drinks table at the back of the room. Jonny winked back.

A slightly dazed Eric Diva took to the podium again.

'Wow . . . Well! What a way to start a show, right? But now, ladies and gentlemen, I give you, from the deepest, southernmost depths of the Deep South, the extraordinary mistress of deception, I give you *Mizz . . . Belinda . . . Vi-i-i-ne!*'

He stepped back from the podium and led the clapping as Belinda swept forward, like she was about to accept her Academy Award, in a delectable, shimmering, rainbow silk-and-chiffon outfit. Sophie usually paid as much attention to fashion as a platypus pays to nuclear physics, but even she had to admit Belinda had got it exactly right. Look glam at your first appearance, then dial it up even higher when it really matters.

Belinda got to the podium and leaned forward slightly to breathe into the microphone.

'Hi, everybody, how are you doing?' Belinda's gentle Southern tones trickled round the room like sap filling the grooves of an ageing tree. 'It is so lovely to be here, in the oldest hotel in the world with some of the oldest folk in the world – I presume!'

Everyone laughed. It was impossible not to be charmed by the hypnotic Belinda Vine. Even President Pickle cracked a brief but genuine smile.

Eric Diva was halfway back to his seat when she called his name.

'Oh, Eric!' She pronounced it *Ay-uh-rick*. 'Don't sit down yet!' (*yay-uht!*) She picked up a roving microphone from the podium and waggled it. It was a large, lollipop type with a massive bulb on the end. 'I have a little job for you!'

Eric Diva looked around as if to say, 'Who? *Little old me?*' Like *anyone* ever had to cajole him into popping back up onstage.

Sophie's eyes narrowed. She remembered their brief meeting in the Dealers' Hall earlier. Was this the set-up they had been planning? Surely Belinda was more sophisticated than that? Or perhaps Eric Diva was just such a bad actor that even when he was doing something perfectly normal he had the air of the oiliest of well-greased stooges.

'Fix,' murmured Zack, clearly having the same thought. He pulled a pair of theatre glasses from out of thin air and studied the two onstage carefully.

'Now,' Belinda said, while unclipping the podium mic from its stand and handing it to Eric so they both could be heard, 'Eric, I would like you to go round this room from table to table . . .'

The Young Magicians looked at each other, wide-eyed, as Belinda described what Eric Diva was to do. To their utter delight, it sounded a lot like the Minds in Harmony mind-reading act of Ron and Nancy Spencer that Sophie had described earlier! Wow – had Belinda worked out the secret? If anyone was going to get to the bottom of such a deceptive plot, Sophie thought happily, it would be the brilliant Belinda Vine.

Eric Diva looked a little baffled as he stepped down off the stage and went to the nearest table. He began with

President Pickle and Cynthia, while Belinda pointedly turned her back on the audience, the wire from her microphone trailing gracefully, threading round her fingers like an overly familiar snake. Sophie made even more mental notes. Somehow Belinda managed to keep all eyes trained on her, even with her back turned.

'OK,' Eric Diva said into his mic, a little uncertainly. 'Mr President, do you have any small object about your person?'

President Pickle felt inside his pocket and handed something over. Eric Diva held it up so that anyone close enough could see. He put the mic to his mouth.

'OK, Belinda, President Pickle has shown me . . . what?'

All eyes fell on the rear of Belinda Vine – so to speak.

'Hmm, let's see . . .'

Belinda began to pace about on the stage, her head bowed, always with her back to the audience. The Young Magicians studied the back of the stage carefully from where they were sitting. It was all curtains – no mirrors, nothing reflective she could have used to see what was happening behind her, no hidden cameras, no earpieces.

'It's . . . a pen!'

There was polite applause, but everyone had seen a stooge act before.

'What kind, Belinda?' Eric Diva asked.

Another pause while she paced about a bit more.

'A . . . biro.' And then, 'Red.' And, 'Slightly chewed at one end, and there's a crack in the plastic near the point,' she finished.

The applause was louder now – some members still evidently recovering from what they'd witnessed during Resurrection. How on earth was she managing it? The applause grew louder still as Eric Diva, with increasing bravado, went from table to table, picking objects that Belinda identified flawlessly, even down to the smallest detail.

The Young Magicians watched in a kind of daze, though by now Sophie was smiling from ear to ear. So what if she had spotted something going on between Eric and Belinda? Even if he was in on it, whatever the secret code between them was, she had never guessed it would be as good as this! This really was Ron and Nancy's act, brought up to date for the modern age.

Zack had his face jammed into the theatre glasses. Something in what he was seeing didn't add up.

'Are we absolutely sure everyone else here isn't a stooge?' Jonny asked, half joking, but clearly at a loss for any other explanation. Sophie shook her head.

'It's more than that,' she said. 'There's lots of ways you can appear to read minds using a stooge, but the stooge always has to know what's coming next.* This is just too random. And too quick.'

---

* Like this, for example. Everyone writes a word on a piece of paper and folds it up and puts it in a hat. The stooge writes, say, *apple*. You draw the first piece of paper out at random, and you hold it to your forehead, and maybe you wave your hands over it, and your voice goes all spooky and you say, '*This says . . . apple! Did anyone write apple?*'

OK, she knew from the Dealers' Hall that Belinda and Eric had possibly planned something – but how could they have planned all this?

'Size six!' announced Belinda's voice. They looked up. Belinda had guessed a woman's shoe size, based on what was printed inside it, so that it was only visible when the woman took it off and gave it to Eric Diva to hold.

'Or . . .' Sophie paused, then grinned. 'There's the way I did it when Belinda was thinking of the false tee–'

'Hardy Amies.' Belinda's voice interrupted them again.

'Impossible!' Zack squeaked. 'That man tweaked his jacket back just enough for Eric Diva, and him only, to see the maker's label inside.' He peeled the theatre glasses from his face. He had been looking so hard that, when he took them away, he had little red rings around his eyes like he was wearing a thin set of scarlet spectacles.

'But there was no stooge when you did your trick with Belinda. It was just you and B–'

Sophie grinned at him and the penny dropped.

'Oh wow!' Zack breathed. It wasn't often that Zack was genuinely awestruck, but it happened now. '*Belinda* was a stooge?'

Your stooge acts all amazed and says, '*Yes, I did!*' So you unfold the piece of paper to check that it really does say *apple*. In fact, you are now reading what the next person has said, say, *radioactive isotopes*. Then you take a second piece of paper from the hat, do the same act and say, '*This says radioactive isotopes. Did anyone write radioactive isotopes?*' And so on.

Sophie nodded happily. She dug in her pocket and produced the nail-writer.

'I made her an *instant* stooge. Remember I gave her the napkin?' she asked.

Wheels turned in the boys' heads as they worked it out.

'You wrote *false teeth* on it?' Zack asked. Sophie nodded.

'And that's what she drew. When she underlined the drawing, she was crossing out my words. She's a pro – she knew exactly what we were both doing and she helped me out! And that's what makes her the best!'

Jonny whistled.

'No wonder you looked terrified!' He held his hands up together, palms out, and lowered them again like he was worshipping. 'I bow down. I really do. That kind of boldness takes nerves of steel.'

Alex was still watching the show.

'But then what about this?' he said. 'This is almost . . . real!' The four of them looked on, hopelessly baffled. It was a wonderful feeling.

Sophie's mind was whirring so much that she barely noticed that Steve and Jane had now taken to the stage with their infamous Ying and Yang act, which was as colourful as it was horrendous and repetitive. And that was before Steve even opened his mouth and attempted his undoubtedly dubious 'foreign' accent.

She still hadn't worked out Belinda's method a few tricks later, even when the first act of the second half came on: live from Moscow . . . *Konveyyernaya Lyenta*, which apparently translated as Conveyor Belt, and was a truly amazing juggling act with three men and three women: tennis balls, skittles, drumsticks, rings and knives, all flying through the air from hand to hand, left to right on top, right to left below, switching direction with two of the women at either end.

But that's as much as Sophie took in, still in a daze. *How. Had. Belinda. Done. It?*

Then there was the 'Nothing Up My Sleeve' act, which – depending on precisely where you were sitting – was either made easier or a whole lot harder by the fact that the magician was wearing a T-shirt.

Come on, Sophie's mind raced. *How, how, how?*

Then it was the Levitate-Several-Members-of-the-Audience trick, which would have been a fitting finale had it not so obviously turned out to be the Levitate-Several-*Pre-selected*-Members-of-the-*Council* trick. And only the thin ones – minus President Pickle, who now would have been an obvious candidate for this, but who had refused to come onstage on multiple occasions over the course of the evening, obviously not wanting to make himself any kind of further target.

It was a little before 9 p.m. when the Gala Show ended. The last of the applause died away as the audience gradually shuffled to its feet, many of them already grumbling about the quality of the seating, how it was already time for bed, or about the price of the nibbles – there were nibbles? Where were the nibbles? – or the loudness of the playout music, or the . . . sorry, what was that?

'Well, if they're all going to bed . . .' Zack said, rubbing his hands together.

'It leaves the field clear for us to do our thing!' Jonny immediately saw where Zack's mind had gone.

Cynthia was picking her way through the crowd towards them. The Young Magicians turned to face her, smiling, hopeful, awaiting her go-ahead for them to launch some through-the-night investigation.

But Cynthia waved her hands to gather all of the junior members together.

'Now then, all of you need to be back in your rooms by nine p.m., please. No exceptions!'

Everyone's faces fell. Cynthia gently waved down the protesting chorus of 'buts' and . . . well, it was a hundred per cent 'buts'.

'We've another exciting day tomorrow,' she assured them, motioning for them to leave.

With every adult eye in the room on them, the Young Magicians (and indeed all the lower-case young magicians) didn't have a choice. They had to shuffle towards the exits, mingling with the stream of grey faces intent on either hitting the sack or hitting the hotel bar, which – for some – amounted to almost exactly the same thing.

Cynthia had started to make her own way out. She turned ever so slightly to the right, signalling surreptitiously for the Young Magicians to hold back. Hope beat in their hearts. Cynthia knew President Pickle wanted them to help. Maybe she was going to give them permission to stay up!

'Well,' she said cheerfully, 'I hope you'll make the fullest use of this opportunity . . .'

They beamed happily back at her.

'. . . to have a really good think about the clues so far. You can tell me what you've come up with in the morning. Don't stay up too late chatting about it!'

Four faces fell.

'B-but . . . we'd like to take the chance to *look* for clues now,' Zack said. 'You know – having a good poke about?'

She smiled sadly. 'You still have the letters? Then you know everything I do. I'm sure you were all paying attention during the show, so maybe you saw something else that will fall into place if you all put your heads together. But poke about? I'm sorry but no. You have to remember that all of you here – *especially* you four – are the future of magic, and are my responsibility. And, for that reason, I must absolutely insist that you stay in your rooms while you do your thinking. It's safest there.'

Cynthia was torn, but she would no sooner put her junior members in danger – even if it meant saving her dearly beloved – than she would adequately perform a buzzsaw illusion.

Their jaws all dropped like someone had released a pin in their mouths.

'But . . . OK.' Sophie made a decision. Cynthia had told them what she knew. It was only fair to do the same in return. 'Cynthia, we found the latest note, torn up. Um, in reception . . .'

'Oh, *that* one.' Cynthia's face took on a very unusual expression for Cynthia: anger. 'And you worked out what it meant?'

'It meant someone was planning to slip him cyanide at the banquet!' Jonny exclaimed.

Cynthia nodded.

'Exactly. And they failed, clearly, as Edmund is still alive. So they're just going to be even more determined, aren't they? We've had threats, we've had flying swords . . . If it was dangerous before, it's extra dangerous now. Yes, I wanted him to ask you four to find out who might be behind these lurid letters – but not to put yourselves at risk! At this point, I'm sorry, you really have to leave us adults to deal with it. We'd be irresponsible if we involved you any more. Steve and Jane here are going to escort you all to your floor, and will patrol to make extra sure that you stay there. I know you want to help, but I can't let you endanger yourselves. Goodnight anyway, and sweet dreams!'

Dejected, the four friends followed after the other junior members, while Steve and Jane brought up the rear like pantomime police officers.

'Never mind, little'uns!' Steve called out cheerfully behind them. 'I remember all the high jinks I used to get up to when I was your age, and look at me now! If that isn't a life lesson, I don't know what is . . . Off to bed now!'

He started to burble about all the jinks he had got up to – high, low and several intermediate – when he was a lad. The four friends made eyes at each other without him seeing. Steve had no idea what was at stake here.

'Don't worry, it's going to be great!' Deanna breezed cheerfully, slipping her arm through Sophie's and – unusually – picking up on Sophie's crestfallen look. 'We can have a girls' night in together! I've got *so much* to talk about!'

'Wonderful,' said Sophie, trying to sound like she meant it and that her hopes for the night weren't in fact quite the opposite of a girly night in with Deanna.

'Maybe I can help you work on your . . . you know – your overall look. Because it's a bit . . . all over the place, isn't it?' Deanna added with such sincerity it could almost be taken as the nicest thing anyone had ever said about anyone. Ever.

Alex, Zack and Jonny slowly started to edge away, fully expecting a small mushroom cloud to appear over Blackpool's neighbouring regions any moment now and wondering how much shelter they would get if they just hid behind, say, Jane. (That OK, Jane?)

Sophie gazed sorrowfully into Deanna's eyes.

'Oh, Deanna, that is so *kind*! But aren't you feeling a little bit . . . sleepy?'

She held Deanna's gaze, projecting her will into the other girl's confused eyes.

'You've been hiding it so *bravely*, but I can see *you're tired*!' Sophie went on. 'You give so much of yourself to others. You're such a friend to everyone! It must be exhausting . . .'

Deanna gave a little whimper of agreement and nodded. Sophie had it right. As far as Deanna was concerned, everything she did was for other kids. After all, she told herself every day, what could be better for anyone than more Deanna in their lives?

'But you forget the one person who really matters – *you*!' Sophie was relentless. She had the other girl totally in her power. Whatever Sophie said became true in Deanna's mind. 'You must have burned so much energy since we got here. I bet your legs are like jelly. You must be *worn out*!'

Deanna bit back a sob.

'I am. You're right. I give so much . . .'

'I bet you can barely stand on your feet right now!'

Sophie had to move quickly to grab Deanna as her knees crumpled.

'Hardly at all!' Deanna wailed.

'And your eyes look so heavy . . .'

'So *very* heavy!'

Sophie took Deanna's hand and patted it gently.

'You need a good lie-down, Deanna. That's all. A good night's sleep.'

Deanna had almost collapsed where she stood. Sophie took her shoulders and steered her the rest of the way while she stumbled along, gazing at the floor.

Sophie winked at the boys. They gazed back with open admiration. Wow, that was even faster than the time she'd hypnotized a brutish security guard at Scotland Yard!

'I hope housekeeping paid attention to my complaint,' the friends overheard Hugo braying to his companions. 'I couldn't believe how badly my bed was made! I mean surely people know to provide freshly starched sheets, with one corner turned down at *precisely* forty-five degrees. Anything else and –' he sighed dramatically – 'I just can't sleep!'

'No chance he could make his own bed, I suppose?' Zack grinned.

'And starch his own sheets!' added Jonny, imagining the severe starching a poor cotton sheet might get under Hugo's watch.

There were too many junior members for them all to use the lift at once. They all shambled up the stairs in a group, Steve and Jane still following closely behind, pointedly taking up positions to cut off any attempt at getting back the way they came.

'We've got to get out of our room,' Alex said quietly. The others looked at him excitedly, always delighted when confronted with this mischievous side to their friend. 'The AGM is less than twelve hours away now!'

'And, like Cynthia said, there may be a frustrated and angry poisoner around,' Jonny agreed. 'We have to look for clues. If whoever is responsible thinks we're in our rooms, maybe they'll get careless and give themselves away.'

'We'll think of something,' Zack said confidently, but not so loudly as to wake Deanna.

It still felt weird for Zack to be all fired up about helping President Pickle.

'We have to find a way to get past Steve and Jane, though,' Alex pointed out.

'True,' Jonny agreed. 'In fact, if they split up, then that's two people to sneak past unnoticed. So two tricks. Hmm.'

'Oh,' Sophie said, suddenly happening on an idea. 'I can manage one. Just leave it to me!'

'More hypnosis?' asked Jonny excitedly.

'No, something much more fascinating to watch!' added Sophie cryptically.

'OK.' Jonny smiled. 'If you won't tell me your ideas . . . I won't tell you mine!' He grinned to show there was no offence, and scooted up the stairs ahead of them on his long legs.

By the time the others reached their rooms, Jonny was already waiting outside room 207. He and Sophie gave each other a 'challenge accepted' sort of smile: yes, they each had a plan, and no, they weren't sharing the details with anyone else! There is such a thing as showmanship.

Sophie steered Deanna in through the girls' door at 208 while Zack unlocked the door to the boys' room, still mystified, along with Alex, as to what either of the other two was planning.

One thing was for sure – they wouldn't be getting much sleep that night!

'Night, Steve, night, Jane!'

Yeah, right!

13

9 P.M.

'So where do we look first?' Zack asked.

'And,' Jonny added sensibly, 'what exactly are we looking *for*?'

Zack paused for a moment, then nodded unhappily, his way of saying quietly that yes, knowing exactly what they were looking for was kind of a crucial part to all this.

They were all in the boys' room, Sophie having quite literally dropped Deanna off next door in 208.

'I think we should start on the ground floor,' Alex answered. 'All the rooms up here are just bedrooms. Downstairs is where the clues will be.'

'But we don't know what we're looking for,' Zack said in frustration. 'I mean . . . a room with pens and paper in it? A weight-loss chart? A signed confession?' He pushed the fleshy bits of his thumbs up into his teeth (the incisors, to be precise). 'But, if there are clues to be found,

Alex is right. They'll be downstairs. At the very least –'
he jabbed a finger at the bedroom door – 'on the other
side of *that*!'

Jonny grinned widely.

'OK, Sophie, I believe you had something planned to
get us past our gorgeous guardians?'

'On it!' Sophie strode into the middle of the room and
stood, feet apart. She flexed one arm, then the other, and
cricked her neck. She twirled her wrists about before gently
putting both sets of fingers to her temples and closing her
eyes.

'*Deanna-a-a-a!*' she intoned. '*K-i-i-c-c-k . . . of-f-f!*'

The others stared at her, mystified. Could Sophie really
control one of her subjects while in a different *room*? She
opened her eyes and grinned before crossing over to the
adjoining wall and bashing hard.

'Wait for it . . .'

Sophie went to the door and cracked it open a few
centimetres, her ear to the gap.

'*Wait for it . . .*'

Sounds:

– The door to number 208 being flung open.
– Familiar footsteps stomping down towards the end
  of the corridor, carrying the heavy weight of
  ATTITUDE.
– A moment's protest from Jane. 'Deanna dearest, you
  really aren't allowed –'

– And then the glory that was Deanna kicking off, full tilt, all systems go, all rockets firing, like a rhino powered by nuclear fuel, back to full strength.

'WHY HAVE WE ALL BEEN CURFEWED LIKE THIS?' she demanded loudly, her voice ringing down the corridor.

'It's for your own safety –' Jane tried to protest.

'BUT DON'T YOU UNDERSTAND THAT OUR LIVES DEPEND ON THIS!'

'I don't see how it's *that* dangerous, sweetheart.'

'I MEAN OUR *PROFESSIONAL* LIVES! LIFE IS ALL ABOUT WHO YOU KNOW AND WHO YOU MEET! HOW ARE WE EXPECTED TO MEET ANYONE *IF WE'RE LOCKED UP IN OUR ROOMS, LADY?!*'

'No one is locking you up – it's just time for bed!'

Sophie poked her head round the door to see Jane with her back to them. She quietly slithered out and gestured for the others to follow. She could explain to them exactly how she'd managed to pre-programme Deanna to do her bidding and kick off at *precisely* the right moment in a bit. But, for now, they had Jane and a whereabouts-currently-unknown Steve to sneak past first.

'OUR FUTURE IS *TICKING AWAY*!' Deanna's voice began to rise, higher and higher up the scale. 'ARE YOU TRYING TO *RUIN* US? IS THIS *DELIBERATE*? *DON'T YOU UNDERSTAND*

THAT YOU ARE SINGLE-HANDEDLY DESTROYING THE HOPES OF THE NEXT GENERATION OF MAGICIANS?'

Sophie, Zack, Jonny and Alex just had to go a few more footsteps round the corner and they'd be out of sight.

'OK,' Zack whispered, having finally worked out what must have happened. 'So Sophie planted a suggestion for Deanna to kick off on cue – which is genius, by the way. I mean *total* genius! But presumably Steve is lurking somewhere round this next corner by the stairs and the lift, yes?'

They all knew this was true – unless Steve was running to rescue his wife from a now truly incandescent Deanna, which would have been a showdown worth staying for if it didn't go against everything they were trying to achieve right at that moment.

The friends crept forward delicately. Alex shuffled his way to the front and clicked his fingers. A dentist's mirror shot down from one of his supersized sleeves. He held it by the handle and gently poked it round the bend of the corridor, like he was invading some giant mouth.

Steve, as Zack had suspected, was in a chair by the stairs and the lift, reading a book and eating crisps, pointedly ignoring the Deanna noises echoing down the corridor.

Alex withdrew the mirror.

'So how do we get past him, Jonny?' he whispered.

Jonny hadn't stopped grinning since they left their room.

'OK, come on, mate. Care to share?' Zack murmured.

Jonny knocked gently on the nearest door. The one that didn't have a number on the front. The one with the plaque that read PRESIDENTIAL SUITE, the words so large that the plaque took over most of the door.

Hugo stepped out in a padded silk dressing gown, tied at the waist with an elegant sash. He and Jonny nodded coolly at each other, and then without a moment's pause Hugo started to complain – like a wounded seagull – as he stepped purposefully round the corner and strode towards Steve.

'Right. Here is my full list of grievances to present to management!' they heard him say. Alex followed his progress in the dentist's mirror.

'One, my sheets were *not* starched, contrary to my specific requirements on the booking form, and the turn-down angle was more like thirty degrees than the full forty-five. Here, look at this . . .'

Hugo fished out a hanky that was, naturally, spotless. He folded it in half, corner to corner, so that it made a perfect isosceles triangle.

'That's more like the kind of thing I'd like to see. Here, take it. Give it to the nearest maid. Do they have maids here? I'm also a touch hungry. Is there room service? Actually, I'd like to speak to the head chef first . . .'

Jonny crouched down so that he could also see the mirror.

'He's good at this, isn't he? Anyone would think he's done it before!' he whispered cheekily.

The moment Steve's back was turned, Jonny gestured for everyone to follow while Hugo continued to chirrup like a battery-powered choirboy.

'Next, the mint on the pillow was *completely* substandard. I expect a *quality* brand, something that Harrods stock at least, not something from some bumper-fun selection box. God forbid those things still even exist. And where oh where, oh where are my evening chocolate-and-ginger biscuits made with real stem ginger and ninety per cent cocoa?'

Oh no! Sophie, Alex and Zack spotted the problem immediately.

There were two flights of stairs, one leading down and one leading up, with the lift in between. Hugo had lured Steve away from one flight of stairs – great – but he was standing right next to the other – the downward flight! Steve was bound to notice them now, surely!

'Third,' Hugo declared, ticking the points off on his fingers, 'the bathroom. The *bathroom*! If you can call it that. The water is too unpredictable – one minute it's ice cold, the next it's boiling hot. No one can live like that, it's too stressful!'

And as Hugo was shifting on to his fourth point – something to do with the distance between the panes in the double glazing being inconsistent – Jonny quickly diverted his friends *up* the flight of stairs to the next floor.

They all had to work hard at not bursting out laughing as soon as Steve was out of sight below.

'OK,' Zack gasped. 'First off, how on earth did you manage to convince Hugo to be on our side? Best magic trick I've seen all weekend!'

'Well, I thought we might need a distraction if we could work out how to get this far. He was pretty cheesed off about being sent to bed early too, so he was happy to join in.'

'Really? That was all it took to convince him?' Zack said, raising a semi-sceptical eyebrow. Jonny shuffled his feet and looked down at the floor. Hmm. Arguably not the best poker face, Jonny!

'OK . . . Plus, I might have promised him shares in all future Young Magicians merchandise as well.'

The others couldn't help but laugh!

'Anyway,' Jonny went on quickly, 'now we're up here, we can just take the lift all the way down to the ground floor.'

Sophie pretended to bow down, like he had done to her earlier.

'Not bad, mister!'

The four friends filed into the lift and hit the button for the ground floor. The doors clanked shut and the lift started to descend before stopping abruptly . . . Exactly. One. Floor. Down.

The doors opened to reveal Steve standing (thankfully) with his back towards them while Hugo continued: 'And finally MY ROOM SMELLS OF EGG!'

Zack pushed the ground-floor button what felt like a million times, hoping beyond hope that this would spur the doors into closing just that little bit quicker than normal, but knowing deep down that this never worked and, if anything, only served to aggravate the electronics.

Hugo peered round Steve, spotting the four looking desperate, and instantly started to freestyle further complaints to prevent Steve from turning round. 'Plus, the carpet needs replacing, the sink needs unblocking, the curtains are teeming with life and I'd like to put some pictures up. Now SORT IT OUT!'

The lift doors closed teasingly slowly as the four breathed a sigh of relief.

I mean, you had to hand it to him. For all his faults, that was a GREAT save – thanks, Hugo!

14

10 P.M.

Alex knelt and gazed at the door handle through his thick glasses. To the average passer-by, one might reasonably conclude that this was the first time the boy had ever set eyes on such a thing. A door with a handle? A *handle*, you say? Are you completely mad?!

But, deep inside Alex's brain, images of locks whistled past as he ran through his own private database. Then he smiled slightly, and nodded to himself, and – with several deliberate flicks of both wrists – produced a long, thin metal spike with a hook at the end, in one hand, and a thin metal shaft in the other.

The bits of metal were a pick and a rake – classic housebreaking tools which could possibly have got Alex arrested, or at least questioned with serious intent, if a police officer had decided to search him – which would never happen because, to the outside world, Alex looked like a harmless, studious urchin, and sometimes – just sometimes – it was very useful to preserve this image. The items were both stored inside the sleeves of his blazer, in little compartments that he had sewn in especially. His mum would have had a fit had she known . . .

'That blazer is meant to get you places, darling! It's not for tinkering with,' she would have said.

'And it does get me into places, Mum,' Alex murmured to himself as he slid the two pieces of metal into the lock. Tinkering away.

The thin shaft was lined with metal ridges that engaged with the pins inside the lock – the bits that actually kept the lock locked. Alex moved the metal gently back and forth until something went click inside, more felt than heard.

Alex twisted the pick, the bit with the hook, and the lock went clunk.

Something or someone moved down the passage and Alex glanced quickly round. Zack was coming out of another room. Their eyes met and Zack just shook his head, his lips pursed.

If there were any clues to be found at all, the friends had decided their best chances of finding them were in the network of function rooms and offices on the ground floor, between reception at the front and the Montpellier Room at the back. After all, this possibly wasn't just the work of one person. This could be a far-reaching plot, and a plot required people to meet and plan . . . ideally in secret, and maybe even to stash their secret stash.

Alex had been making his way from room to room, unlocking each door so that the others could follow in his stead and conduct a search. This was the last room before the large lobby area that led to the bar and the dining room.

Behind the increasingly dejected-looking Zack, Alex saw Sophie and Jonny coming down the passage, which meant they were all done too.

'Nothing,' Zack muttered.

'Zip,' from Sophie.

'Nada,' from Jonny.

Alex shrugged, and tugged on the handle of the last room. The door swung open and he stepped in, quickly followed by the other three.

'Yep. And I think this one's going to be just the same, sadly,' Jonny said as his eyes searched desperately for clues, but only fell on dingy, scuffed carpet and piles of old chairs – the kind of battered plastic ones that you get in primary schools, which smell slightly of sick (correction: smell one hundred per cent of sick). Nope, no clues here. Not today. Not ever.

'Only one thing for it,' Zack sighed. 'We're going to have to search the bedrooms.'

'All one hundred and eighty of them!' Jonny groaned.

'Well, one hundred and seventy-eight,' Alex pointed out. 'We know there's nothing in our two rooms. Unless Deanna is behind all this!'

Jonny held up his hand for silence, his head cocked like a lovely tall doggy.

The sound of approaching footsteps. And the turn of a door handle . . .

By the time the door opened, the Young Magicians had all vanished behind stacks of chairs, each conveniently choosing a height similar to their own, save for Jonny who was now bending his knees while keeping a straight back, and hoping his core strength would last the next few minutes. None of them had the foggiest idea who had entered the room. From his cramped position, all Alex knew was that a man's legs had come in (woven leather loafers, trendily shabby jeans), followed by a woman's (high heels, colourful, floor-length skirt). The man was laughing, fit to bust.

Alex's eyes went suddenly wide. Oh no, they weren't all about to witness – he blushed – any of, you know, *that* going on, were they? Not with the four Young Magicians as hidden observers. That would really be hashtag *AWKWARD*!

Sophie's eyes also flew wide open as the woman spoke, filling the room with the sultriness of the Deep South and fried green tomatoes.

'Are you all right? (*ahl-rayuht?*) I thought you were having a fit!'

'Oh my, I never thought we'd get away!' Eric Diva wheezed. 'One more anecdote about Pickle's early days and I was going to spontaneously teleport, if no one else could do it for me. The number of times he said, "When I was young"! When Pickle was young, he was entertaining the other cavemen by pulling baby mammoths out of a hat!'

Jonny grinned at Alex. So Eric Diva's nice-guy image was . . . let's just say not entirely accurate – but then this was a magicians' convention, and everyone knew you shouldn't take anything at face value.

'Oh, Eric, you are unkind!' (*ahn-kayuhnd!*)

That's Belinda in a nutshell! Sophie thought. *Defending a man who isn't here.*

'But yes,' Belinda continued, 'maybe the Magic Circle is long overdue a new president. We're doing the society a favour.'

Sophie frowned. *Okkkkkkkay*, Belinda wasn't exactly defending President Pickle ... But maybe she was just being realistic.

'*Long overdue?*' Eric Diva snorted. 'Belinda, you know there are telescopes that are so powerful they can look back in time to the furthest reaches of the universe? But let me tell you, we are so *long overdue* a new president that not even one of those telescopes could spot *due* from where we're now standing.'

Surely it couldn't be that these two were somehow behind the plot?

Could it really be *that* easy?

'Well, patience, Eric dear, patience. We have to wait for the AGM before –'

'Before what, Belinda?' said a voice. A third voice. An impossible voice.

The jaws of the Young Magicians simultaneously hit the floor. How did *he* get in with no one noticing?

'Oh wow, Mr President!' Eric Diva exclaimed. 'Didn't see you there! How are you?'

If the discovery that Belinda and Eric Diva might possibly be behind this plot had been mind-blowing, then this was the mic drop to end all mic drops. Where had President Pickle even come from?

'Belinda.' President Pickle's voice sounded calm and friendly. 'Eric. What are you two doing skulking in here? Rehearsing some clever trick, like that quite astonishing telepathy act you did earlier?'

The four friends looked at each other as best they could – Alex to Jonny to Sophie to Zack – as their minds collectively whirled, desperately trying to make sense of everything ... How had President Pickle managed to appear on a whim at precisely the right moment? Or the wrong moment, depending on whose side you were on.

They were absolutely certain no one else had come into the room – in particular Alex, who could see the door, and who had actually watched two people, and two people only, enter.

The only other explanation was that President Pickle had been hiding here all along. So why hadn't they spotted him? In fact, why would he have been hiding in here at all? And why hadn't he emerged to tell them off for sneaking around? No, none of this added up whatsoever.

But, even if you put that to one side, the other question was, how much had President Pickle heard of this potentially mutinous plot from Belinda and Eric? From his affable tone, it sounded like nothing at all.

'Mr President.' Belinda oozed concern. She sounded just like the woman Sophie had thought she was. 'Are you sure you should be walking about on your own? We know about the letters – we'd hate anything to happen to you.'

'Happen to me?' President Pickle started to bellow with laughter. It was a mad, deafening sound – the audio definition of unhinged.

'Oh dear! Oh, dearie me. I'm obviously much better at magic than I thought, if I was able to get it past the likes of you two!'

Silence. None more so than from four watching, waiting, worried young magicians.

'What you don't understand is . . . there is no plot!'

The friends gaped at each other.

It sounded like Belinda and Eric Diva were just as gobsmacked.

'No . . . no plot?' Belinda whispered melodramatically, like this was the rehearsal for some dodgy stage play.

Another bark of laughter from President Pickle. 'Not the faintest sausage of one! I made the whole thing up from scratch! I wrote those letters to myself and even spiked my own food with a bit of saltpetre to get those authentic-looking cramps.'

'But why –?'

'The Young Magicians!' President Pickle screamed. 'Those intolerable, overhyped, untalented brats!'

Who you asked to solve this mystery? Each one of the Young Magicians thought the same baffling thing.

He calmed down, took a couple of breaths and continued in a voice that was almost normal. 'I . . . I have given my *life* to the Magic Circle, I am president of one of the most respectable and honourable societies in the country, maybe even the world, and yet when I say *Magic Circle* what do people say back? They say, *oh yes, those clever children*! They say, *that elongated marionette . . .*'

Jonny bit back an indignant 'Hey!' when he realized President Pickle was talking about him.

'Plus, *the girl-thing*.'

Sophie's eyes narrowed.

'And *the cocky little twerp with the haircut*.'

Zack felt a sudden red-hot fury grip his heart. This from the man they had been trying to save! Talk about ingratitude!

'And *the one who looks like an owl*.'

Alex shrugged to himself. Fair enough. Some people had said that about him and he couldn't wholly dismiss it as a pretty reasonable approximation of his look.

'They say, *you must be so proud of them*! And I – I have to grin like a constipated skeleton, nodding like a screw has come loose and say, *yes, of course, SO proud*, because what else can I do? But I'm going to show the world what they really are! A bunch of kids who got lucky with the Crown Jewels plot, but who don't really know a thing. They'll never solve this new mystery because quite simply . . . there *is* no mystery to solve!'

A stunned pause.

'Well,' said Eric Diva after a moment, 'that was – um . . .'

'Most unexpected,' Belinda filled in for him. 'Will you be stating all that at the AGM, Mr President?'

'I certainly shall! I think it'll make quite a stir, don't you?'

'*Okaaay* . . .' Eric Diva still didn't sound like he knew how to process what he'd heard. Had the president finally well and truly lost it? Talk about going down in a blaze of glory. 'Well, um, Belinda and I are going back to the bar . . . Would you like to come along too?'

'No, you two run along now. I'll stay here with my thoughts for a while.'

There was a pause, and then the sound of footsteps. Alex counted the legs walking past him again, in the other direction. One, two, three, four – two male, two female, the same as before. The door opened and closed.

Zack could contain his fury no longer.

'Overhyped!' he raged. 'Untalented!' He leaped up from behind his stack of chairs. 'We were trying to save y–'

His words dried up as the others all jumped to their feet, ready to confront this meanest of men.

But they found Zack standing stock-still, rooted to the spot, staring round the room in total amazement.

Amazement that they all felt . . . because the room was now as empty as they had found it. Apart from four totally baffled Young Magicians!

15

11 P.M.

They searched the room again, high and low, pulling back the carpet and knocking on the walls to check for any hidden doors. Jonny was tall enough to reach up and rap on the ceiling, just in case a hidden ladder might fall, revealing President Pickle's secret passageway. But no, this particular Pickle-shaped riddle appeared to be frustratingly solution-less.

Eventually they made their way back to the boys' room, still so baffled that they could barely spare the brain cells for small tasks like breathing and walking without bumping into each other. Their thoughts were so awhirl that they forgot about Jane and Steve at their sentry posts – until they found the two of them fast asleep in their chairs, Jane mid-knit and Steve with a copy of *The Stage* draped over his face, rising and falling slowly in time with his snoring, animating the picture of some old-time thespians like they were mid-soliloquy.

They sat on the boys' beds and looked at each other, still keeping their voices down in case the sound made its way through the walls and triggered Deanna's Sophie-proximity-alert.

'I mean,' Jonny said helplessly, 'it has to be some kind of trick, obviously, but how . . .'

'Agreed,' Zack sighed, equally helpless. They'd been floored by decent magic before, but then they'd never expected it to come from the likes of President Pickle, whose go-to trick was usually the one where you made it

look like your thumb had come off. 'But there's something about this that still doesn't add up.'

'Well, the main thing is we've cracked it,' pronounced Jonny with as much chutzpah as he could muster for this somewhat small victory, 'in that there wasn't really anything to crack in the first place! We should at least tell Cynthia, though. Clearly she doesn't know that her vile husband is the one who concocted this whole plot.'

Zack's face clouded with anger again as he remembered how President Pickle had talked about them, and the lengths he was clearly prepared to go to, to humiliate the Young Magicians. Talk about petty!

'Why just tell Cynthia?' he grated. 'Let's tell *everyone*! You know, at the AGM. Bring it *all* out.'

'Yeah, but President Pickle would just deny it, wouldn't he?' Jonny pointed out. 'He'd be all, "You think I'd give up *food* just to get at these four?" I mean, *I* can't even believe he'd give up food just to get back at us, so you can bet no one else will.'

'*Hr-r-r-r-m-m-m* ...' Zack growled and sank into contemplation, scowling at the corner of the room, resting his chin on his hand.

Suddenly he looked up again, more thoughtful. He shook his head as if physically removing the idea from inside it.

'What?' said Jonny in an instant, knowing that this particular movement from Zack often meant he was on to something.

'Well,' began Zack, slowly mulling it over, 'I wonder if there's a connection . . .'

'Between?' asked Sophie immediately, also keen to catch Zack's train of thought mid-flow. She was with Jonny on this one. These were undoubtedly the moments when Zack's inside-out thinking was invaluable.

'Between this and the inexplicable act Belinda did in the Gala Show. I just feel there might be a connection between what we saw earlier this evening and President Pickle's disappearance . . . I just don't know what, but something tells me there's a missing link!'

'Well, maybe we shouldn't start here then,' said Jonny thoughtfully.

'And instead you'd suggest . . .?' Zack encouraged him to go on.

'So Belinda's act was a re-creation of Ron and Nancy Spencer's, right?' Jonny continued. 'Presumably people have been talking about it, and writing about it, for years. And everything they wrote will be in the Magic Circle library, back in London. So that's where we start. Solving Ron and Nancy means solving Belinda, which means solving President Pickle.'

He smiled happily at them, waiting for them to congratulate him on his genius.

'The Magic Circle library?' Zack said. 'The Magic Circle library back in London? The Magic Circle library that's approximately a three-hour train journey away? *That* library?' Zack started to smile as he peered at his oldest friend, his mouth widening into a classic Zack-shaped grin. 'You've got an idea, haven't you?'

'Damn right!' Jonny grinned back. 'We phone a friend!'

They looked at him.

'Alf!' he exclaimed as if they were all totally stupid for not realizing. 'He's back at HQ, there's no one else around because they're all up here, and he's got access to the full Magic Circle library, records – absolutely everything!'

They all had to admit that this was a pretty good idea and, if anyone could help them get out of a sticky situation, it was Alf Rattlebag. And to think they had only been talking about him that morning!

'But,' Sophie pointed out, 'without our mobile phones, how . . .?'

'Way ahead of you!' screamed Jonny, almost knocking himself out on one of the bed posts as he leaped up in a move that was designed to impress but had EPIC FAIL! written all over it.

Steve and Jane were still fast asleep as the four cautiously tiptoed past them down the stairs towards reception. As their eyes adjusted to the gloomy-green light of the exit signs, they spotted the huge, sarcophagus-like desk they had all hidden behind earlier that day, brooding in the corner like a giant sleeping beast. Jonny was right: there was a phone!

All of a sudden, a shadow swivelled towards them, causing the four Young Magicians to make a noise between them that was indistinguishable from the sound of a velociraptor playing a prank on a chimpanzee being watched by a group of audibly appreciative gazelles.

The green lights shone on the face of . . . the receptionist. But now with a different hairstyle, plus he'd lost the fanboy T-shirt. Maybe this was his night-time look?

'That's rather a long shift, isn't it?' Sophie asked boldly, trying to hide how startled she'd just been. 'Weren't you on reception this morning, when we got here?'

The man blinked slowly.

'I'm the night porter,' he announced, like it was the saddest fact in the world. 'The one you saw this morning was my twin brother.'

'Ah! The evil twin!' Jonny tried to make a joke of it, but soon regretted the attempt as the man's head swung slowly round.

'No, I'm the evil one,' he uttered dolorously.

'Please can we use the phone?' Alex asked, getting to the point of why they were there and not wanting to dwell on why this man was self-proclaimed evil.

The head swung slowly back and forth between them as the night porter just as slowly chewed the idea over.

'Now that's a bit of a conundrum. You have to remember I'm evil. So, *being* evil, should I say yes or no? Using the phone is plainly something you want to do, so I'm inclined to say no, to spoil your fun.' He shrugged. Slowly. 'Evil, see? Of course, you could be up to some kind of mischief that will cause no end of problems for everyone, and the evil side of me – which is, to be frank, all of me – would quite like to observe and actively encourage that, so, on that basis, I'm minded to say yes.'

'Great, thanks!' Jonny reached for the phone. With surprising speed, a long-fingered, claw-like and surprisingly strong hand clamped itself round his wrist.

'Ah, but your faces all lit up so happily at that moment,' said the night porter, 'that I'm afraid it's tipped the balance. I'm inclined to disappoint you. So the answer's no, you can't.'

The man let go of Jonny's wrist, and Jonny rubbed it thoughtfully.

But, before the night porter could fully withdraw his hand, Sophie reached out and took it in both of hers. He stared at her with a tiny facial twitch that, by his standards, meant extreme surprise. Sophie's touch was precisely calculated: not so hard as to be unpleasant, not so soft as to be annoying. Firm, warm, almost feline. She ran both hands up his forearm as she locked eyes with him.

'You really don't mind, do you? We can use the phone, can't we? Of course we can. You don't mind. If that's what you want.'

Sophie's biggest strength, her main skill, her *thang* was mental magic. And her ability to access another person's subconscious and sync it with her own was now second nature.

The night porter smiled, creepily, and gently plucked her hands from his arm like he was picking off a couple of gangrenous scabs.

'I can see you're trying to use some form of power of suggestion on me. Sadly, you need a subconscious for that to work, and I don't have one.'

Sophie stared at him, for once totally flummoxed.

'Not even an evil one?' she managed at last.

The night porter tapped his head with a bony finger.

'Oh, it's all evil in here, but there's no subconscious. Nothing is sub anything. Everything's on the top level, as it were. What you see is what you get. Hyper evil but nothing less.'

'Can you stop us going outside?' Jonny asked suddenly.

Another slow blink as the night porter turned the idea over in his head.

'What, four against one and me at my age? I doubt it.'

'Will you raise the alarm if we do go outside?' Jonny clarified.

'Will you be going out to cause mischief?'

'No end of it,' Zack assured him.

'Will people be angry you've gone?' For some reason the question was directed at Sophie.

'Almost certainly.' She nodded vigorously.

'Will you get into trouble?'

Alex nodded so fast that his glasses were in danger of coming off, though he had no idea why Jonny wanted them to go outside.

'Absolutely no doubt,' he said. Two bony, pointy shoulders shrugged through the gloom.

'Then off you go,' the night porter said.

The moment they stepped through the hotel doors, it was as if someone had switched on a fan the size of an aeroplane propeller, poured two or three buckets of freezing cold water into the airstream and blasted the icy mix directly into their faces.

No one was actually there, of course. It was just the beautiful Lancashire coastal weather reasserting itself and reminding them what a good idea buildings were, especially buildings with walls and windows and central heating, and especially, especially on a night like this.

They huddled together in the hotel porch, like emperor penguins on the south polar icecap, keeping each other warm by sheltering their friends with their bodies. Except that emperor penguins are all about the same size, and there are usually several hundred of them, and they rotate to take turns on the outside of the pack to minimize ever getting too cold. Four humans of assorted sizes huddling together were not going to have the same effect, and they soon worked this out for themselves.

'So where are we going?' Alex asked as they stepped out of the porch, drizzle instantly blurring his glasses.

Jonny was already striding down the potholed drive with his coat billowing behind him like the action figure of a cloaked wizard. He paused and looked back with a grin.

'Remember that World War Two communications post? The key word is *communications*. I bet it's still got equipment in there!'

'That's miles away!' Zack protested.

Jonny was already walking again. 'Then we'd better get a shift on, hadn't we?' he called, his voice trailing off with the wind.

'Actually,' Sophie called, 'it's about half a mile.' Jonny paused and looked back. Sophie jerked a thumb in a completely different direction.

'If we take the cliff path,' she added with a smile.

16

Midnight!

CLIFF PATH
EXTREMELY DANGEROUS (OBVS!)
DO NOT PROCEED PAST THIS POINT
(EVEN MORE OBVS!)

The Young Magicians paused at the edge of the hotel property, staring. There was just enough light from the hotel windows to make out the faded lettering.

'I'm sure this sign's out of date now,' Jonny said, trying to sound hopeful. 'They might have fixed it up by now.'

He strode forward in a desperate attempt to look confident as, one by one, the other Young Magicians put their heads down into the wind and rain, like Arctic explorers, though not suitably dressed, and traipsed towards the cliff edge.

The light from the hotel was soon gone. The path twisted and turned in the dark, over-soaked and spongy

moorland, running between vast banks of heather and gorse bushes, the only things that were willing to grow and survive the cold, salty blasts from the sea. Everything was just lumps of grey in the dark of night, with the rain doing its best to further blind them. The only way to navigate was to listen to the sea on one side of them, roaring and raging against the foot of the cliffs, determined to wear them down molecule by molecule even if it took hundreds of thousands of years. (Which it would but the sea is patient. Always bet on the sea. It wins in the end.)

'*Whulp!*' (or a noise very like it) Jonny exclaimed, and his gangly grey shape suddenly vanished. The friends hurried forward, and quickly found out – each in their own way – that the ground was laced with roots and brambles that could trip you up at a moment's notice.

'Maybe I'll take it a bit slower,' Jonny muttered as he picked himself up off the soaking wet ground, feeling rather than seeing a long, wet muddy streak running from his knee and up his leg and waist and ribs along the side of his face to the top tips of his hair. The others mumbled their agreement as they picked their way through the saturated dark a bit more carefully than before.

They made a sort of diamond shape – Jonny still ahead, Zack and Sophie side by side and Alex bringing up the rear, grateful for his thick, heavy, oversized blazer, which gave pretty good protection to most of his body. It was just a shame that it didn't include a hood: his vision through his glasses was just a blur. It was like his prescription had just doubled within the space of fifteen minutes. Thanks, wind and rain!

'So how did you work out this way is better?' Zack called to Sophie over the sound of the wind.

'I looked at the map,' she called back. 'The road up from town curves round this area. The cliff path is more direct.'

Zack remembered Sophie's memory-palace trick with the hotel map, and the promise to show him how it worked. So he trusted her memory. It was just, 'I didn't see any map,' he said.

'Oh, it was in this book in our room. You know, one of those tourist guides to the area, full of interesting folk tales and stuff. Did you know, this is where they had the most recent sighting of the Ribble Render?'

'The Ribble what?'

'No one knows!' Sophie said cheerfully. 'It's this legendary animal, like the Beast of Bodmin and the Portishead Predator and the Fiend from Fangfoss. The guide says it's probably an escaped wild cat from a circus. There's a sighting every few years up and down this part of the coast and they always find the body of an eviscerated sheep lying around nearby.'

'An *eviscer-what*?'

'Eviscerated. It means all its guts scooped out.'

Zack tried to smile but his imagination was already running wild.

'Ah. Heh. Right. Funny, I don't remember seeing any sheep on the way up here.'

'Maybe it was extra hungry. And then there's the banshees.'

'The who?'

'No, the banshees. The book said they've definitely been seen –'

'And banshees are what exactly?'

'They're spirits that come and perch on the roof of a house where someone's going to die, and scream,' said Alex behind them, nervously glancing left and right.

Well, he thought, *if the Ribble Render is some kind of cat, it'll be indoors. Cats hate the wet.* But then again maybe the Ribble Render was different to other cats. A cat that liked to EVISCERATE livestock.

'What do they scream?' Zack asked nervously.

'The book didn't say,' Sophie admitted.

'I suppose, if someone's going to die, then screaming "call an ambulance!" would be a good idea,' Jonny joked from up ahead.

The friends trudged on behind Jonny, with Alex and Zack trying to put the folk tales of predatory wild cats and screaming banshees to the back of their mind. They had a mission – contact Alf – and it was better to focus on that than fall prey to some monstrous . . . COME ON NOW, FOCUS!

'*Whoa!*'

Alex stumbled blindly down the slope for a second, arms waving madly to keep his balance. Something caught his foot and he toppled – *splat!* – face forward into cold, slick, liquid mud that immediately started to close over him.

'*Ach!*'

Alex spat out a mouthful of bitter, brown, grainy goo – hoping beyond hope that this was purely decomposed plant matter and not something that originated from the back end of the Ribble Render. He tried to stand up, but his legs were now held firm, floating inside the sticky, swampy mess.

'Help!' he shouted. 'I think I'm in a bog!'

Even though Alex had read that the worst thing to do when trapped in a bog was to kick and scream, it was all he could manage. Even when he began to sink further and further down into the smelly slime, like he was slowly being absorbed into the earth, like he was melting into it, he did not stop kicking and screaming. Because what else was there to do? Sing? Have a bite to eat? Do the morning crossword? No, if there were ever a time to kick and scream, it was when being eaten alive by the ground. And, if this was the way Alex was going to go, he sure as hell wanted people to know about it.

'HELP!'

And then Jonny was there, crouched in front of him, holding out a long arm, like a superhero.

'Here! Hold on!'

Jonny and Alex closed their hands round each other's wrists as if they were forming a pact. Sophie wrapped her arms round Jonny's waist, Zack wrapped his round Sophie's, and together they hauled Alex back on to dry – well, as dry as could be expected – land, like he was some enormous turnip.

'Are you OK?' Jonny asked anxiously.

Alex could now feel the cold mud soaking into his shoes, clogging up the fibres of his socks and trousers. But it was the tricks inside his blazer that he was more concerned about. He pulled out a dripping brown deck of cards from his pocket – like he was about to advertise a brand of washing powder. 'I'll live,' he said, smiling back up at them. He had to admit, sodden magic props aside, that things could have gone a lot worse.

'Still, if you hadn't nearly died, we might have walked straight past it – look!' said Sophie. Alex turned to where Sophie was pointing. It hardly seemed like the cosiest of places, but the communications post was a damn sight better than the boggy home Alex had last resided in. They had made it!

They all squelched their way over, Alex moving a little slower than the rest, now carrying over half his weight in mud and water trapped inside his blousy blazer.

It wasn't raining inside, fortunately, and it did offer some respite from the wind, but other than that it was as bleak as one might expect an ageing, concrete World War Two communications post on a blustery Lancastrian night should be. Still, minus a slight detour, they were here, and they had a job to do!

'Hello, what's this?' said Jonny in the dark. They heard him grunt with effort. Then there was a metallic click and a snap and a clunk, and a dim light from an old-style incandescent bulb flooded the interior. Jonny's hand was on a large circuit-breaker switch that he had just pulled down.

'And there,' he exclaimed happily, 'is the phone! Told you!'

Sophie, Alex and Zack had almost forgotten what they had come here for. Wasn't their Lord of the Rings style epic trek along a cliff face enough?

The phone looked more like a prop than something that had insides and actually worked. A big black box clamped to the wall, with a handset connected to it by a curly cable, so massive that you needed to practise with weights to lift it, and a rotary dial, and a couple of other knobs and wheels and switches.

Jonny lifted the handset and held it to his ear.

'Completely dead . . .' he said thoughtfully. He studied the rest of the equipment. 'I mean, at this point in films someone usually just turns a wheel to generate enough charge for a connection and they're away . . .' Jonny matched his words with actions and spun the nearest metal wheel near the circuit breaker. He tentatively held the phone back up to his ear and his face split into a massive grin.

'You're kidding!' said Zack, his smile mirroring Jonny's.

'And we have a dialling tone! Wow, I love being me sometimes!' The others laughed out loud . . . Jonny's bonhomie was infectious.

He reached out for the rotary dial with a finger, and paused.

'Oh cripes. Anyone know the number for the Magic Circle?' One look from Sophie told Jonny he needn't worry. 'Course you do!' he beamed.

Sophie began reciting the number digit by digit from memory, as Jonny dialled it in. For every digit he had to stick his finger into the right hole on the dial, move the dial round as far as it would go clockwise and release it. The dial clicked its way back to its starting point, and then you repeated the next digit, and so on. SHOUT OUT TO ANY ADULT READING THIS AND NOW GETTING SHIVERS DOWN THEIR SPINE!

'Wow, how did anyone even make calls back then? It must have taken them ages!' Zack wondered.

'Yeah, and no video, only audio . . . Forget things like FaceTime!'

At last the dial spun itself back to zero as the final digit was entered. The friends gathered round the handset, each of them straining an ear to catch what was going on down the line.

Buzz.

Click.

Buzz-zzz-zzz . . .

Whir.

Squawk!

And then, finally, no, it can't be . . .

Ring!

17

1 A.M.

If you've ever seen *The Phantom of the Opera*, then you might have some definite ideas about theatre ghosts.

In particular you might have decided that:

1. every theatre should have one, and
2. they hang out in a vast underground lair mostly filled with a subterranean lake and thus are at HUGE risk of contracting legionnaire's disease.

Only one of these is, in fact, true.

And that was why the Magic Circle's theatre ghost – or Alf as he was known to his friends – did the exact opposite of live in a damp subterranean lair.

In the five years since he had moved down south, Alf had kitted out a space in one of the attics of the Magic Circle's London HQ as his own private apartment. He had a bed, a chair, a small bathroom and a little kitchenette. He had lined the roof above him with pillows and cushions, so that when warm air rose (mostly from the nostrils of magicians) through every floor of the building below, it pooled in the attic and gave Alf free, cosy central heating. It was snug and dry and it was all his own. And he was at ZERO risk of contracting legionnaire's disease.

Alf had led a mixed life, and had undoubtedly made sacrifices, some because he wanted to, some because they were forced on him. For the last five years, though, Alf had finally felt he was somewhere he *belonged*. He was the happiest man in London.

And, because he had never felt the need for one, Alf had never got round to installing a phone. Which was why it took a long time for the distant ringing from five floors below to penetrate his sleeping subconscious.

(Two hundred and fifty miles away, Jonny was starting to grow anxious.

'Come on, come on . . .'

'How long does a charge last on that thing?' Zack whispered, so as not to wake the banshees.*

'Dunno. Give it another spin. C'mon, Alf, pick up!')

First Alf dreamed he was awake, which didn't help as he lay there sleepily, eyes open, and waited for the ringing to stop. Except that the ringing wasn't going to stop, and his eyes weren't open – they were shut tight, as he was still fast asleep. WAKE UP, ALF!

---

* *Who's forgotten about the BANSHEES already?!*

Slowly, eventually, Alf forced his eyes open, one at a time, then his ears, and finally his brain as he finally admitted to himself that – yes – someone really was ringing the Magic Circle at –

'Oh, good grief,' he mumbled, glancing at the illuminated face of his traditional wind-up alarm clock and throwing back the bedclothes.

Alf wasn't obliged to answer the Magic Circle's phone – in fact, as a professional theatre ghost, he wasn't obliged to do anything apart from vanish when he needed to vanish and, well, that was kind of it – but it was in his nature to do anything to help the society. And some gut instinct – probably based on the way the phone kept on ringing – told him that this wasn't just a wrong-number call from an insomniac insurance salesperson. This kind of persistence in letting the phone ring at 1 a.m. told him it was urgent.

Alf yanked at the string that opened the hidden trapdoor and let the ladder down from his apartment. He was already sliding down it even before its feet touched the landing below.

(Jonny sighed.

'Come ON, Alf!'

'I mean, will Alf even remember who we are?' Sophie asked.

'Of course he will!')

Alf hurried along towards the stairwell. No time for stairs. He swung his leg over the banister and started to slide. Face forward, because that was how he liked it, full throttle and barely touching the sides.

('I don't think he's going to answer.'

'Sorry, Jonny. It was worth a try.')

Alf leaned into the bends as they came up so that his gangly body whipped sharply round at ninety degrees before starting its next plunge – much like a Pendolino train, if trains could navigate stairs, that is. Third floor. Second floor . . .

Right at the end of the banisters, on the ground floor, was – for some inexplicable reason, known only to whoever decorated the Magic Circle back in the seventies (that is, the 1370s) when this kind of thing was acceptable – a large, knobbly, decorative, carved wooden thing that was probably some kind of fruit or vegetable, made by someone who had never seen a real whatever-it-was, but had heard a lot about them.

Towards which Alf is speeding at about thirty miles per hour.

In the dark.

Closer and closer Alf gets. First-floor bend, and then the final straight, down to ground level and the lurking, lethal legume (possibly a pineapple . . . possibly) that is now hurtling right towards Alf's – well, don't make me spell it out. (Just say that if I did, Sophie would roll her eyes, Alex would blush, and Zack and Jonny would snigger.)

('OK, five more rings and then I'm hanging up. One . . .')

But this is not Alf's first rodeo. He is already reaching out with both hands, wrists together and palms spread out, like a wicket keeper. His hands slap into the thing and in a flash he has vaulted over it, like the leapfrog to end all leapfrogs, landed on the tiles of the ground floor, and is running to the ringing phone in the front office.

(*'Two, three, four, five. He's not there. We'll have to think up something else. Sorry, guys. Hanging up.'*

Click.

'Hello?')

At the other end, Alf heard a sudden scrambling sound as four pairs of hands tried to reverse the inevitable fate of a phone that had commenced being hung up on its hook. They were too late. In the lonely, windswept communications post on a distant, damp clifftop, the receiver landed back on its stand.

And was immediately snatched up again.

'Hello?' Jonny shouted. 'Alf? Are you there?'

'Still here,' Alf said calmly, smiling warmly.

Because Alf was old enough to remember how old-fashioned landlines worked. Unless both parties hung up their receivers, the call was still ALIVE. Do with this fact whatever you will. Or ignore it completely.

'Is that . . . Jonny Haigh?' said Alf, both startled and a tad delighted to hear the young lad's voice coming through loud and clear, chocks away!

'YES!' Jonny shouted in relief. 'I mean, yes, we're all here. The Young Magicians,' he added unnecessarily because Alf certainly couldn't imagine him meaning the Pickles at 1 a.m. 'How are you, what have you been up to?! Sorry, actually, don't have a ton of time. We need to know something really urgently.'

Jonny quickly rattled off the details of their query.

'Right. Yes. Vanished into thin air? OK . . . Oh, Ron and Nancy Spencer! Yes, absolutely, they're one of the greats . . .'

Alf sounded like he was jotting all this down. In fact, he was just remembering it, storing it in cursive copperplate at the front of his brain.

'Got it,' he said eventually. 'OK, if the answer's anywhere, it'll be in this building. Give me an hour or so and I'll call you back. Same number? Got it. Bye for now.'

Alf silently hung up and looked at the receiver thoughtfully. He loved a challenge – even in the dead of night – and helping out the Young Magicians was fast becoming a particular forte of his.

'What have you got yourself into now, young'uns?' he murmured, smiling.

'Well, if you find out,' said a voice, creeping up behind him, 'you'll be sure to let me know?'

Alf whirled round. There were very few people in this world that could successfully sneak up on a ghost and cause them to gasp, but then this person standing before Alf had been known to deceive even the sharpest of minds.

'What are *you* doing here?'

18

2 A.M.

The interior of a World War Two communications post doesn't have much in the way of in-house entertainment, unless you're entertained by the sight of a very tall, gangly boy pacing impatiently back and forth while waiting for a phone that hasn't rung in seventy-five years to ring.

Zack squatted down next to Sophie, looking at her expectantly as Alex continued to tend to his sodden blazer, cautiously removing his tricks from the waterlogged pockets like they were fledgling chicks.

'OK then,' Zack said with a grin, 'memory palaces! You promised to tell us how they work!'

'What, now?'

'Well, we've certainly got the time. Or we could go for a lovely clifftop walk in the moonlight instead?'

An extra-strong gust of freezing spray whistled past the entrance as if to reinforce the point. Sophie smiled.

'OK, free tutorial. Right. First you need your palace, which doesn't have to be an actual palace, just a place you know well. Like your home. I presume you know your home well enough to find your way around blindfolded, right?'

'Sure,' Zack said, like it was normal for someone to be able to navigate their house, get dressed and cook while blindfolded.

'Next, you get the things you want to remember. Maybe it's a series of numbers or names. Maybe it's instructions for a recipe . . .'

Zack laughed. 'My kind of recipe hardly needs a memory palace. Open tin. Pour into mouth!'

'OK, bad example. But say you want to memorize pi to twenty digits . . .'

'Three point one four one five nine two six five three five eight nine seven nine three two three eight four six,' Zack said promptly.

'OK, very impressive, but say you want to memorize something that you haven't already committed to memory!' Sophie was getting exasperated. 'Like the serial number on a banknote. In your head, you visualize putting each of the digits – in this case – into specific bits of your memory palace. Say, for example, I imagine walking from the living room to my bedroom . . . I would literally put a big fluffy number two as I opened the door going into the hallway. At the bottom of the stairs I'd visualize a flashing number three, with a number five waiting for me at the top of the stairs. And so on . . .'

Zack handed Sophie a couple of notes from his wallet. She stared at them briefly, before recounting both sets of numbers from memory, plus the sum of all the digits.

Zack sat back, agog.

'I mean, obviously I haven't got a calculator to check whether that sum is correct,' Zack managed, wondering if there were any limit to Sophie's mental capabilities – but also not forgetting to take the notes back.

'Good,' said Sophie, 'because I just made that last bit up, but it was worth it for the look on your face!'

Zack threw his head back and laughed. Sophie sure did like her bold methods – hit them with something sure-fire at first, then befuddle them with something entirely fabricated after!

On the other side of the communications post, Alex had located a semi-dry pack of cards and had started to go through the strange dealing routine Zack had spotted him fumbling with twice now.

And, whatever he was meant to be doing, it *still* wasn't working.

Zack and Sophie wandered over.

'What's up?' Zack asked. Alex looked up at them and blinked.

'Remember how I dealt the cards on the train?' he asked innocently. Zack grinned.

'And did me out of a slice of choccy cake? Of course I remember!'

Alex held out the pack in his palm, face down, and showed them the top card.

'Seven of spades,' they both answered.

Alex put the card back on the top of the pack.

'Say a number between one and fifty-two,' he told them.

'Thirteen?' Sophie suggested.

Alex's hand flicked back and forth over the pack as he dealt out thirteen cards on to the floor, counting them out one by one. Then he took the top card off the pack again and showed it to them with a smile.

'Still seven of spades,' Zack said, grinning.

'Again, in slow motion?' Sophie asked, her eyes narrowed in concentration.

Alex smiled and put the cards back together again before holding them up.

'Left hand holds the pack,' he said by way of explanation, 'while the right hand deals.'

Alex slowly started to deal the cards again, one by one. Zack and Sophie fixed their attention on Alex's hands.

As Alex's right hand moved across the pack to take hold of the top card, it briefly and partially obscured the pack from view. Alex had the thumb of his left hand resting on top of the pack. As soon as his right hand came over, Alex pressed down with his thumb and slid the top card to one side, so that the fingers of the right hand now took hold of the *second* card down. Alex dealt the second card, and at the same time moved the first card back to the left again with his thumb.

'It's called the second deal,' Alex said shyly, 'because you deal the second card without anyone noticing. Or at least that's what it's meant to look like!'

'Smooth as anything!' Zack agreed admiringly.

'On the train, I dealt the top card to Jonny as normal,' Alex went on. 'You'd put the king as the second card, so after Jonny's card that meant it was on top. So I just dealt you and Sophie the ones after it, and kept the king for myself.'

'How did you make sure I got the ace?'

'That was just a very fortunate coincidence. I got lucky, so I pretended it was all part of the routine!' Another devilishly good ploy!

'It couldn't have gone better if you'd planned it!' Sophie laughed.

'So why do you keep dropping cards? It's the second time I've seen it happen now,' Zack said, intrigued. 'You've clearly got the second deal sussed.'

'I'm working on the centre deal now,' Alex explained, 'where you deal the card from the centre of the pack without anyone knowing – and it's a lot harder!'

'I bet. Though why would anyone want to do that?'

'No idea. But, once I've tackled that, I'll move on to mastering the bottom deal.'

'Which, presumably, is where you deal cards out of your bottom, right?' Zack sniggered.

'That's a Jonny joke,' Sophie chided him.

'True,' Zack admitted. 'I should think more carefully about stealing other people's material –'

Jonny came barrelling between them, making a grab for the handset as the phone began to ring . . . like he'd almost sensed it in the air.

'*Alf!*' he shouted into it, before catching himself. 'I mean, um, Alf? Hey! No, of course I haven't been pacing back and forth waiting for you to call back! So – did you manage to . . .?'

He trailed off, and the friends saw his whole body stiffen with surprise.

'Sorry,' Jonny said, not quite believing his ears, '*who* did you say is with you?'

The Magic Circle's library was somewhat of a unique space in the magic world.

First the architect had been given a lower-ground area the size of, oh, let's call it about the size of Wales. Then someone had shown them all the different kinds of books that would be going in. Hundreds of thousands of them, from the size of a miniature pack of playing cards (that would fit inside a Christmas cracker) to the size of a dining-room table. And a big one at that.

Then they had said, 'Find a way to fit all that in.' So the architect – who liked a challenge, but was already feeling a bit overawed – immediately started to think: balconies. Spiral staircases. Ladders. Delicate, curly-wurly wrought iron everywhere. *Massive* bookcases. Wiggly ones, lopsided ones, skew-whiff ones – whatever it took.

Then it had been explained to the architect – whose brain was by now starting to melt slightly – that the filing system would be based on a special method thought up by the then-President of the Magic Circle. Less Dewey Decimal, more Decidedly Deranged.*

The one thing that could be said for it – because many magicians are eccentric, but very few are outright stupid – was that the books were arranged alphabetically. Once you knew which section you wanted, it wouldn't be hard to find the works of a particular author. But finding the section in the first place – that would be the hard part.

Let's just take it as read that there were no terminals, no soft-play areas, no children's corner, no DVD section. Though some wished there were.

Accessibility? Never heard of it. Good luck, was the Magic Circle's response to that one.

There were also one or two built-in security systems the Young Magicians had come into contact with when they were last together, but we won't go into that right now because they didn't so much matter to Alf as he ran back and forth, hither and thither, piling up reference material

---

* Dewey Decimal: the search-engine system for treeware. Invented by Melvil Dewey, who actually did have a life, it's a way of assigning each book in a library with a unique decimal number that not only tells you what subject the book is about, but where to find others like it on the shelves nearby. Mr Dewey would have had a headache bringing his system to the Magic Circle, not least because books there may be classified based on Roman numerals, the Mayan calendar or other strange counting systems.

in the central reading area and trying not to lose his bearings. Truth be told, Alf didn't know this place half as well as he would have liked.

But – then again – he had a guide.

'So what's my grandson got embroiled in this time?' Ernest Haigh asked jovially. 'Telepathy *and* vanishing, I heard you say? It sounds like quite the act.'

Ernest wasn't as gangly as his grandson because he had grown into his height over the course of an impeccably

long life, and his hair – what there was left of it – was the purest white, like on top of a drawn-out snowy owl. Apart from that, he looked like Jonny would if you fed his photo into one of those programs that can artificially age your image and show you what you might look like in a hundred years' time. He moved slowly, with a stick. His joints were old and sore now, so he tended to stay in one place when he could help it. Just like he was doing now, sitting next to Alf's ever-growing pile and using his stick to point out handy sources of information.

Alf had taken about half a second to decide whether or not he could trust Ernest. He too had been surprised and hurt by what Ernest had done. But Alf knew that, deep down, Ernest had only had the best interests of the Magic Circle at heart . . . plus, the bloke had gone to prison for it. As far as Alf was concerned, he had paid his debt to society and wasn't it enough that Ernest had lost the love and respect of his grandson already? And who was Alf to judge?

Alf continued to fill Ernest in on what scant information Jonny had divulged over the phone.

'Well, bless my heart,' Ernest laughed. 'If they can solve the Spencers' act, there'll be no stopping those youngsters. It's baffled me to this day.' He waved a bony hand at the pile of dusty books Alf was slowly forming into a small mound. 'There's plenty of theories, of course, but none of them really hold water. Do you know, I've just remembered there was a particularly good review of their act in the society scrapbook around October 1926 . . . I believe in that pile there, if I recall correctly.'

He waved his stick to indicate.

'This whole Pickle vanishing feat, though,' Ernest murmured while Alf continued to rifle through the mix of books and old society magazines. 'That seems most mysterious . . . but perhaps useful in some way. I just don't know why or how!'

'It hit young Jonny hard, what you did,' Alf commented, without looking up, as he continued to leaf through pages.

'I know.' Ernest bowed his head and was silent for a few moments. 'I had to make a decision – the good of my grandson or of the Magic Circle. I still don't know if I chose the right one. My one consolation is that it hurt me to hurt him even more than it hurt him to be hurt by me.'

Alf had to take a moment to figure his way round that last sentence as his fingers ran over the headline of the October 1926 issue of the *Magic Circular* now facing him:

STUNNING BLEND OF OLD AND NEW TAKES MAGIC CIRCLE BY STORM

The latest technology met with the most ancient of magical arts in the Magic Circle's Grand Theatre on Thursday 5th. For once, even the oldest and most infirm members present did not have to strain their ears to hear, due to the installation of

Mr Marconi's astonishing electrical sound-amplification system at great cost over the last few months. The curtain rose to show a lonely microphone on its stand in the middle of the stage. From either side came the Spencers: Mr Spencer in hat and tails, Mrs Spencer led on by her nurse, because the one thing anyone could be certain of in this evening of marvels and illusion was that Mrs Spencer is certifiably, medically blind . . .

After that, the review pretty well described what Sophie had already told the other Young Magicians, though somehow it sounded even more baffling, for this was undeniable written proof that Sophie hadn't been making it up, or passing on a story that had already been embellished by multifarious mouths in the intervening decades. This was the real deal from someone who had been there, and it was just as astonishing as Sophie had described. The certifiably, medically blind Nancy Spencer had turned her back on the audience, Ron Spencer had gone into the audience and thereafter she had correctly described whatever object an audience member had given her husband, infallibly, with one hundred per cent success rate.

Mr Spencer travelled all the way round the theatre, even to the very highest seats from where his wife was just a dot onstage, relying on the amplification system for his words to be heard below. The finest, keenest eyes of the magical world were upon her, yet no one could divine the secret of Mrs Spencer's astonishing, unbroken success rate.

Alf and Ernest spent some time flicking through the rest of the material, checking they hadn't missed any extra detail, or any other mention of the act.

'Nope, I think we have all that we need,' said Alf, pleased to have something to report back to the Young Magicians waiting for him patiently (yeah, right!) at the other end of the line.

'I agree,' intoned Ernest, looking up at Alf with sad eyes. 'It's nice to be of help, in what little way I can.'

Alf plucked the decaying society magazine from the table and headed for the door as Ernest began to hoist himself up the metal stairs, his walking stick tap-tapping on the floor all the way. From downstairs, they made their way back to the front office. Alf picked up the phone and dialled a number.

'Impressive,' Ernest said behind him. For someone so antique – his words – the elderly man was certainly quick. 'I was watching you take down their message and you didn't note down the number. Maybe you're a mind-reader too?'

Alf smiled.

'I've always had a good memory! Like Father d–' He didn't have time to say anything else because the phone had already been picked up at the other end and the sound of Jonny talking at him now wobbled his earlobes.

'Um, yes – so your grandfather and I found something . . .' Alf began to reply. He paused. 'Your grandfather. Yes, that's right. Ernest has been helping me out . . . No, I don't know how or when he got out either, but . . .'

There was a long silence.

'Hello? Jonny?'

Alf frowned and put his hand over the bottom end of the handset.

'He's there. I can hear him breathing. He's just not saying anything.'

'Just tell him what we found,' Ernest advised gently. 'I don't think he's ready to let me back into his life just yet.'

Alf nodded gravely. Despite everything that had happened, Alf still trusted Ernest, even if Jonny wouldn't and couldn't right now. They had been through too much together.

'OK, here it is,' Alf reported. 'There's nothing on the disappearing act, I'm afraid, at least nothing you don't already know. And no clues on the telepathy method itself, but I do have a review of the Spencers' act . . . You know, like an eyewitness account, if you want me to read it out? OK then. Are you sitting comfortably?'

Alf winced and held the phone away as four voices told him emphatically that they were presently in a freezing cold, concrete World War Two building with no furniture or anything that would ever meet the criterion for 'comfortably'.

'OK, well, quickly then,' said Alf, smiling.

He read them the review, fast enough so as not to get another earful, but clear enough for them not to miss any of the key details.

'So . . . was that helpful?' he asked hopefully.

The silence that followed gave Alf an indication as to what the answer was.

'Yes. Maybe,' said a voice thoughtfully out of the blue. Alf imagined the others staring at Zack, and Zack holding up his hands defensively. 'Hey, I don't know! There was just something in the description that made me think the solution to this whole thing was staring us in the face. I just don't know precisely what, though!'

A mighty yawn seized Alf. It was close to three in the morning after all.

'Well, if there's nothing else right now . ... You'll be sure to let me know how it all turns out, won't you? And yes, lovely to hear from you all again too. Until next time!'

Alf hung up and turned to face Ernest, his half-formed words drying in his mouth as he realized that Ernest had vanished. Alf cocked his head to one side as he heard the unmistakable sound of the old man's stick tap-tapping away into the depths of the dark building, fading away into nothing.

Alf shrugged. Well, the old gent was entitled to come and go as he pleased, now that he was a free man. Another ghost to add to the collection!

19

3 A.M.

Some places look romantic by moonlight – a place where star-crossed lovers might secretly meet on the first day of the rest of their lives.

Some look magical, like they have sprouted from the ground fully formed, for one night only, full of mystery and promise. And at considerable expense!

Some look scary, like ancient Eastern European aristocracy with big teeth and a taste for blood should be flying round the turrets, their cloaks flapping like bat wings.

It would take more than one moon to have any kind of effect like that on Tudor Towers. Two or three moons, a ringed gas giant and maybe a nearby supernova in the sky might just do something, but there was none of that on this particular night. To the Young Magicians, as the hotel front loomed before them, Tudor Towers was just the place they were coming back to after failing in their task. For all their efforts they hadn't learned anything new.

'I was so sure Alf would be able to help,' Jonny moaned. The surprise of hearing that his grandfather was out of jail had been a knock. He wasn't sure if he felt hurt, or relieved, that Ernest hadn't let him (or, he presumed, his parents) know of his release. Still, he forced it to the back of his mind, for he had better things to lament . . . Their plan – his plan – had, to all intents and purposes, failed. They knew nothing more about Ron and Nancy Spencer's act, and – crucially – no clue as to how President Pickle had managed to appear and vanish seemingly at will.

Alex yawned and looked forward to drying off his soggy, wet feet and resting them in bed. Sophie just stared at the ground, wrapped up in her own thoughts.

'We're close,' Zack said, rubbing his temples. 'It's . . . *there*. Somewhere inside my head. I feel like we've got all the facts, it just needs to – I don't know – sort itself out.'

They pushed through the doors and into the gloom of the lobby.

'Did you manage anything evil?' a dolorous voice asked out of the dark.

''Fraid not,' Jonny said glumly. The night porter tutted.

'Ah well. There's always tomorrow.'

The hotel was deathly quiet now. As far as the friends knew, they were the only ones still up. They mooched sleepily and silently down the corridor to the lift.

'Do you think –?' Zack began. The others looked at him. 'Do you *honestly* think this is a deliberate set-up by

President Pickle? I know he's got it in for us, and I know what we all heard him say – but do you think he'd *really* deliberately set this up, along with the fake death threats and going without food and all that, just to make us look even more stupid? It seems unnecessarily elaborate. Surely he's got better things to do?'

'Even if that's true, it doesn't explain how he appeared and vanished in plain sight,' stated Alex, rubbing his eyes under his glasses. 'Nor why he would make something up like that to Eric and Belinda either.'

'Right,' the others agreed, all after a slight delay.

The lift took them up to their floor. Even Steve and Jane had turned in for the night, obviously under the impression they had successfully warded off any illegal extraneous expeditions.

They got to their doors and paused, looking at each other. Then, with a silent four-way shrug, they pushed their way into their rooms.

'Sophie! I simply HAVE to tell you this!' sounded a familiar voice.

Sophie rolled her eyes in the dark, and turned the light on. Deanna was sitting up in bed and staring at her, seemingly wide awake.

'Deanna.' Sophie looked down at herself. Outdoor clothes spattered with rain, legs dotted with mud splashes. 'I didn't know you were still up.'

'Buffalo wings!' Deanna exclaimed.

Sophie stared back at her, confused.

'Buffaloes don't have wings! It should be buffalo *tentacles*!'

'Because . . . buffaloes totally have tentacles?' Sophie ventured.

Deanna continued to stare at her, a bit wild-eyed.

'And no one ever carries a dog on the escalator even though it says dogs must be carried!'

Sophie frowned. 'Not really seeing the connection, but –'

'Do you think it's illegal to make fun of seagulls? It totally should be because roundabouts are so cool.'

Sophie leaned in closer, peering into Deanna's eyes. They weren't quite focused. She waved a hand: Deanna didn't blink. Sophie smiled and breathed out in relief.

Deanna was asleep. This was just sleep talk.

Still, Sophie thought as she got ready for bed and Deanna talked about her plans for building a mosquito trap on the clifftops, she hoped Deanna would shut up eventually. Even better, *very soon*.

Then Sophie realized that, if Deanna were asleep, what was coming out of her now was her subconscious. Deanna was just dreaming out loud. The top levels of her mind weren't even switched on.

Which meant that the route into the back of her brain lay wide open.

'Deanna,' Sophie said in her most assured mentalist voice, 'go back to sleep.'

Deanna's voice dried up like someone had turned off a tap inside her. She keeled over and lay on her side with her eyes closed. A few moments later, she started to snore.

Sophie tugged Deanna's duvet over her, then got into her own bed and turned the light off.

But sleep was a long time coming, as she lay awake in the dark, staring up at the ceiling and running President Pickle's astonishing disappearance through her head, over and over on a continuous loop, not to mention Belinda Vine's earlier performance of Ron and Nancy Spencer's mind-boggling act.

Could it have been some kind of hypnosis? Making the Young Magicians think President Pickle had disappeared when in fact he had been there all the time?

Sophie was very good at short-circuiting other people's minds. With a bit of distraction and confidence, and the right tone of voice, she could make them think things were different to how they were.

But it was only ever for a second or two. With her kind of magic, you had to do the trick and then move on, quick, before the mark realized. It wasn't like you could hypnotize someone and keep them under your spell as they let you into the loose change vaults of the Bank of England.

Plus, you can't hypnotize someone who doesn't even know you're there. The Young Magicians hadn't known

President Pickle was there – and Sophie was certain he hadn't known they were either. Otherwise he would have said something when they came in. Conclusion: it wasn't hypnosis. But what was it then . . .?

It was a very stared-at ceiling that night, or it would have been if the lights had been on for anyone to see it. In the dark of the room next door, in their own beds, the three boys were doing exactly the same thing.

How would I do it? Jonny was thinking. And the immediate answer that came to him was: *Well, with a gadget, of course.* That was what he was good at after all. Making things.

OK, so how had President Pickle vanished with a gadget?

There was no trapdoor. They'd checked.

Jonny's eyes narrowed as sleep hovered round the edges of his mind and his thoughts began to run into each other with less discrimination than they usually showed when he was fully awake. Hmm, a backdrop! A backdrop, hanging from floor to ceiling, painted to look *exactly like* the back of the room – with some really high-quality airbrushing by someone with a good grasp of perspective. President Pickle just stands behind it. At the right moment, he presses a button and the backdrop whips up to the ceiling. To anyone not looking directly at it, he just seems to appear. Then he reverses the process to disappear.

Except . . .

One, no backdrop could be that good when you were up close to it. If it existed, it would have been within a couple of metres of the four friends. They would have noticed.

And even if you ignored that – they had explored every inch of that room. They would still have noticed. They would have bumped into it.

(Sorry, Jonny, not even close, though it would make a neat trick at another time, if you can work on it.)

Networking, Alex thought. His mind was on Belinda and Eric Diva's act. Eric Diva loved to chat and be friendly. It was what he'd been doing all convention. *But then what if . . . every time he chats to someone, he notices something about them and commits it to memory?*

Hmm. Alex frowned a little as it started to come together in his head. This *guy has a blue Nokia phone,* that *guy has a Casio watch . . . Ooh, and maybe he uses a nail-writer to secretly make a list as he goes. Which he passes to Belinda. Which* she *memorizes. And then . . .*

Alex's heart began to beat a little faster. He was so close! He could feel it!

Then Eric Diva goes round the audience, from person to person, in exactly the same order as before, *and gets them to hold up the items he's already made a note of, and Belinda just goes through the list off by heart . . .*

Alex's face fell.

Except that everyone had got changed for the Gala Show. They had put on suits and ties and posh frocks and glad rags. How could Eric Diva know that they would all have the same items on them later that day? Or how could he have stopped them from producing something else from their handbag or pocket or whatnot when asked?

And how did any of it relate to or explain President Pickle's vanishing act? *No, I'm way off.*

But . . . Sleep was closing in. *What if* . . .

(A rather good trick in the making there, Alex – you could probably set up your own telepathy act along those lines if you work on it and get over your dislike of schmoozing with strangers. But, like Jonny, you're barking down the wrong plughole, if you'll excuse the mixed metaphor and to steal a saying from Deanna's dreamy diatribe. Let's see how Zack is doing . . .)

Over in his bed across the room, Zack clenched his fists to dig his nails into his palms. He was going to get this and sleep was not going to get the better of him! Not even if it came with a big, soft, warming, cuddly, snooze-inducing, cosy and welcoming, fluffy . . . *STAY AWAKE!*

OK. If the method behind Ron and Nancy Spencer's act was the same as Belinda and Eric Diva's, then there were certain things that needed to be true in both cases.

(Good start, Zack. Keep going.)

So what did the two acts have in common?

They had both been in theatres, in front of a live audience (the use of the word 'live' here might not strictly be accurate for certain members of the Magic Circle, but let's not get hung up on technicalities just now!).

They had both had the main performer up onstage and the assistant in the audience, moving around with a microphone. Zack smiled slightly at that. It had been kind of cute, that the 1926 reviewer had been so overawed by the awesome new technology – the ability to make sounds louder! Welcome to amplification, world!

They had both had performers who couldn't see the audience. Belinda had had her back turned. So had Nancy Spencer, plus she was blind to boot. So they both relied on the assistant's voice to have any idea what was going on.

Zack shivered, despite the duvet. He was still feeling a little chilly from their night-time walk. He would warm up soon, but the shiver brought back memories of the interior of the communications post. The dank, damp smell of cat pee, Jonny burbling technospeak as he made the call.

No video, only audio . . .

'WELL, DUH!' Zack shouted into the dark. From different places in the room came the sound of two bodies – one quite short, one very long – elevating from their mattresses, convulsing with surprise and getting tangled up in their sheets.

Zack just lay there, grinning. Jonny fumbled for his bedside lamp. One of his long arms swung round in the darkness and knocked it off the stand with a crash.

'Oops!'

Alex was more successful in turning on his bedside light.

'OK, spill – you've thought of something, haven't you!' Jonny swung his long legs out of bed and sat on the mattress, hands together, eyebrows raised as he looked at his friend.

Zack grinned at them, then, without warning, jumped out of bed into the middle of the room, where he struck a pose.

'I've only solved it!' he said. 'I have only *gone and solved it*!' He wiggled his hips from side to side. 'The *world famous*, the *amazing*, the *one*, the *only* Zackary Q. X. Harrison –'

'Those aren't your middle initials,' Jonny objected.

'Who cares, it sounds good! Because *I* have only gone and simultaneously solved the most titillating telepathy puzzle *and* the most vexing vanishing act in the history of the world! Ladies and gentlemen: I have *done it*!'

Alex and Jonny looked at Zack, then at each other, then back at Zack.

'There's no ladies here,' Alex pointed out.

Zack strode over to the wall and thumped it.

'Hey, Sophie!' he shouted at the wallpaper. 'I solved it!'

There was an immediate thump from the other side of the wall, which to anyone who could understand the ancient and oft-derided language of Thumpish basically meant, '*I'll be right there!*'

Alex poked his fingers behind his glasses to rub his eyes.

'OK,' he said sleepily, 'talk us through it?'

20

4 A.M.

The corridor had the eerie quiet that only comes for a couple of hours in every twenty-four, when absolutely everyone else is in bed and the promise of a new day still feels like an eternity away. Zack strode confidently out of the boys' room into the night-light gloom.

'Hurry! The AGM's in four hours.'

The Young Magicians crept back through the corridors of Tudor Towers.

'Why are you in such a hurry to get to the AGM? Like you say, it's in four hours!' quizzed Jonny, smiling, and falling into step beside Zack. 'Are you really that keen to hear President Pickle humiliate us in front of everyone?'

'I really doubt that's going to happen,' Zack said confidently.

The other friends looked at each other with a mounting sense of excitement. No, they didn't understand either, not a single drop – but then this was Zack all over. They'd understand soon, but in Zack's own time.

(Zack, you could have just explained it all there and then in the bedroom, couldn't you? But you're a born showman. Some things just *are*. Water is wet, the world is round and you're going to do it this way. Let's take it from there.)

Soon the friends were in the corridor outside the sets of double doors that led into the ballroom.

'The scene of the crime ... to be,' Zack whispered mysteriously.

Behind the doors, the room was a dark, empty space. The friends fumbled around to find some light switches. They managed to turn on a few spotlights that threw direct beams of photons out haphazardly, and grudgingly gave up enough illumination to cast a half-light over everything else. The stage was now a dim cavern surrounded by curtains. The tops of the tables and chairs all laid out for the show were lit up, but the light didn't reach the bits in between, so the theatre was laced with a random pattern of lines of pitch-black shadow. This was the kind of theatre that deserved to have a ghost, and a real-life one at that, with a far spookier agenda compared to Alf!

'This way,' Zack said, and he led them down towards the stage. 'Right, everyone find somewhere different to sit.'

Zack hopped up the steps at the side of the stage and disappeared into the wings for a moment, looking around for what he knew had to be there. He came back a few moments later, twirling something casually in his hand.

It was one of the lollipop mics that Eric Diva had carried around with him so that he could be heard as he moved about the audience during Belinda's act.

Zack turned round, with his back to them.

'Each of you pretend you've got one of these. OK, so I'm onstage and I can't see you. You're down there. How do you make it seem like we've got telepathic powers, so that I know what you're thinking?'

Alex went back to the ideas whirling around in his head during his ceiling-staring exercise in bed.

'You already know what the other person is going to say?' he suggested. 'Because you know in advance what belongings they have on them. Because the one thing we know this definitely *isn't* is telepathy.'

'Close, Alex,' Zack said with a grin over his shoulder. 'But it would be very complex, managing so many people in that way. And it wouldn't be sure-fire. What if someone pulled a different object to the one you'd already noted down out of their pocket?'

'Yeah, I thought that too,' Alex admitted, still bewildered.

'That's a great big microphone you're holding . . .' Jonny's eyes narrowed. 'Microphones can be a lot smaller. Maybe there's a *third* person, who can see what the assistant is seeing . . . but no one in the audience is looking out for them and they whisper it into their own mic . . . and Belinda picks it up in a hidden earpiece, and . . . *Ach!*'

He shook his head. Jonny knew how it was sounding – way too complicated. Why involve a third person, even if they were unseen? That's just one more person who might be tempted to give the game away or spill the real secret – it's simply not worth it. And anyway how did this third person get to see the up-close details that only Eric Diva could see, like the writing in someone's shoe, or the inscription on someone's brooch?

'Back in the bedroom,' Sophie said thoughtfully, 'you said you'd simultaneously solved the telepathy puzzle and the president's disappearing act. Have I got that right?'

'Sure!' Zack said with a grin. 'At least, I *assume* it's how the Spencers did it too. Of course, they were geniuses and they might have come up with something even simpler and cleverer. But I've definitely worked out how Belinda and Eric Diva pulled off what we saw yesterday evening – but only because first I worked out how President Pickle vanished from that room. Why don't we go back to where it happened?'

'Oh, sure,' Jonny sighed as he got to his feet. 'I just love to revisit the scenes of past humiliations.'

'My mum says you can never revisit exactly the same place,' Sophie said with a smile. 'Either it's changed, or it's changed you.'

Jonny felt his head with his hands. 'That's too deep for this time of the night . . . or do I mean morning?!'

The four friends retraced their steps up to the next floor and the function room adjacent to the Montpellier Room. They had already searched it once, very thoroughly, a few hours ago, and nothing had changed since.

'There's nothing,' Jonny sighed. 'In fact, there's no evidence any of us were ever here at all. Not us, not Eric Diva, not Belinda, not President Pickle. There's *nothing*!'

Sophie and Alex had to nod and agree with him. Zack grinned and patted him on the shoulder.

'Which just goes to show *exactly* how they did it!'

21

5 A.M.

Zack wasn't saying any more than that, so the four friends made their way back to the stairs, Zack leading the way and trailing a wake of smugness behind him for the others to bob about in like buoys in a calm sea.

With any other group of friends, Zack's behaviour might have been quite irritating, arrogant even. But not to the Young Magicians. They knew he was just toying with them ... knowing that each of them was hanging on his every word. And they all knew each of them would be acting exactly the same way if they had been the one to work it all out! This was Zack's moment. Though Jonny also silently noted that Zack had had a very similar kind of moment solving the Crown Jewels plot last time – greedy-chops!

They reached the lift lobby – and familiar voices came down the stairs towards them.

'*Ay-uh-rick* ...'

And there were footsteps descending too.

The friends froze for half a second and looked quickly around for somewhere to hide.

(And why did they want to hide? Well, not only were little human beings like these four meant to be confined to their bedrooms at this unearthly hour, but surely only people who were up to something – as the Young Magicians could personally testify – would be wandering around the hotel at five in the morning. And people who are up to something never want to be caught out by other people who are up to something.)

The only ways out were the corridor leading back to reception (too long: Belinda and Eric Diva would get to the bottom of the stairs and see them before they reached it), the lift (too noisy to be subtle, even if it reached the ground floor in time), or . . . the other stairwell.

And so the four friends waited just long enough to be sure that Eric Diva and Belinda were coming down the left-hand stairwell, and popped up the right-hand one. Not all the way, just far enough to be hidden from anyone on the floor above or the ground floor.

'I hate (*hay-ut*) early-morning starts,' said Belinda's voice as they reached the ground floor.

'Likewise, but needs must,' Eric Diva's voice answered. 'We have to give the ballroom a final check before there's anyone else about.'

'I need my beauty sleep.'

'After today, my dear, we won't *need* early-morning starts – and besides you do not need any kind of extra beauty!' Eric Diva declared. 'The one you already have is overwhelming!'

Halfway up the right-hand stairwell, the Young Magicians rolled their eyes. None of them knew very much about dating, but they were pretty sure that, when the time came, they could manage better than *that*. If this was Eric Diva's idea of flattery, no wonder he was single!

Still, now they knew where Belinda and Eric Diva were going, it was easy to follow them. There were so many corners to turn en route, they could always lag just one corner behind and stay out of sight.

The area outside the ballroom was completely dark when the Young Magicians got there, with only a thin ray of light spilling out of one of the sets of double doors, which had been left slightly ajar. Eric Diva and Belinda were now down by the stage. They had found the switches for the house lights and the whole room was lit up.

And that made it very easy for the four friends to lurk outside, unseen, Zack and Sophie poking their head round one of the double doors, Jonny and Alex round the other. Darkness is the illusionist's friend. When you're in the dark, looking into the light, you can see everything clearly. When you're in the light, looking into the dark, it's much harder.

Eric Diva was on the stage behind the speaker's podium. Belinda was at the table nearest to the stage, legs crossed, arms folded in front of her.

'Once he's made that admission in public,' Eric Diva was saying, 'in front of hundreds of witnesses, Pickle will be potted permanently. He'll never live it down, even when he starts denying he said any such thing. And then we'll move in, for his own good, for the sake of the society. This time tomorrow, my dear, we shall be running the Magic Circle! Our wilderness years will be behind us.'

'Finally!' she agreed. 'It might not be as big as some of the outfits back home, but it's old and it's famous and it's just the right size for us. For now! But let's not forget that Cynthia hired the Young Magicians to find out what was going on. Those are four bright minds – do you think they'll smell a rat?'

Eric Diva snorted. 'Yes, but Cynthia doesn't know she hired the Young Magicians to investigate completely the wrong thing! Don't worry, my dear, the Young Magicians will be putty in our hands!'

The hands of the Young Magicians tightened on the edges of the doors, as four sets of eyes narrowed. So Belinda and Eric had their own agenda this weekend and were up to their necks in this plot! They just needed to catch them out somehow.

'They're not stupid, Eric.'

Eric was fiddling with the microphone on the podium, fitting a foam cover over the end of it – the same kind the portable lollipop mics had. If you looked at it from the right angle – for example, from Belinda's position – it obscured a good portion of his face.

'No, they're not,' he commented absently, 'but they need us as much as we need them. Sure, they're famous, but they're just kids. They need the guiding hands of grown-ups to help them achieve their full potential – and that will be us. President Pickle won't give them the time of day, while we'll give them everything they could possibly ask for. We'll keep them too busy getting what they want to ask questions. They will rise to the top and lift us up the way a rising tide lifts a boat . . .'

He paused and squinted thoughtfully down at where Belinda was sitting.

'Problem, Eric?' she asked.

'I'm just looking at the front row of tables. Do you think they're too close to the stage? How do I look from where you're sitting?'

'They can't be too close, that's for sure.' Belinda got up and repositioned herself on the front row. 'Do you think we should move them all back?'

'Couldn't hurt . . . just half a metre or so . . .'

And it was then that something went *ping!* in Jonny's head. His jaw dropped and his eyes glazed.

'Oh, now that's clever!' he whispered.

Ping!

Ping!

The idea leaped from head to head, Jonny to Alex to Sophie and then on to Zack, who already knew it, and so the idea just shrugged and stopped pinging. Job done.

The friends looked at each other. Then they stepped back, away from the doors, into the dark, and walked carefully round the pool of light splashing through from the ballroom so that they would stay unseen from the stage. They reconvened at the back of the corridor and gazed excitedly at each other in the gloom.

Now they knew how Ron and Nancy Spencer had done their act. Which meant they knew how Belinda had done hers. Which meant now they knew what had happened, back in the room where President Pickle vanished, or at least seemed to vanish, in front of their very eyes.

And from that they could work out that the threatening notes were all part of an act – misdirection. Even the near accident in the Dealers' Hall had been just that – a near *accident*, though handy for the plotters to add fuel to President Pickle's paranoia. His life had never really been in danger. And, as much as it pained Zack to say it out loud, President Pickle wasn't the bad guy in all this.

'You've worked it out then?' Zack whispered.

'It's so simple!' Jonny agreed.

'Totally,' said Sophie. 'Totally. And . . .' She scowled. 'Vicious. Nasty. Cruel.' All the words she would never have dreamed of ascribing to Belinda Vine, with her elegance and grace and kindness.

'But there's just one thing . . .' Alex pointed out, almost apologetically. They looked at him. 'We know *what* they're going to do, and we sort of know *why* . . .'

'You mean cash in on us?' Sophie said bitterly. The others looked at her, at the way her face was set, her teeth clenched, her breathing slow and steady – like someone trying very hard not to scream or burst into tears or totally erupt with rage.

Jonny put a kindly hand on her shoulder.

'I'm sorry,' he said sincerely. 'I know she was your hero.'

Sophie just nodded. She'd get over it, she vowed. She would not let Belinda Vine get away with this.

'Go on, Alex, continue,' she said eventually.

'We just don't know exactly *how* they're going to do it yet, do we?' Alex finished.

Sophie considered their situation for a moment.

'And, for that reason, we can't tell Cynthia,' she concluded. 'There's no proof until they actually do something. If we say what we've worked out, they'll just deny it. We need them to think everything is as it should be and let their plan play out until the last minute.'

'We've got to let the AGM go ahead without saying anything, so we can get the last piece of the puzzle and catch them out in the final few seconds,' Zack agreed.

'And you know something?' Jonny added. 'It's going to be a whole lot of fun doing so!'

Sophie paused, then nodded again.

It might be fun for Jonny. For her, it would be *justice*.

22

6 A.M.

The Young Magicians got back to
their rooms and *finally* slept.
For precisely and exactly one hour.
MORNING!

23

7 A.M.

'Matchsticks,' Zack croaked. His face was pressed into the tablecloth that smelled of 50,000 shades of breakfast, and his eyes were barely open.

The Young Magicians weren't the only ones who were not, let's say, as spritely as a freshly showered Clive Gore on a crisp Christmas morning. Conversation at the other tables was notably muted by the throbbing heads and dry mouths of the older members – some as a result of an excessive stay in the tiny hotel bar, some just because this was what mornings were now like. Even the rattle of cutlery on china sounded apologetic.

The other junior members were fine. Deanna hadn't got up yet. The remains of Class Act were at one table, immaculately groomed, ties neatly Windsor-knotted and business suits spotless, tucking into something green, minimal and macrobiotic. Max and the now thoroughly corrupted Mayhew and Jackson were at another table.

Max's new friends had ditched their jackets, their collars were hanging open, and Max had introduced them to the wonders of the full English breakfast, getting eggy stains on their clothes for good measure. From their half-closed eyes and dopey expressions, the taste of bacon of a morning was like a new religious experience.

The only adult exceptions were Belinda and Eric Diva – who must have been charged with energy at the thought of the impending overthrow of President Pickle – and Steve and Jane (well, who'd have guessed!) who had missed out on the bar due to their sentry duty, and were their usual chatty, chirpy selves. Which just made the people they were being chatty and chirpy at feel even worse. At least the Young Magicians had the best reason for not being fully on top of it. One hour's sleep after a busy night. *Wheesh!*

'Are these matchsticks for a new trick?' Jonny mumbled round the rim of his large mug of coffee, which he wouldn't usually have had the taste for, but then anything for a swift injection of painless caffeine.

'No, I just need to keep my eyes open,' Zack admitted. 'Oh, thanks,' he added as a box landed in front of him, put there by Alex. With a huge effort, Zack strained with his hands and lifted himself into an upright position. He took the box and fumbled with it so that the matches spilled out on to the tablecloth.

'Well, get on with it,' said Sophie. 'We need to keep our eyes on those two.'

She nodded across the dining room to where Eric Diva and Belinda were cheerfully chatting with some of the council members on the top table, and totally not looking like they'd been up before five, applying the finishing touches to their devilish plot. President Pickle was next to them, moodily pushing a full English breakfast around with his fork like it was still alive. He had obviously loaded it on to his plate out of (bad) habit before he remembered he wasn't meant to be eating. He didn't yet know that the Young Magicians had worked out most of the plot and were just waiting for the last pieces to fall into place. He still thought the nasty notes he'd received might have been real.

The Young Magicians had seated themselves on the same side of their circular table so that they could all get a good view of the top table. (The savvy among you may wish to complain to the publishers of this book – in writing – that there is indeed no 'side' to a circle. AS YOU WERE!) Alex absently took a match from the spilled pile, held it up, and ostentatiously wrapped an invisible piece of thread (invisible because it didn't exist, not because it was invisible) round the top with his other hand. He gave the invisible thread a yank and watched the top of the match fly off. No one else noticed. Alex sighed and focused his attention back on the top table.*

* First choose your specially prepared pre-burnt match carefully. Hold it upright between the thumb and first two fingers of one hand, while you wrap the invisible thread round it with the other. When you tug the

Cynthia appeared in front of them, unintentionally blocking their view. She didn't notice when they all subtly leaned to either side of her to see past.

'Well, dears?' She gave them a friendly, hopeful smile. 'Have you got any closer to finding out what's been going on? Who's at the bottom of these threats against Edmund?' She spoke in a kind of hushed, rushed whisper: a sign that she wasn't sure whether she wanted to receive positive or negative news at this stage.

'As a matter of fact, we have.' Zack grinned excitedly. Remembering their mission and addressing Cynthia so directly had somehow boosted his energy levels. Cynthia's face lit up.

'*And?* Please, please tell me! Poor Edmund is at the end of his tether, but he's so determined to go ahead with the AGM. He has the agenda all prepared, and he does love a good agenda. The one he read out on our wedding day actually lasted longer than the ceremony.'

The friends looked at each other.

'Well – we just need to let it play out a little bit longer,' Sophie said. 'We know what's going to happen, we're just not sure how and, until we do, we won't really have anything to tell you that we can prove.'

Cynthia's face fell. 'But – the death threats, the poisoning . . .' This didn't sound like a solution at all!

---

invisible thread, at the same time give the base a gentle flick with your third finger. The vibration makes the top of the match snap off.

'We can absolutely guarantee President Pickle's in no danger,' Jonny assured her. 'That – in fact – is all a brilliantly placed piece of misdirection.'

'Oh . . .?' Cynthia perked up a little and – magician to the core – even looked slightly interested. 'Well, if you're *absolutely* sure . . .' she added slowly, trying to fathom whether she'd made the best decision to rely on these young – undoubtedly brilliant – four. But maybe this was an ask too much.

They assured her that, if she would allow them a few more hours, everything would become clear. Cynthia was just turning back to the top table when Alex surprised himself by blurting out a question that had been bothering him since he first set foot in the Magic Circle.

'Why doesn't President Pickle like children?'

He flushed a burning red when he realized what he'd done, but words said can't be unsaid. The others froze, staring at him, then at Cynthia.

Cynthia's shoulders had braced as if an enormous weight had just dropped on her. Then, slowly, she turned back to face them with a sad smile.

Cynthia sighed. 'Oh dear.'

She pulled back a spare chair at their table and dropped herself into it.

THE STORY OF CYNTHIA AND EDMUND

It was rather sad how it had all turned out.

They had met at the Circle many moons ago, both relatively young and junior magicians, at one of its infamous Easter buffets – a kind of all-you-can-eat affair, or at least that's how Edmund had approached it – starting in adult life as he meant to go on, really. He'd been performing close-up magic at the table when his and Cynthia's eyes had met over the two of hearts.

Several romantic days (and nights) later, Edmund clumsily produced a rose out of his top pocket, which accidentally caught on the lining and was torn to shreds, sending the engagement ring he'd stored carefully and precisely in his waistcoat flying and causing him to chase it round the floor of the medium-swish restaurant (Edmund's compromise between what he *wanted* to spend, what his instincts said he *should* spend and how much he *could* spend) like an odd snuffling pig, sussing out its latest truffle. Eventually, though, and covered in bits of food, he proposed.

And from then on Cynthia was forever Mrs Edmund Pickle, a regular at high-society gatherings, always on display, always polite, a permanent addition to Edmund's arm – a beaming example of magical excellence as Edmund shot straight to the top of the conjuring hierarchy, from a mere councillor at his local club, to President of the Magic Circle itself – taking Cynthia all the way with him (whether she liked it or not). It didn't matter that their life now revolved around society dinners, benevolent events and endless conventions. This was Edmund's calling and Cynthia would accompany him throughout. It was her lot.

And then they'd tried to have children.

It was the one thing that they were truly united on. For the first time a journey that they could embark on together on a purely equal footing. I mean, creating offspring was about as equal as it could get in terms of footings! They entered into it passionately, excited – delighted! – by the prospect of starting their very own magical dynasty. A little baby.

They'd tried for two years before they sought some kind of medical reassurance, and the result was crushing. It was no one's fault. It was just . . . one of those things. And quicker than a magician might vanish a small, beautiful dove, Edmund and Cynthia had to deal with the fact that they would never have children.

From then on, Cynthia had devoted her life to forging some kind of junior arm to the Magic Circle, desperate to attract children from all walks of life, desperate to help, desperate to surround herself with the children she would never have. Edmund, on the other hand, was utterly bereft, stunned into uncharacteristic silence that there wasn't something he could do, or say, or pay for to help. It was like constantly receiving some dreadfully sad news that sat at the back of his mind, festering, bubbling away – unquashable, always there. When he thought about it, he couldn't even finish his chocolate bread-and-butter pudding with extra custard. And so he stopped thinking about it, out of a sheer need to survive. Plus, he really, really liked chocolate bread-and-butter pudding with extra custard.

Until slowly, like it was the only way to rid himself of this affliction, he began to turn against the very idea of children. Putting himself above the idea, cringing at the very mention of them, wincing every time he heard one of their whiny voices. Wherever they were, at the theatre, at a restaurant, at special occasions. If he couldn't have his own little family, then why should anyone else get to have one? Silly little children. What a waste of time. No, fate had magnificently intervened, he would tell Cynthia – *We've dodged one hell of a bullet there, haven't we, darling!*

And, if one thing was certain, there was no way his wife was going to rub his nose in it even more by allowing a junior faction of the Magic Circle to exist and pervade the society he'd worked for all his life. Yes, he knew there were more members dying off at the older end than were coming in. But so be it: the society would die with them in that case. These children would only cause mayhem and run amok. That was all snotty brats were good for.

The clinking, clanking, toasty breakfast buzz of the dining room came back as if someone had just turned up the volume. For a few minutes there Cynthia's voice had been all that the Young Magicians had heard.

Cynthia blinked and jerked her head up, as though she'd been in some kind of trance, just reciting the words under a spell.

'Well, my goodness!' She gave a nervous laugh. 'Do you know, I've never told that to anyone. Oh, my! But it does feel good to have said it out loud.' She smiled, even though she was dabbing at the corner of her eye with a napkin. Then it was all over and she was the Cynthia they knew again, forever cheerful, forever bustling, forever fussing.

'So there you are, Alex,' she said. 'President Pickle doesn't have anything against you personally, so please don't take it that way. Now would you look at the time!'

Cynthia quickly pushed her chair back and hurried over to the top table while the Young Magicians just looked at each other. For once – and note this occasion well because it had never happened before and has very rarely happened since – none of them knew what to say. But, then again, none of them needed to. For what Cynthia had confessed to them, as sad and as tragic a tale as it was, now made abundantly clear why President Pickle acted the way he did towards them. It was all just his way of . . . dealing with an awful situation.

The four watched from their table as Cynthia bent to whisper something in President Pickle's ear. From his expression, she could have been reminding him of the date of his own funeral. Maybe he thought she was.

'I don't suppose she'll tell him we've worked something out?' Jonny mused.

Sophie shook her head. 'She knows he wouldn't believe her – in fact, it might just make him feel worse.'

'But we're still going to do this, right?' Zack checked, and the others all nodded.

Across the room, President Pickle pushed his chair back and tapped a spoon against his glass for silence.

'Ladies and gentlemen, the AGM will commence in five minutes in the ballroom,' he said, sounding like he was announcing his own execution. Without looking left or right, he walked out of the room to face the firing squad while Cynthia hurried after him. She flashed the Young Magicians a final, flustered, hopeful smile, and then was gone.

All around the dining room, people were hurrying to finish their breakfast – scooping up their food, chucking their teas and coffees back, burning their old-as-the-hills throats – and standing up.

The Young Magicians looked at each other, and then Alex shyly held his clenched fist out over the table. He had seen other kids do this and wasn't quite sure how his friends would react, but it was worth a try.

Without hesitation, the other three bumped their fists against his.

'Endgame,' Zack said, and they pushed their chairs back – in chorus – to join everyone else.

PS GO ALEX!

24

8 A.M.

The ballroom was already filling up by the time the Young Magicians got there as the older contingent trudged in like zombies, already moaning about more things than there were physically possible to moan about. The front row of tables – the ones that had so concerned Eric Diva and Belinda earlier – was now reserved for council members, and even the ones behind those had begun to fill up. The four friends would have liked to be closer to the front, but still at least . . .

'Sophie! Over here!' Deanna called. She must have skipped breakfast and come straight here. Her eyes were wilder than usual, her hair was a web of blonde and it didn't look like she'd slept well at all. But her Sophie-DAR was evidently up and running perfectly this morning.

'How does she *do* that?' Zack murmured.

'Yeah, you should probably disable that tracking device at some point, Soph!' added Jonny.

Deanna had kept four seats free for them. Which may go down as one of the most practically useful things Deanna has ever done. At least without assistance.

'Thank God you're OK!' Deanna gushed, looking up at Sophie with huge, tragic eyes as they filed over. 'I dreamed I kept waking up and you weren't there! It was *awful*!' Deanna held her haunted expression for about ten seconds too long, which undoubtedly meant she wanted – hell, needed – a response.

'Probably just a dream!' Sophie joked, tapping Deanna on the head. Deanna slowly turned to face the stage, shocked into silence by the possibility that perhaps Sophie *had* been out all night. Without her.

The clock at the back of the stage was just ticking the final seconds to eight o'clock. On the dot of eight, Eric Diva jumped up on to the stage and rapped a gavel on the podium, much lighter of touch than President Pickle, but just hard enough to prove that he still meant business. He had changed out of his so-cool-it-hurts-actually-these-are-genuinely-too-tight jeans and T-shirt outfit into a grey business suit but with a fluorescent rainbow tie . . . as if to reinforce the fact that his personality was STILL THERE!

'Ladies and gentlemen, honoured members of the Magic Circle, young and old.' He beamed at the audience, but this time there were no *bing-bongs* or other sound effects.

'I declare the Annual General Meeting of the Magic Circle to be open.' He gave the podium a final *thwack* with the gavel. 'Pray silence for your president and mine, Edmund Pickle.'

President Pickle stood up from his chair as slowly as if he had lead weights in his pockets. For all the differences they had had, even Zack suddenly felt sorry for him. Even without knowing what Cynthia had just told them, you couldn't dislike someone who looked so utterly, utterly miserable. Zack almost wanted to run down the aisle and give the man a big hug.

But he couldn't do that. Not yet.

Just a bit longer, Zack promised telepathically, though he of all people knew that telepathy was just a big illusion. *Just a few more minutes . . .*

The four friends leaned forward in their seats, tense and poised for action, with their eyes flitting from President Pickle to the podium to the back of the stage to the backs of the heads of the council members at the front – anywhere or at anything that might provide the final piece of the puzzle. Belinda and Eric were going to enact their plan and take over the Magic Circle. That much they knew. But precisely how was yet to be determined.

President Pickle tapped his sheaf of notes for his speech on the podium in front of him.

'Ladies and gentlemen . . .'

His voice came out as a wheeze. He coughed, and then took a sip from the glass of water in front of him.

Zack slapped his knee gleefully as the last piece of the puzzle fell into place.

'It's the glass!' he exclaimed quietly, so that only his friends could hear. 'It's the *glass*!'

President Pickle spoke. His amplified voice could be heard plainly around the ballroom.

'First of all, thank you for your support at this difficult time. Some of you might have heard rumours of what I was up against. Poison-pen letters, even death threats . . .'

There were sympathetic nods and murmurs from the audience. Onstage, President Pickle was becoming a little agitated, moving from side to side.

'However, it gives me great pleasure to tell you . . . None of it was real! None! I had you all completely fooled!'

Now there were gasps of shock. Every member of the council, most especially Cynthia, was sitting bolt upright, staring at him in disbelief.

'This whole thing was my plan to make you all – yes, all of you, every single one of you here – realize that the Young Magicians – Zack Harrison, Jonathan Haigh, Sophie Yang and Alexander Finley – are just a bunch of *jumped-up upstarts* with *no* talent and *no* respect for their elders, who couldn't even solve a problem like Maria, let alone anything else!' President Pickle yelped. Even though the four had heard bits of this over-rehearsed speech before, hearing it delivered – first hand, as it were – in front of a room full of their contemporaries wasn't easy.

Now President Pickle seemed to be dancing a little jig, shaking the podium back and forth. He gave the microphone a couple of thumps.

Cynthia's face had started to crumple as her eyes filled with big, globby tears. She was shaking her head slowly from side to side, devastated by her husband's humiliating public breakdown.

Zack saw it, and his heart filled with burning anger. She was such a sweet soul and she didn't deserve this.

'Let's end this,' he said, and he stood up, the others with him. Deanna watched in awe as they started to pick their way through the tables towards the stage.

'But let's not be too harsh on them!' President Pickle almost screamed. 'They are young, and easily led. Easily led by *you*, honoured members of the Magic Circle. *You* gave them all this recognition and adulation. There's even ... *merchandise*! *You* must bear some of the blame here. You had *me* – a man who has given his life to your service, to our glorious and magical Circle, who has been here for you for literally decades, through thick and thin, always at your beck and call, never complaining, never asking for anything – and you dared to turn your back on me and look to *them* as the future of magic? But no, apparently, not one of you was intelligent enough to see through their act! So let me ask, sincerely and honestly, just between ourselves – are you all *really* that stupid?'

President Pickle plucked the microphone from its stand now and started to pace about the stage, rocking from side to side like he was on deck during a frenzied storm. The throng of conventioneers watched, agog, the odd bit of dribble falling from their mouths on to their knobbly knees, as their once-respected hero rattled on as if he had gone positively mad, now almost chewing on the microphone like it was a Cornetto.

'And I'll tell you what else you are too. *Jealous!* You're jealous of me and the successes I've achieved during my tenure as president of the Magic Circle. Oh, don't deny it! I can see it in all your eyes. All you hopefuls and possible president-elects. You're all hoping to ride on the coat-tails of the Young Magicians into positions of power!' President Pickle ranted. 'You want me out of the way so that you can take the Magic Circle in your own "modern" direction!'

Belinda and Eric Diva had both left their seats and gone on to the stage by the staircases at either side. They approached President Pickle from different directions.

'Well, I think I've proved that I am completely on top of things, don't you? I've shown you who's boss –'

Belinda gently plucked the microphone from his hands.

'I think that's quite enough, don't you, Mr President?' she asked kindly.

President Pickle's face was beetroot red. Without the microphone, he seemed to all intents and purposes to be struck dumb, gesticulating wildly with his arms like a giant chicken desperate to fly. Belinda handed the microphone to Eric, gazing sorrowfully into his eyes.

'Well . . .' Eric Diva turned to face the audience. His face was suddenly ashen and his voice shook, like someone in a soap opera who had just received the worst piece of news of the entire series. 'That *was* unexpected. Ladies and gentlemen, I have no choice but to propose an emergency motion. I can't offer a medical opinion, but it's clear President Pickle has suffered some kind of mental breakdown. It's a sad thing to happen to such a fine and magical mind, but he obviously cannot continue as our president under the circumstances. I propose that President Pickle be relieved of his duties with immediate effect.'

Even at a time like this, even knowing what he was doing, Sophie had to admire the showmanship. The act was perfectly timed. Eric Diva was riding the wave of sympathy and confusion in the room perfectly, bringing order to a scene that had suddenly erupted in all the wrong directions. People instinctively sought order over chaos. They wanted certainty. His tone was firm and definite – he wasn't giving orders, just speaking with quiet assurance, as though this were the most natural thing in the world, that even these seasoned magicians couldn't object to it. It was almost like hypnosis!

Eric Diva had never shown this talent so explicitly before, Sophie thought – but then that was the sign of a great magician. If he didn't show it, no one would know he had it in him, and the trick would come out of the blue.

'Seconded,' Belinda said sorrowfully. President Pickle wheezed and groaned and twisted in her grasp, but he couldn't break free of her grip.

'All in favour?' Eric Diva asked, and such was the grip of his magnetic spell that, one by one, the hand of every person in the room went up.

Except five.

Cynthia – who was too busy sobbing quietly into her hanky.

And four fine Young Magicians, who had their hands firmly in their pockets, except Zack, who jabbed in fury with a rigid finger at the stage.

'NO!' he bellowed. The shout echoed round the room and startled people out of their daze. If anyone was still a bit groggy from breakfast and hoping for a sneaky doze during the AGM, even if they had somehow managed to nod off during the ravings of President Pickle, then their hopes were almost certainly dashed now. Zack strode down the aisle, backed up by Alex, Jonny and Sophie, as murmurs and questions arose around them.

'Passed, I think,' Eric Diva said calmly, pointedly ignoring the oncoming wave of Young Magicians, 'in front of all these witnesses. Hardly worth counting the nos.'

'This is a stitch-up and you know it!' Zack raged as he clambered on to the stage to face Eric Diva.

'I really don't think so, Zack. We all heard what he said. Uh – Belinda?' Eric Diva turned to face his companion. 'Could you escort *ex*-President Pickle out the back? I think he should have a lie-down before we get him the medical help he so obviously needs.'

President Pickle seemed to have slumped into a silent heap. Days of going without eating had left him broken and defeated. He turned to look at the Young Magicians, as Belinda started to lead him to the back of the stage, with anguished, bloodshot eyes that begged for help.

Alex, Sophie and Jonny quickly ran across the stage and blocked Belinda's way. Perhaps if she'd been without a wilting ex-president in her arms she might have squeezed past, but even though President Pickle had lost a lot of his interior mass, he still had a rather impressive and bulky frame. No matter how much these people starved him of his puddingy treats, you couldn't diminish the size of the man's bullish bones. And that meant that Belinda Vine was well and truly trapped.

With her back to the audience, no one but them could see Belinda's expression. Her usual charm, with its hints of magnolias and sultry warmth, was stripped away, replaced with cold, icy, intoxicating rage. The glare between Belinda and Sophie could have stripped the nuclei from the atoms in the air.

But it was Zack who was left to go toe to toe, nose to nose with a coolly smirking Eric Diva.

'*We all heard what he said?*' Zack snapped. 'But President Pickle didn't say any of that, did he? Because he can't say *anything*!'

'Please!' Cynthia begged. She climbed onstage, still dabbing at her glassy eyes, but determined to be brave. 'Please, for the love of digital dexterity, will one of you just explain what's going on?!'

Cynthia gently but firmly lifted Belinda's hand from her husband's shoulders and guided President Pickle over to

the side of the stage, his eyes still bulging, his lips writhing as strange gurgles erupted from between his lips. Was the man now having a fit?

'I'll show you,' Zack said. 'I didn't know exactly how you were going to do it – until I saw the glass.'

He snatched the glass of water that President Pickle had drunk from off the podium, pressed his palm against the rim and held it up. He splayed all five fingers wide so that everyone could see that he now wasn't holding on to it – but somehow the glass stayed hanging from his hand.

'It's glue!' said Zack. 'Glue around the rim, which got on to his lips when he drank from it.' He scanned the audience. 'Alton, are you out there? Did you sell Eric Diva some of the glue you were showing us yesterday?'

Alton Davenport slowly stood up, suddenly aware that every eye in the ballroom was on him, and that, even if none of the other magicians present understood quite what was happening, this was all a whole lot more fun than the usual AGM, and they expected him to continue with the entertainment.

'Um . . . yes?' he admitted, fumbling his hands together, a glint in his eye hoping that this might end with a pitch so that he could sell some more of the damned sticky stuff for double the price now that it had been tested on the lips of a president, no less!

'Then how do you get it off?' Cynthia demanded. Alton shrugged.

'It wears off very quickly. It's only meant to last for as long as your act. If you want it off sooner, it just needs a solvent. Which I don't sell. But simple nail-polish remover will do it. Not that I paint my nails,' he added with such speed and force that he might as well have just come out and said *I paint my nails*. And who cares if you do, Alton!

Without further delay, Cynthia led President Pickle off the stage and back to her table, where her handbag was waiting, full – thankfully – of all manner of items, including the much-needed, aforementioned nail-polish remover.

'So . . .' Belinda finally spoke. Her arms were crossed defiantly. 'If President Pickle was unable to say all those horrible things . . . how did we all come to hear them?'

'We heard them the same way you and Eric did that amazing telepathy act – and Ron and Nancy Spencer before you!' Sophie spat. 'Because President Pickle didn't say anything just now. Just like how *you* never said anything in *your* act either.'

She turned to face the audience.

'All the time . . . it was *Eric* doing the voices,' Sophie explained. 'One of the first things Eric said to us was how he's a rubbish impressionist and an even worse ventriloquist – well, now we know that was all a lie! In fact, he's brilliant. At both! Last night, when Eric was going round the audience, getting people to show him objects, we were all so focused on watching Belinda that we never saw Eric impersonating Belinda's voice impeccably, and all without moving his lips, straight into the microphone – such that the voice came out of the speakers. We all assumed it was Belinda speaking because that's just what we *expected* to hear. Meanwhile, Belinda stood with her back to the audience so no one could see that her lips were in fact perfectly still.'

'Well!' Belinda affected an outraged pose, hands on hips. 'That is certainly a fine theory, little lady, but oh dear, *where* to start picking holes in it?'

'For instance,' Eric Diva smirked, 'during the act last night, I was holding a microphone – but just now President Pickle was up onstage and I was down there, in the audi– Hey!'

Because while he was so busy smirking at Sophie, Alex – small Alex, not-usually-noticed-in-public Alex – had come up behind him, reached under the collar of his suit jacket and plucked out . . .

'A lapel mic!' Alex announced. 'Discreet and hidden!'

'*I couldn't talk!*' President Pickle suddenly screamed from the back. Cynthia had been dabbing at his mouth with nail-polish remover – which you shouldn't do unless it's a real emergency, because apart from anything else it tastes disgusting – and the glue sealing his lips had finally dissolved. He pushed his way back onstage.

'*I couldn't talk!* You robbed me of my *voice*! My dearest possession, and you corrupted it! You *monster*!'

He glared at Belinda.

'Monsters,' he amended, and then he frowned at the Young Magicians. 'How on *earth* did you work it out?'

Sophie smiled. 'Believe it or not, President Pickle, you were the key to all of this.'

'Really? How?' President Pickle almost sounded flattered.

'We thought you disappeared from a room – when, in fact, you were never really there! We *thought* it was you because we could hear you but not see you. But – as with some of the best magic tricks – the simplest explanation was that you weren't there in the first place. It was just Eric practising his imitation of you for this morning's grand performance.'

President Pickle gaped.

'I *literally* have *no* idea *what* you're talking about.'

The Young Magicians smiled at each other. OK, maybe it wouldn't make sense to someone who didn't have all the facts, but *they* all knew to which particular chapter in this whole plot Sophie was referring to.

Then President Pickle whipped back to Eric Diva, with a finger so close to the man's nose that Eric had to hold his head back to stop the long and stretchy digit from going up a nostril.

'Oh, and don't think I haven't guessed your game!' the president hissed. 'Yes, you wanted to replace me, but that was just the start of it, wasn't it? All those little shortfalls in the accounts, and after we'd been bailed out by Her Majesty last year. All the little things that suddenly didn't add up again, and I trusted you – trusted you! – when you told me not to worry about the society finances, and the overspending here and there . . . I see it now! You've had your fingers in the pie all along, haven't you? I *knew* this convention should be making more profit than it showed. Was I asking too many awkward questions, Eric? Did you want me out of the way so you'd have a clear run at the piggy bank? Was that it?'

For the first time a murmur of discontent rippled round the room. The entertainment was obviously over. Maybe, with a bit of fast talking, Eric Diva could have persuaded them all that it had just been an honest bit of fun. No one had been hurt, he could have said truthfully, and he certainly wasn't the only one who thought that, one way or another, maybe the Magic Circle could do better in the – you know – presidential area.

Eric sighed, and stepped away from President Pickle's accusing finger so that he could stand up straight. He tugged on his jacket, straightened his tie – and smiled.

He looked over at Belinda.

'I think the jig's up, my dear,' he said sadly. He held his hands out. Belinda smiled wryly and came over to join him, taking his hands in hers.

'You may be right, Eric,' she added with that infamous drawl.

They stood pressed close together, hands clasped, and turned to face the audience as if they were about to do the romantic reprise from the last act of a musical. Eric looked into Belinda's eyes.

'We got so close. Old Bill Dungworth dying was just going to be the icing on the cake. I'd have made an absolute steal out of the treasurer's job!'

'So much money there for the taking,' she sighed. 'And then the ultimate prize – the presidency itself!'

'But of course they're all forgetting one thing. President Pickle. The Young Magicians. Everyone.'

Every eye was on him as they all tried to work out *what* they were forgetting.

'And *what* might it be that we're forgetting?' President Pickle demanded after an unnecessary amount of time.

'Don't try to truss a trusted trickster who can trip a trap,' said Eric Diva, and he clicked his fingers above his head. The lights flickered, and he and Belinda vanished.

For a moment everyone was staring at the space onstage where they had been, the silhouette of Eric and Belinda's frames still glowing in their retinas.

Then the Young Magicians dropped to their knees and were feeling round the edges of the trapdoor set into the floor of the stage. It was very well made. The crack was barely large enough to see, let alone dig fingers into.

The moment the trapdoor had opened, a spring mechanism had snapped it shut again. *Impressive*, thought Jonny. And no doubt that same mechanism was connected to the electrical wiring, to make the lights flicker right on cue – just when Eric and Belinda would have vanished from sight.* The flicker was an important part of the illusion

---

* Blame – or thank – Galileo for this. He worked out that gravity isn't like in cartoons, where you can continue to hang in the air for a split second before falling. In fact, it's working on us every second of our lives. We are all in a state of constant acceleration towards the Earth's

because, in the heads of any watchers, the brain would make an image of them persist when they were already gone, hiding the fact that they had dropped through the floor and making it really seem that they had just – well, gone.

'*No!*' President Pickle screamed, his eyes bulging so much that a good slap on the back could probably have popped them out permanently. 'Get them back! Track them down! Seek! Locate! Destroy!'

Cynthia was back at his side, calming, soothing.

'Seek! Locate! Destroy!' he continued to scream as she led him away for the second time, like he was a well-disciplined Dalek. 'Seek! Locate! Destroy! Seek! Locate! Destroy . . .!'

The four friends looked up and their eyes met.

'Should we follow them?' Sophie asked.

'Are you kidding?' Zack asked. 'This is what everything's been building towards . . . It's the final chapter! Alex, how do we get this thing open?'

Alex flexed his wrist, and a playing card slid into his hand from his sleeve. He started to work it into the

_____

core, at a rate of 9.8 metres per second (give or take, but which either way is really pretty fast). The only reason we're not *actually* falling is that usually the ground is holding us up. The moment there's nothing there beneath us, we *instantly* go to 9.8 metres per second. A second later, we're going 9.8 metres per second faster, and so on. So, the next time you trip over and bang your knee on the ground, take a moment to thank it for saving you from a much worse fate. Be grateful to the ground. The ground is your friend. Thank you and goodnight. NO, keep reading!

crack, but the space was still too tight and the card just crumpled.

'OK, we need something stiffer,' he said. 'See if anyone's got a credit card.'

'On it.' Zack hurried off the stage into the audience to see if anyone there was willing to lend their credit card to a fourteen-year-old boy with a reputation for being a thief. The other three stood up and looked at the trapdoor thoughtfully.

'Let's try to think this through scientifically,' Jonny said as he leaped up and down on it hopefully.

'Oh, dead scientific,' Sophie said with a grin, clearly still on a high from having outed Belinda and Eric so publicly – and once again cementing the Young Magicians' reputation as no less than the very best in the business at foiling mischievous magical plots.

Jonny smiled ruefully. 'I suppose it could take both their weight, so it's unlikely to open just because I'm jumping up and . . .'

He trailed off and looked up. The other two followed his gaze. Jonny lifted a hand above his head – and suddenly he wasn't there. The room erupted with further surprise. This AGM was turning out to be an absolute riot!

'What happened?' Zack asked as he came hurrying back, explicably credit cardless.

'Jonny worked it out – somehow,' said Sophie.

'He was looking up there and then suddenly . . . Ah! Got it!' Alex exclaimed.

He ran to one side of the stage and peered up. There was a tiny red dot of light on the wall about a metre above his head, like someone was shining a laser beam on to it. He looked back across the stage to where it was coming from. Yes, there was a pinprick of red light on the other side too.

'There's some kind of beam cutting across the stage,' Alex said. 'I bet it triggers the trapdoor mechanism. Remember when Eric clicked his fingers? He held his hand in the air that's how he must have set it off.'

Alex reached above his head and waved his hand, but he was the shortest of the Young Magicians and not quite lined up properly.

'Let me tr–' Sophie started, and suddenly she was gone too. The now-enraptured crowd went wild!

Alex and Zack looked at each other.

'Shall we?' Zack grinned, gesturing towards the space where Sophie had been standing.

Alex went to join him as Zack reached his hand into the air, clicking his fingers just like Eric had done minutes earlier.

Whoosh! Thud! Ouch!

Zack and Alex found themselves tangled together, all the breath knocked out of them, on the padded landing mat that Eric had put out precisely to prevent any broken bones on the hard concrete floor. A laughing Sophie and Jonny helped them to untangle and get up.

'Welcome to the underworld!' Jonny said in his best spooky voice.

In fact, they could quickly see it was a room the exact size of the stage, but underneath. Most of it was lined with shelves and cupboards full of the most truly intriguing bits of scenery and stagecraft that they had ever seen, and on any other day they would all want to come back here and explore for hours. But the most important thing now was that neither Belinda nor Eric were here.

A pair of double doors towards the far side of the backstage area hung slightly ajar, almost teasingly. *Nothing to see through here*. Yeah, I bet!

'So they could be anywhere in the hotel,' said Jonny. 'Come on, we'll stand more chance of catching them if we split up –'

'*Stop!*' Sophie said suddenly. 'Think how Eric's misdirected us up till now. "Oh, look how bad I am at ventriloquism!" No one leaves a door open like that when trying to escape, it's just too obvious . . .'

The four friends quickly started to search the room for other ways out, running their hands along the walls, trying to locate a groove or latch that might open up some further hidden passageway.

'Unless,' said Zack, wrapping his fingers round the handle of a small cupboard door, 'they never left in the first place and are still . . . here!' He pulled open the door with a mighty tug and almost fell back as a blast of moist sea air blew into his face. The door led straight out on to the slope below the hotel! Well, they'd certainly been *there* before!

The Young Magicians burst through to the outside, the gale from the previous night still billowing and howling all around them almost as if to say, *Welcome back, friends!*

'This way!' screamed Zack as he made out a faint path in the scraggly seaside grass showing where it had just been trampled.

'The chase is on!' Jonny whooped, and he set off, his long legs eating up the distance while the others scrambled up the grassy slope practically on all fours.

Alex had to grit his teeth to pump his legs hard enough to keep up with the others as they fought their way further uphill. The only consolation was that if this were tiring for them, it would almost certainly be tiring for Belinda and Eric too. Plus, as he recalled, Belinda was in high heels and a flowing skirt, and he was almost certain you couldn't run fast in either of those, and my oh my, if that flowing skirt got caught in the wind, then the lady might even take off like a hot-air balloon! But then, if anyone could predict which way the wind might blow, it would surely be the delectable and brilliant Belinda Vine.

'Come on! *Come on!*'

Jonny was waiting for them at the top of the slope, hopping up and down with impatience.

'Where are they?' Zack gasped.

'Can you see them?' Sophie started scanning the area around them with narrow eyes, her chest heaving up and down. Jonny pointed down the hotel's drive. In the far distance, he could just make out the grey blur of Eric Diva's suit and the bright splash of colour that was undoubtedly Belinda's outfit and hair singing against a backdrop of mid-morning sea fog and drizzle.

'Well, come on!' The sight gave Zack a renewed burst of energy and he started to run after them, dodging between the potholes. Sophie reached out to stop him with a hand on his chest.

'Wait, let's think this through,' she said. 'Where do we think they're going?'

'They probably have a getaway car,' Alex panted, leaning on his knees and fighting to get his breath back. 'They'd obviously planned an escape route out of the hotel, just in case things went wrong, so they must have a vehicle hidden away somewhere!'

'What's down the road?' Jonny asked. 'I mean, it's a long way into town.'

'The communications post?' Zack suggested.

'You think those two would ever choose somewhere so untheatrical?'

And it was then that all four of them remembered something with chilling clarity. The only other place on the road nearby.

'The creepy funfair!'

Ferdinand's Fantastic Festival of Fun – that dank, sinister collection of rusting fences and dilapidated, rotting buildings.

'The road curves round,' said Zack excitedly, 'so if we cut straight across the coastal path we might catch them up!'

'Well then, why don't you three get your six little legs pumping and let's go!' Jonny laughed.

They hurried off along the top of the cliff, skirting the EXTREMELY DANGEROUS sign, each of them giving it a mocking nod of approval as they went past. *Sorry, don't mind us . . . again! Coming through!* It was easier to see their way ahead this time, but that only meant you got a better view of how treacherous the path was and how lucky they'd been the previous night not to fall into the fizzing and hissing sea beneath them.

Soon the communications post was looming up ahead. Zack grinned and pointed at a hollow in the path, filled with sludgy brown goo.

'Hey, Alex! Fancy a quick dip to cool down?'

'Not funny,' Alex grunted.

They came over a slight rise and – as if by magic – Ferdinand's Fantastic Festival of Fun appeared through the gloom like someone had dropped it from a great height where it had landed, splat, on the sodden moorland. They were just in time to see the fugitives disappear through the gates.

'Got 'em!' Jonny exclaimed, catapulting forward ahead of the others.

The throbbing roar of a powerful engine split the air as they ran closer. The rusty gates had been chained shut the last time they saw them, en route to the hotel in the minibus, but now they stood open. The Young Magicians spilled into the funfair and spun round as a motorbike and sidecar came bursting through the walls of one of the booths in an explosion of flying plywood fragments and with a roar as loud as a lion with a hernia.

A helmeted Belinda was at the controls, hunched over the handlebars with her chiffon scarf billowing behind her. Eric was squeezed into the sidecar, knees up round his ears, resplendent in goggles and a beanie. For just a second four young magicians and two older ones locked eyes and time stood still, for the smallest of moments. *Justice*, thought Sophie.

Then Belinda gave the handlebar throttle a twist, the engine howled, and the bike and sidecar shot forward. Half a tonne of petrol-powered metal versus four soft human bodies would be no contest, and Belinda must have been counting on them working that out for themselves and getting out of the way. Or, even worse, maybe she didn't care about the actual outcome! The four scattered in four different directions as the bike zoomed ahead towards the open gates.

Zack started waving his arms and a discarded ice-cream cart suddenly began to move into the motorbike's path. Belinda's natural and automatic magician's reaction – *how did he do that?* – was overridden by the more fundamental and practical reaction of a human being now hurtling at high speed towards a solid obstacle, notably exacerbated by Eric Diva's terrified sidecar screams, which both hinted at exactly the same thing: *Turn!*

Belinda heaved on the handlebars and the motorbike spun round ninety degrees, leaning over dangerously and only staying upright under the weight of Eric Diva – no offence, Eric. It lurched up on to the veranda of the ghost train, where the carriages usually waited for sugar-fuelled kiddies to get on board, and smashed through the double doors into the depths of the ride. The engine popped and gargled and then died entirely.

Alex peered over the top of the ice-cream cart that he had managed to push into Belinda's path, the bulk of the freezer compartment evidently blocking her view of him. Nice work, Alex!

'Crikey! Do you think they're all right?'

'Let's go and see,' Jonny said grimly. They hurried towards the shattered doors. The remains of the peeling paintwork – grinning skulls and constipated ghosts – peered sadly back at them as though they blamed the four friends for what had just happened to their fine looks. We used to look *great* before this!

The Young Magicians peered into the dark.

Just inside the doors the tunnel split in two and headed off in different directions. The motorbike had crashed into the back end of an abandoned carriage, the front wheel now buckled back on itself like the claw of a crow. One thing was for sure: Belinda and Eric wouldn't be going anywhere soon on that.

There was no sign of either culprit.

'Which way do you think they went?' whispered Alex, hoping Jonny wasn't about to suggest that they should –

'Let's split up,' said Jonny. 'This ride is probably a loop that starts and finishes here. If we go both ways, we'll have them cornered and can regroup back here.'

'It's kind of . . . dark . . .' Alex pointed out.

Jonny reached into his pockets, and suddenly a soft green glow filled the space as he removed two glowsticks.

'I've only got two, so one per pair?' he added, his teeth shining green in the strange chemical light.

'OK, this way.' Zack grabbed Jonny and the two of them marched down the left-hand tunnel. Alex and Sophie gripped hands and headed to the right.

It wasn't totally dark. There were wormy holes in the sides of the wooden tunnel that let in pinprick beams of light, egging them on. Skeletons, ghouls, witches and Frankenstein's monsters loomed out of the dark, glowing with luminous paint and almost appearing half alive in the strange light of the glowsticks. Sophie and Alex made their way cautiously down their tunnel, keeping either side of the rails.

'I wonder what this does?' Alex said, bumping into something at the level of his knees. It looked like a lever, the kind that might be used to shift the points on a real railway. He gave it a small, thudding kick.

'Look out!' Sophie shouted as two glowing skeletons came hurtling at them, flying through the air without any apparent support. The skeletons jerked to an abrupt halt just in front of them, juddering and jiggling in delight – like they were thrilled to be finally scaring some punters again after such a long period of unemployment.

Alex and Sophie had both dropped into a crouch, covering their heads with their hands. They straightened up slowly and Alex held the glowstick up to look at the dangling skeletons more closely, which still twitched like they were involved in some nervous dance. With the light up close, you could see that each of them was hanging from a chain, painted black to merge into the darkness, connected to a runner on a rail fixed to the ceiling.

Sophie gave the lever a second kick and the skeletons slowly trundled back the way they had come, pulled back into hidden recesses on either side of the tunnel.

'I guess the front of the train hits the lever on its way through, sending the skeletons out, then something on the back of the train hits the lever the other way and they reset themselves until next time,' Sophie mused, ever the one to know the mechanics behind a good trick, regardless of the circumstances. 'Kind of neat.'

They moved on down the tunnel and it widened out into a large graveyard. The train tracks ran between rows of crooked gravestones, with hungry-looking zombies poised on hidden rollers that would lumber about, arms akimbo, the moment the power was switched back on.

Sophie whispered in Alex's ear. 'We should check behind the graves.'

Alex swallowed and nodded. He didn't like the idea of going up against either of the fugitives in broad daylight, let alone in a shadowy, papier-mâché graveyard!

They moved off in different directions with Alex clutching the glowstick like it was a magic wand as he slowly worked his way round the gravestones, before lunging across to the other side, glowstick now held out like a sword – *en garde*! Its light disturbed several surprised spiders and a couple of centipedes whose body language Alex couldn't really read due to the number of legs getting in the way – but they were undoubtedly annoyed. (Centipedes are almost *always* annoyed.) But there were no hidden humans here. Not yet at least.

Suddenly Alex's heart pounded faster as he realized a figure was moving along the wall a couple of metres away, just beyond the circle of green light cast by the glowstick.

'Sophie? Is that you?' Alex asked, his voice trembling.

'Look out, he's right behind you!' shouted Sophie's voice suddenly.

Alex spun round as a figure came pelting out of the dark towards him. Alex felt his stomach turn to water and readied himself.

'Take *that*!' he howled bravely, putting his head down and charging right into the stomach of . . .

'*O-oo-oo-oo-f!*' Sophie wheezed, collapsing to the ground, all the wind knocked out of her. She heaved for breath. 'What did you do that for?'

Alex climbed on to all fours. 'But you said he was behind me.'

They both understood what had happened at the same time. Alex leaped to his feet and jerked round, just in time to see a square of daylight open up in the ceiling above and the silhouetted frame of Eric Diva as he clambered out, giving them a cheerful wave, before slamming the hatch shut behind him.

'He was throwing his voice again!' Alex realized. 'He was pretending to be you!'

'Well, he's not getting away with it this time,' Sophie vowed fiercely, keen for both Eric and Belinda to face justice. She grabbed a ring set into the wall that led up towards the hatch. They both quickly scrabbled up to the roof and emerged, blinking, into the daylight.

Jonny and Zack advanced cautiously down the tunnel, walking on either side of the railway as Alex and Sophie had done. Zack bit his lip, aware that the daylight was slowly receding behind them; plus, he had no idea how Belinda or Eric would react if cornered. At one point, it had looked like Belinda was more than happy to mow them down with a motorbike, so *that* didn't quite fill him with confidence!

The tunnel was well soundproofed, so that when punters were on the ride there would be no light-hearted distraction from the music and laughter outside. Just the ominous music and sound effects and the noise of their own screams instead. Nice. And now it meant that all the two boys could hear were their own footsteps and breathing and heartbeats and – was that more footsteps?

Zack's heart rate went up abruptly as something soft and slimy slid across his face.

'Oh, that is so old,' Jonny muttered nonchalantly. He brushed whatever it was away from his own face. 'I mean, fake webs? Who is actually scared of this kind of stuff?'

'Beats me,' Zack agreed, grateful that Jonny couldn't see his deep blush.

Light glimmered ahead and the tunnel widened out. The railway ran past what might have been a pleasant picnic scene, if your idea of a pleasant picnic scene included a group of hideous, warty witches and a steaming, glowing cauldron. A sign hung above it in glowing red letters: BUBBLE, BUBBLE, BOIL AND TROUBLE.

'Well, they've got that wrong too,' said Jonny. 'It should say *double, double toil and trouble*. We did *Macbeth* in English last term. It's from the bit where he meets three witches.'

Zack's eyes narrowed.

'Three witches?' he whispered.

'Yup.'

'There's . . . four!'

One of the witches suddenly lunged towards them. A high-pitched scream filled the air – possibly Zack's – as Belinda fled back the way they had come, towards the entrance, in her borrowed witch's robes.

They both leaped after her as Jonny reached out with long arms, desperately trying to grab a handful of the rotting robe now flapping wildly in front of them. Jonny yanked a handful of it back, causing Belinda to decelerate abruptly and Jonny to tumble into her. Zack careened off course, stumbling into the legs of a waxwork mummy, which now slowly fell towards Belinda, arms held out, as if trying to embrace her as it toppled, finally pinning her to the ground.

'Get it off! Get it off!' Belinda shrieked.

Zack grabbed the end of the mummy's bandages and yanked hard. They started to unravel as Zack wrapped them tightly round Belinda's heels.

'You idiots!' she raged. 'Don't you know what you've done? Eric and I were poised to take over the Magic Circle and we'd have taken you with us! You dummies would have had a free ride straight to the top with us in charge!'

'Thanks,' Jonny said, sounding pleasantly upbeat, 'but we don't need a free ride to the top of your greasy pole. We're getting where we're going on our own merits, or not at all.'

Belinda screamed in frustration as Zack tied the final knot on her wrists and stood up.

'Think she can do escapology as well?' he grinned.

'I wouldn't put it past her, but not if we keep an eye on her,' Jonny said as they helped Belinda to her feet. She was still cursing under her breath, her accent out in full force now, though not perhaps with the silky undertones it had had before.

'Come on,' said Zack, 'let's see how the others are doing.'

Sophie and Alex stood on the roof of the ghost train, blinking in the sunshine. There was another flat-topped building next to them, about a metre away, where they had just caught a glimpse of Eric Diva's hand disappearing into a hatch below.

'Which ride is it?' Sophie asked. Alex squinted down, but the front of the building – the bit the paying public saw – was out of sight.

'I can't tell from here.'

'Well, I'm sure we'll find out soon enough.'

They both had to take a run-up to get over the gap between the roofs. Alex thought ruefully how Jonny could have done it without even breaking his normal stride! They reached the hatch and pulled it open. Sophie peered over the edge. Oh no, what new hell was this?!

She was looking out over a geometric pattern of triangles and squares and hexagons. The room appeared to be a maze of little cubicles, about two metres high, each one with three, four or six sides. Every hexagon had a square attached to one of its edges, and every square had a triangle between it and the next one. And the next one after that. Confused yet? Over on the other side, about twenty metres away, she could see daylight shining through the entrance.

'It's . . . some kind of maze, I think,' Sophie reported. She stared at it for a bit longer, admiring the aerial view, before jumping down into the gloom, with Alex right behind her.

Their feet touched the ground and they turned round, suddenly startled. Half a dozen Alexes and Sophies stared, suddenly startled, back at them from a million different directions.

'Ah, so it's a *mirror* maze,' Alex said.

'We have to try to stop him reaching the exit,' Sophie decided, hearing footsteps. 'You go that way, I'll go this.'

They carefully headed off into the most baffling maze either of them had ever set foot in. Most of the sides of each cubicle were formed entirely of mirror glass, but – crucially – others weren't. So sometimes the only way out of a cubicle was the way you'd come in, and other times you could walk in one way and out the other. Yet all the time you were surrounded by an often distorted array of images of yourself, or whoever was in the next cubicle, or sometimes both!

It was confusing, but with a bit of effort Sophie could make herself see past the mirrors and spot the way through. It was actually easier to put the glowstick away, and be guided by the dim amount of daylight, than try to see through the glare of the glowstick, reflected multiple times.

At one point, Sophie looked herself in the eye and moved towards where she thought the exit must be. She froze in surprise and shock, heart pounding, as the reflection *moved the other way.*

Sophie realized she was looking at a reflection of a reflection: a reversed mirror image. In other words, she was seeing herself exactly as she actually appeared. This was the Sophie everyone else saw except her ... It made her feel quite dizzy.

'Sophie! Where are you?' she heard Alex call. She was about to answer when she heard Alex again, more indignant and in a different direction.

'That wasn't me!'

'OK,' Sophie called back, 'he's doing his voice tricks again. But this is the real me.'

'Oi! That's my voice you're stealing!' she heard her own voice shout.

'No, it isn't!'

'Sophie, where are you?'

Something moved in the corner of Sophie's eye and she whirled round. Followed by a dozen other Sophies.

'I think I saw him,' Sophie called.

'Don't listen to him! That's a lie!' came back Sophie's voice.

'It's OK, I can see him!' said Alex.

'No, I can't!' replied Alex again!

Sophie took a breath. One Alex on her left, one on her right.

'Alex, on the train yesterday, what were the cake options?' she called.

'Chocolate or carrot!' shouted the Alex to her right, sounding very pleased. Well, there's no way Eric Diva could

316

have known about the cake, Sophie reckoned, so that meant he was standing . . . Sophie started heading left.

'You ask me something,' she called.

'Um – OK,' the real Alex answered. 'What stopped you crash-landing over the wall at Buckingham Palace, when you jumped from the zipwire?'

'A pile of compost!' both Sophies suddenly shouted.

Eric Diva grinned to himself. The story of how the Young Magicians had got into Buckingham Palace was already a minor legend within the magic community. Alex himself had scraped the pile of compost together for the other three to land in safely. Oh, silly Alex, you should have asked the girl something else!

'OK, let me try another – when did you last see an evil twin?' Alex called.

Eh? a baffled Eric Diva thought.

'Last night!' Sophie laughed.

Now Sophie knew roughly where Alex was and where Eric Diva was, based on their joint shouts of 'Compost!'; plus, she knew where *she* was. In her mind's eye, she had put the pattern of mirror cubicles that she had seen from above into a memory palace. Now she was slowly working through it again, room by room, cubicle by cubicle. Sophie started to move, slowly and surely closing in on where she knew Eric Diva must be hiding.

On the other side of a mirror, Eric Diva froze. How had she got that close? It shouldn't be possible! Was she navigating by radar, or something? He turned round, and froze as he found himself staring at Sophie.

Sophie was the first to unfreeze. She ran forward but went slap into a mirror.

'*Ow!*'

She stumbled back, clutching her nose, her eyes streaming.

Eric Diva quickly ducked out of the cubicle before Sophie could get her bearings. *No, no, no . . . that was close*, he thought. *Much too close.*

'How you doing, Sophie?' Alex called anxiously.

Eric Diva didn't bother imitating the littlest Young Magician again. He was close to the exit. Another couple of cubicles to go and he'd be free . . .

Suddenly he was facing the reflection of a man. He moved, but the man moved in a different way.

Not in the different, real-world way that a reflection, or even a reflection of a reflection, might move. This ghoulish man moved in a *completely* different way altogether, striding confidently towards him, arms outstretched. Eric Diva froze and screamed as he came face to face . . . with a real-life ghost.

'What is it?'

'What happened?'

Alex and Sophie stumbled in from opposite directions to find Eric Diva lying unconscious on the ground with the figure of another man crouched over him. The figure turned, looking up, and his lugubrious features split into a grin.

'I believe that the showiest of showmen, Eric Diva . . .
just fainted,' said Alf.

Alf, Sophie and Alex escorted a recovered and squirming
Eric Diva out of the Hall of Mirrors, Eric now having at
least worked out that he wasn't being manhandled by an
actual ghost.

'Who the hell are you?' he gasped. 'Do I know you? I'm
sure we've met . . .'

The three friends smiled at each other. Alf's portrait
was on display back at Magic Circle headquarters – or
at least the portrait of a man who looked very like him
was, with the caption ALF RATTLEBAG, PATRON SAINT
OF STAGEHANDS, 1892–1923. (It's a long story. READ
BOOK O– . . . Oh, I'm sure you've got the picture by
now, haven't you? Especially if you've got *this* far!) Eric
Diva had probably walked past the painting a thousand
times.

'Let's just say *I* know *you*, Mr Diva,' Alf told him,
straight-faced.

Out in the daylight they found Zack, Jonny and a truly
trussed-up, balefully glaring Belinda waiting. Her eyes
met Sophie's. Sophie slowly smiled and Belinda looked
away, scowling into the middle distance.

'*Alf!* When did you get here?' Jonny exclaimed in delight.

'I couldn't get back to sleep after your call last night,'
Alf said. 'And I knew you were either getting into trouble
or you could do with a hand – so either way I thought

I could do more good up here than down there. So I got the Magic Circle van out and – well – here I am.'

He nodded over to a corner of the fairground where a very, very old, very battered, very Ford Transit was parked, with the words MAGIC CIRCLE in glowing, seventies-style letters on the side.

'But how did you know to come to Ferdinand's Fantastic Festival of Fun?' asked Alex.

'Well . . . I was on course for the hotel, but I couldn't just pass by without dropping in to pay my respects. You don't get places like this any more. Plus, something told me that if there were ever a place you lot might wander off to, given your penchant for little errands and theatrical detours, then this one would surely tick a lot of boxes. Then I heard the two of you shouting at each other in the Hall of Mirrors. So why were you chasing Mr Diva, and what's wrong with this lady?'

'Right, well, it's a long story,' Zack grinned.

'It's preposterous,' Belinda snapped. 'I don't know who you are, but I can tell instantly that you're a reasonable guy – it's a gift I have. These four children have concocted the most *ridiculous* tale –'

'And I don't know who you are either, ma'am,' Alf interrupted politely, 'but you ought to know that if I have to choose between believing these four, or a complete stranger who's tied up in mummy bandages, I will always go for the former four.'

'It's not worth it, Belinda,' Eric Diva muttered. 'It's over.'

'Anyhow, we can easily sort this out,' Jonny said. 'Let's take the van back to the hotel, and then President Pickle can vouch for everything.'

'There you are then,' Alf agreed. 'Not something I'm prone to say, but let's leave it up to the wisdom of President Pickle as to what to do with you!'

And with that he started to march Eric Diva towards the van.

9 A.M.

President Pickle was back at the podium and trying to restore some kind of order. This was still an AGM after all. And, as far as he was concerned, an agenda was an agenda, especially at an AGM, and, apart from the small technicality of at least a couple of serious crimes being attempted and thwarted, he, personally, still had a *lot* to get through. In fact, if it weren't for the agenda he was now clutching – neatly typed, double-spaced, twelve-point Palatino (he detested Times New Roman) – the whole AGM so far might have gone seriously to pot with all its disruptions. His thoughts were still so muddled that the thin sheet of A4 paper was his only link to what ought to be happening.

Every time they finished off an item, he drew a neat line through it with a sense of destiny and satisfaction. He had just crossed off 'Approve the Minutes of the Last AGM'. Ahead lay the glorious sunlit uplands of:

- 'Matters Arising from the Minutes of the Last AGM'
- 'Matters Arising from Matters Arising from the Minutes of the Last AGM'
- 'Election of Officials of the Magic Circle'
- 'Matters Arising from Election of Officials of the Magic Circle'
- 'Matters Arising from Non-election of Unsuccessful Non-candidates Previously Hoping for Election as Non-officials of the Magic Circle'

And so on.

Those times when President Pickle was chairing the AGM, and when his lips weren't glued together and a cunning ventriloquist wasn't sabotaging his career, were the times when Edmund Pickle was actually, clearly, positively happy. He had a purpose. He had a plan. He was achieving something. To some people, an AGM is a tedious task. To Mr President Edmund Pickle, it was a holy duty. AND NOW HE COULD EAT AGAIN! It was like he'd been handed a new life. The prospect of diving head first into the buffet as soon as this AGM came to a close was almost starting to make him physically vibrate.

He rapped his gavel on the podium and called for order. Then a flicker of movement made him look up. He froze, and the sound in the ballroom slowly died away as the members followed his gaze.

The double doors at the back of the room swung open of their own accord, framing Belinda Vine and Eric Diva in the entrance.

Standing behind them on one side, and head and shoulders above, Jonathan Haigh. Standing on the other, Zack Harrison. And then popping out from behind the doors – because of course they hadn't opened of their own accord, that was just for effect – Sophie Yang and Alex Finley.

'We got them, Mr President!' Zack said cheerfully, and the four friends started to usher their two captives down the aisle, prodding them in the back like they were herding cattle.

Alex suddenly noticed something. He glanced quickly around.

'Hey, where did Al–?'

Alf had come with them as far as the doors to the ballroom – but had quietly vanished, just as real-life ghosts ought to do, when no one was looking.

'Shh,' Jonny advised in a whisper, and Alex remembered that, as far as most of the Magic Circle knew, Alf didn't actually exist. And dear Alf certainly wasn't going to do anything to spoil that illusion either.

'Where did the other guy go?' Belinda demanded.

'What guy, Ms Vine?' Sophie asked breezily, and met Belinda's scowl with such a blank look, you'd have sworn that not in a million years could there ever have been a time when Sophie looked up to this woman.

They escorted their captives down the hall towards the stage. Nearby, Deanna was sending enough gigawatts of hero worship at Sophie to power a small city, with Hugo generating enough frosty cool to freeze one.

'Seize them!' President Pickle ordered grandly from the podium. The nearest Magic Circle officials, who were Jane and Steve naturally, closed in on the small group, then looked back towards the stage for verification.

'Um – you did mean these two, Mr President?' Steve asked. 'Not the Young Mag–'

'Of course I mean those two, silly man!' President Pickle spluttered.

Steve and Jane took charge of Belinda and Eric, and wheeled them off into a side room, there to await the pleasure of Pickle's judgement, and leaving the Young Magicians and President Pickle gazing at each other.

Which was when something amazing happened.

The scowl that President Pickle generally displayed whenever he was looking at the four friends relaxed. Just a bit. Slightly less than a glacier moves in the course of a single heartbeat, of course, but still. A bit.

'Thank you,' he said. 'You've been . . . quite helpful.' And then, before anyone could faint with surprise, President Pickle proclaimed pointedly, 'And now, *if* you've *quite* had your fun, I have an AGM to run, so kindly take your seats.' He waved his piece of paper at the four friends. 'As you can see, we have an agenda to follow! Where there is an agenda, there is order! And the agenda says you must now sit down so that I can carry on.'

The Young Magicians looked at each other – shrugging and smiling – and sidled towards the nearest free chairs.

President Pickle opened his mouth to continue, but was interrupted by yet another figure standing in the doorway. A wave of gasps flooded through the hall, making the four look up. Their jaws dropped in unison at the sight of the figure shambling towards the stage.

Skinnier even than Jonny, and approximately a million times older, he looked like he had died and been buried in his best suit and had dug his way out of the grave – still wearing the suit – and had come now to wreak revenge on those who had betrayed him in this mortal life.

But, to be fair, that was how Bill Dungworth usually looked.

President Pickle gaped at the apparition, clinging on to the sides of the podium for support.

'Bill? But – you . . . *died*!'

However, there was no doubt in anyone's mind that this was Bill Dungworth, the lately late treasurer of the Magic Circle, though now not so much late . . . just a little delayed.

'I. Was. ASLEEP!' Bill gasped. He lumbered the last few steps on stiff legs and extended a trembling finger like a long, knobbly twig at President Pickle. 'I was just having my usual lunchtime nap and they buried me!'

'I mean, the funeral director went through several formalities first, B–' President Pickle tried to say, before being interrupted again.

'I asked who called the medics and they said . . . it was you!'

'Well, of course it was me!' President Pickle protested. 'It was me who found you, after you'd been lying there for a week.'

'It was just a nap! You didn't think of checking me for life signs?'

'Of course I did! And I watched the medics run all the usual tests, Bill,' President Pickle blustered. 'You know . . . reflexes, temperature, heartbeat!'

'I am going to *sue*! Do you hear me?! I am going to start at the very top of this society and sue my way down, and the top, Mr President, is *you*!'

At this point, following a sentence that had taken nearly ten whole seconds to say without once drawing a breath, Bill gasped and staggered over to lean on someone's chair for support.

'Sue,' he wheezed.

'OK . . .' President Pickle took a few deep breaths. 'If someone could help our good and happily undeparted friend Bill to his seat, we can deal with this under Any Other Business.'

He looked down at the full length of the agenda as his tummy began to rumble like a thunderstorm.

'Although . . . maybe it might be better for all if we just . . . I declare this AGM closed – for now!' he announced with a half-hearted tap of his gavel and a strange beaming smile that could only mean he was thinking of food.

'Perhaps our respect for keeping to the rules is brushing off on him,' joked Jonny as the room began to surge to its collective feet.

An anxious-looking Cynthia intercepted the Young Magicians as they exited the room.

'Sorry. Jonny dear, may I have a word?' She threw a look at the others. 'In fact, I know how close you are, so maybe you should all hear this?'

The Young Magicians looked at each other as she led them into one of the function rooms – in fact, it was the very one where they thought they'd heard President Pickle laying out his cunning plans before he'd vanished. How different that room looked now they'd got to the bottom of everything! But Cynthia was looking so serious. What was up?

Cynthia closed the door, and turned to face Jonny. She gently reached up – quite some distance, it must be said – to clasp his shoulders and gaze up into his face. Jonny stared down at her in bafflement.

'Jonny dear, I'm afraid I have some very bad news for you. It's just that . . . oh dear. This is rather hard.' She dabbed at her eyes with a folded hanky. 'He was such a good friend and asset to the Magic Circle over the years, though I know he and you parted on quite sour terms . . .

Look, there's no easy or kind way to say this. Jonny, your grandfather was moved to the prison hospital and, um, at three p.m. yesterday afternoon, his nurse found him . . . Well, he's passed away. I am so sorry, dear.'

There's no right way to react when you hear of a loved one's death. You can't practise it like a trick. You just feel as if an enormous weight has swung down from the ceiling and given your body a massive, full-frontal *thwack*, so you're aware you've been hit by something – and you know you should be feeling it – but the blow has knocked every single emotion out of you so you're not sure what that feeling should be. All you can do is stand there, numb.

Jonny was vaguely aware of his three friends gathering round slowly, not sure themselves what they should be doing, but knowing their tall friend needed them. One by one, Sophie, then Zack, then Alex pulled Jonny into a hug while he stood there, towering above them, face blank, trying to take in everything that Cynthia had just said.

In the midst of his whirling, numb thoughts, Jonny realized Zack was saying something to Cynthia.

'Um – you did say three p.m.? That's three p.m. *yesterday*?'

'Oh yes, dear.' Cynthia gave her eyes a final dab. 'I'm sorry it took so long for news to reach us up here. Well . . .' She gave the four friends a brave smile. 'I can see you've got each other, and I have to get on. Don't hesitate to come to me if you need anything, Jonny.'

Cynthia left the room, while the meaning of Zack's question gradually sank in – to Alex, to Sophie, and even eventually to Jonny. They pulled slowly apart and stared at each other.

'So, if Granddad died yesterday –' Jonny began.

'At three p.m. –' Zack repeated.

'Over twelve hours *before* we called the Magic Circle from the lookout post –' Sophie added. Alex finished off the question.

'Who was that helping Alf in the library?'

Acknowledgements

The hugest thanks to the children's fiction department at Penguin Random House for their constant support, humour and understanding of why this book was delivered so late! Particular thanks to Ruth Knowles, Wendy Shakespeare, Ben Jeapes and Robert Kirby for making everything so fun – I owe an awful lot of this book to them! And to Noémie Gionet Landry for bringing so much of the chaos that was in my head into such clarity by way of a single drawing. It is a skill I can safely say I will never have!

And to the magicians and non-magicians young and old who enjoyed the first book enough to give this second one a read . . . I hope Zack, Sophie, Jonny and Alex won't fail to disappoint. They're a little older than the first time we met them and Brexit hadn't happened, but not much else has changed.

And finally to B, b, F, A and PD who remain my absolute everything.